Asandra

For Kathy!
Enjoy the adventure!

Jessie

Asandra

Asandra

Book Two of the Xsardis Chronicles

By
Jessie Mae Hodsdon

Adventure with a purpose

Text Copyright by Jessica Mae Hodsdon

All rights reserved. No part of this book may be reproduced or transmitted in any form or by any means, electronic or mechanical, including photocopying, recording, or by any information storage and retrieval system, without written permission from the publisher. For information contact Rebirth Publishing by mailing PO Box 1006, Bangor, Maine, 04402; or by emailing rebirthpublishing@issym.com.

ISBN 978-0-9843386-1-0

Cover Art by Ande Binan

Published by Rebirth Publishing, Inc.

Printed in the United States

Visit www.issym.com

Acknowledgements:

In the whirlwind of what has happened since Issym was released last November many people have supported and encouraged me. Thank you all!

To my editors: Judy, Julie, Loretta, Alyssa and Chuck—thanks for all your dutiful hours, your rushed projects, your late nights and your early mornings.

To Charlie: your behind the scenes help was amazing. Thanks for everything, Brother.

To Sarah, my dear, understanding roommate: thank you for all the times you let me walk in and explain a publishing problem that really got under my skin. Even though you may not have understood a word I said, you made it all better. Your constant understanding this semester has kept me going through the craziness. Thanks.

To Kate: you have been my constant friend, despite the distance. Your quiet way of getting me to talk out a story before I write it has been so helpful in plotting my series. Your love, Sister, has been so helpful in plotting my life! Bonum Est Amari.

And to God: looking back I can't figure out how we got here. Your hand has guided along this path. Without you, this truly would not have happened. Praise Your Name forever!

Asandra

To my mother,

>Who taught me how to paint a picture,
>Who believed in me
>Who never gave up on me
>   And
>Who worked beside me

>   Thanks!

Asandra

Introduction

With great anticipation, Joppa watched his niece's intense work. Many times she had begged him to let her write the history books that he kept, but this was the first time that he had granted her request. As a tear slid down her cheek he wondered if he had made the right decision. She was very close to this story. "Reesthma," he called to her softly.

She had to look at her uncle's broken frame to distinguish who called to her. "I hardly recognize you anymore, Uncle Joppa," she answered, putting down her feather pen and wiping away the tear. Joppa had once lived unbothered in a mighty tree where he preserved the truth. He had sacrificed himself to save her and that history, giving himself up to be carried to the prison fortress, Maremoth. Though his life had been spared and he had recovered, he was still very different. His body was bent and his voice was coarser.

"Why does my first book have such an unhappy ending?" she questioned.

"Often a story seems like it has ended badly, but there is always a future. Remember," he used the same tone he had always used when reading to her. "After months at sea, the mighty warrior and the fair princess reached her home. The castle towered above them as they drew the eyes of the people. Jherek, the dark-skinned sailor who had proven his loyalty during the voyage, drew their attention from the princess with his warrior's posture, bare feet and richly colored clothing. He walked a few paces behind Issym and Asandra.

"Upon entering the throne room Issym stepped back as Asandra was swept into the embrace of a man her age. 'My beauty, you have returned!' he exclaimed. 'We had given you up for dead. Just like...' his voice trailed off and Asandra pulled back. She took Issym's scarred hand and pulled him forward. 'Lord Commal, this is Issym—my rescuer and my betrothed.'

"'Asandra, Princess. Your father... he's been murdered.' It took a few moments for Lord Commal's words to be understood. Then, Asandra sunk to the floor and clung to Issym's arm as she wept. Issym's own heart broke as he watched her in agony.

"When Asandra had finally fallen into an unrestful sleep, Issym sought out Commal. His warrior's instincts told him not to trust the lord, but he needed the man's knowledge. 'You have brought us back our princess. We thank you,' Commal spoke first as they stood in the empty hallway.

"Issym learned that Lord Commal had been Lord Protector in the absence of Asandra. He would continue to rule until she chose a king. The men who were responsible for her father's death had fled into the mountains, but the army had not been able to pursue them.

"'They will be brought to justice,' Issym vowed.

"He left Asandra before she rose the next morning, committing her safety into Jherek's hands. Asandra wept all the more, believing that she had lost her love when she was told how strong the forces in the mountains were. Weeks later, Lord Commal confirmed the rumors of Issym's death. Left with a broken country, the princess had to choose a leader and accepted the proposal of Lord Commal.

"But Jhereck knew this to be an even graver than danger than her death and went to the mountains to find Issym. He approached a camp and saw Issym's bound form thrown into one of the tents. In the night, he freed his friend and together they fought their way out of the camp.

"Tending to Issym's wounds, Jhereck then learned that Issym had allowed himself to be captured in order to learn who was behind the kidnapping and attack. He had discovered that it was Lord Commal. When Jhereck told Issym of the lord's plans to marry Asandra, they left the camp's occupants in their treachery and returned to the castle—just in time to stop the wedding and expose Commal. Issym led the army to capture the camp in the mountains. When he returned, he and Asandra were married."

"Don't you see Reesthma? This was not the only time Issym was believed to be dead only to be found alive again."

"But Uncle Joppa, I don't think our heroes are dead. I *know* they are."

"Tell me everything, then."

Reesthma handed him the book she had been working on and he began to read:

Chapter 1

They moved with joint precision. Running through the forest with a silent haste, the two teenagers increased the distance between them and their pursuers. As soon as they were certain that they were out of sight, the boy dropped to the ground and opened a hatch that was covered with plant life. The girl hopped into it and he followed, pulling the leafy cover over them.

The two stopped moving and tried not to breathe. Their enemy passed above them, but did not stop. "That was a close one!" the teenage girl almost shouted with enthusiasm. She seemed to enjoy danger.

"Mom is going to kill us..." the boy murmured.

"Come on, Ev. You didn't find that even a little fun?" his sister teased, punching him on the shoulder and dislodging some of the dirt from his tattered tunic.

He shook his head.

"Don't look so nervous," she chastised. "We're safe now."

They stood and began to walk through the tunnel. It grew so dark that the boy could not distinguish the form of his sister, but they continued without slowing their pace. They knew these passages well. Finally, after a series of twists and turns, they saw a familiar light in the distance. The tunnel widened to make a room, lit by torches with three openings leading away. An alert guard in a well-worn uniform stood in front of each one. The sentry moved aside as they entered the leftmost way.

After passing several doors, the siblings took another left and two more guards stepped aside to allow them entrance to the room they protected. As they stepped in and closed the door, they saw yet again how small the apartment was. It had a torn rug lying on the floor, torches on the walls, a bed, a desk and a chair. It was by far the nicest room in the underground, but even so...

A woman sat in the chair, leaning on her desk as she supported her head with her hand. At the sounds of the teens, she turned around to face them. Her regal dress was pristine; her brown hair was curled and long; a slender crown was upon her head. She would have been strikingly beautiful if concern had not aged her before her time. Looking at them, she questioned, "Had a close encounter with Sasha's men?"

"Yes Mother," the boy replied, ready to get the truth out in the open.

"How close, Evan?" The quietness of her voice was an attempt to mask her sharp focus.

"They did not discover our hiding place," Evan replied. That was what truly mattered.

"But they *almost* did," she surmised. "And what would have happened if they had? How foolish! You insist that I let you go above, but you nearly got us discovered. And this is not the first time."

She shook her head and the weight of her hair left it unmoved as she continued, "We are not just ordinary rebels. I am the rightful queen; you the prince and princess. If we are captured, what do you think will happen to the resistance?"

Evan listened; his sister rolled her eyes. He knew it was his mother's concern for the others in the hiding place that made her speak so. She did not care—she was happy to let her brother take the brunt of their mother's words.

"Did you get what you were looking for, Katarina?" their mother sighed.

Katarina's face lit up as she opened up the muddy bag she wore around her shoulder and pulled out a red gem on a string. "I'm so glad Ian kept it hidden for me. I thought I had lost it."

Evan and Katarina had each been given a gift on the day of their birth—Katarina's was a cord with a ruby on it and tethered under Evan's shirt was a large blue gem. Katarina returned her stone to its rightful place on her neck and fingered it. Queen Juliet had given Evan his and King Remar had bestowed Kat with hers. Oh how the princess missed her father! He had been captured by Sasha, the wicked shape shifter, years and years ago. Her father had always listened to her, always loved her, always cared for her.

Katarina thanked the stars that he had been wearing commoner's clothing the day he had been taken—Sasha had no idea that he was the king.

The queen called her children to her side. Wrapping an arm around each one, she told them, "For many days I have fasted and prayed and I have come to this conclusion: you must go to Earth and bring us back Rachel and Seth, the ones who imagined Xsardis."

"But how will we get to Earth?" questioned the ever-sensible Evan. To him the journey was a logical conclusion. To her, it was a more adventurous decision than she had ever seen her mother make.

"Katarina, hand me your necklace," Juliet commanded.

Kat hesitated, but obeyed. Her mother put it on her desk. Taking the hammer that waited she aimed for the ruby.

"What are you doing?" Kat shouted, fueled by panic. They heard the guards outside the room stir at the sound of her high pitched voice.

"You must trust me," the queen insisted.

"Smash Evan's!" she protested.

"Your brother's is less powerful."

Juliet brought the hammer down and the ruby shattered into pieces. Kat's heart filled with despair, feeling as if she had lost the last part of her father. Then anger took over. How could her mother have done it? Both emotions were suppressed as curiosity took their places. Something was rising from the pieces. It looked like a red, glowing light. The light was smaller than her hand and it floated softly around the room, as if it were alive.

"What is it?" Katarina asked in wonder, as the creature started to buzz.

"An illuminescent," her mother replied.

"I thought those were just legends," Evan voiced, flicking his eyes towards his mother for a moment and then turning his attention back to the creature.

"No," answered Juliet, "they are quite real, but as far as we know, the one you now see and the one in your gem, Evan, are the only ones to have survived."

The queen buzzed something to the illuminescent and it showered Kat and Evan with light. The next time they heard its sound, the teens thought it was trying to communicate something like, "Where am I?"

"There are different types of illuminescents," the queen explained to her children, "but red ones have always belonged with royalty and they have the most extensive powers. Whereas the others only have one ability, red illuminescents have many."

"What can it help us do?" the siblings asked almost simultaneously.

"She can take you two to Earth."

Kat looked towards her mother with anticipation on her face, "When can we leave?"

Evan did not appear as enthusiastic. The queen asked her son, "Why so reserved?"

"Because I know that this task will not be as easy as it sounds."

"True. Earth is not the same as Asandra. Your trip will be difficult and dangerous. Your task will take time; time that Asandra does not have. The longer you are there, the more established Sasha will become here.

"And yet," she continued, "I can offer you very little guidance of how to begin your search. Rely upon your illuminescent. She will adapt more quickly to the new environment, but keep her safe, for she will be unable to blend in. Do not disclose your identities; do not say where you are from. You will begin your search in New York City, New York. That's where Seth lives. Find him and he will help you find Rachel. Remember to hurry."

The queen hugged each of her children. Katarina broke away quickly, but Evan lingered, trying to pass on some strength. He knew that as dangerous as his trip was, it was more dangerous for his mother who was staying on Asandra.

"How does getting to Earth work?" the princess inquired.

"Ask your illuminescent. You need to learn to understand each other."

Kat looked towards Evan as if commanding him to talk to the creature. "Can you take us to Earth?" he tried to say. He had never been much of a communicator in his own language, let alone an entirely new one.

"Yes," the red creature replied simply.

"What do we need to do?" Katarina questioned.

Without answering, the illuminescent hovered above them, showering them with red light. They disappeared.

Chapter 2

Katarina and Evan appeared in the middle of a paved road, as waves of horseless carriages swerved to avoid them and let off loud sounds. Evan grabbed his sister's hand and pulled her towards the path where people were walking. "What are those things?" Kat screeched as the illuminescent quickly dove into her bag.

"Never been to New York before?" asked a friendly old man.

Evan declared, "No."

"Those cabs will run you over if you're not careful."

So the speeding objects in the road were called cabs.

The man looked over their costume-like appearance. Kat's faded green dress was reminiscent of medieval times. The jagged slits in the floor-length fabric revealed her scratched and dirtied skin. The boy's boots were muddy like her legs and caused the New Yorker to wonder where they had come from. His thoughts tumbled from his lips, "You guys from around here?"

Evan wondered how they were supposed to answer such a question. "We're from Asandra," Kat replied, her focus clearly on the strange surroundings.

They received another queer look.

"It's... a pretty remote place," Evan answered, uncomfortable providing too much information. He hoped his sister had not already done that.

"Can I help you find anything?" the man questioned. He turned slightly towards the road, making it clear that he wanted to bring the conversation to an end.

"Do you know Seth Albert?" Kat asked.

"No, I'm sorry... I don't." The man walked away.

The street was loud and people bumped into them as they stood on the smooth, hard path. Sometimes they received odd looks; other times no one would even look them in the eye. Katarina drew her brother into an alley. "How are we supposed to find Seth?" she inquired, gaping at the strange environment. The buildings surrounding them towered into the sky, higher than any fortress wall. Where were the trees? The grass?

Katarina opened her bag; her illuminescent flew out, shooting through the air. Someone walking along the sidewalk stopped and looked intently down the alley. Kat guessed that the person had seen the creature, but the illuminescent had already hidden herself. "What was that thing?" the guy called to them, keeping a good distance.

"What thing?" Kat responded.

"That glowing..."

"I don't see any glowing. Do you, Brother?" It was true. They did not see the creature at that moment.

Evan was not as comfortable with telling half-truths. He simply stared at the man, without answering.

The guy waited a few moments and then moved on. When he left, the illuminescent came out again. This time, however, she tried to hide behind Evan's shoulder.

"You got us to Earth. Can you get us to Seth?" the princess inquired.

The creature gave a short reply, "No."

"Do you have a name?" Evan asked it. He did not like thinking of it as 'the creature'.

"No."

"May we call you Zara?" Evan was quick to pick that name, for he knew Katarina would approve: Zara had been her favorite nurse before she had been taken captive by Sasha.

"Yes."

Katarina looked away. She knew her brother received her thanks. She never had to say it.

"My suggestion," declared the illuminescent, "since you asked for it, is that you inquire of someone from this world how to find a person."

Evan and Katarina slowly walked back to the sidewalk, Zara hiding herself in the princess' bag once more. Evan felt someone hit him from behind. A boy of perhaps twelve, with wheels on his feet, had fallen over beside him. "Hey!" the boy shouted. "Watch it!"

"Sorry," said the prince, ever polite.

The boy was working on getting up. Evan decided to ask him their question. "How do you find a person here?"

"What do you mean?" the kid retorted. "You get in a cab, tell the driver where you want to go, and he takes you!" He sped away.

"How do you get a cab?" Evan shouted after him. No reply came.

Katarina watched a woman walk to the road and wave. A cab stopped and she got in. Katarina walked to the road and held out her hand. A cab stopped.

The two teens climbed in the car. "Where to?" the guy in the front of the cab asked.

"We want to see Seth Albert," Kat told him.

"What's the address?" the driver said shortly and with a heavy accent of some kind.

"I don't know," Katarina replied.

"So where do you want me to take you?"

They did not answer.

"Look. You've got to tell me where you want to go."

"How do we find a person?" Evan asked again.

The man sighed. "Have you tried a phone book or the Internet?"

Huh? Kat and Evan thought simultaneously. "No," she answered.

The driver took pity on them. "Go inside that building there," he pointed as he spoke. "Ask for a phone book. Look up the name."

The teens did as they were told. The room they entered was small. It had a lot of tables and chairs and people crammed in. It seemed to be a popular eating place. They walked up to the glass cabinet which housed some food, cutting the long line, and asked the person behind it, "Do you have a phone book?"

The lady handed them one and quickly began to ignore them. Taking a seat at the only open table, the two teens started turning page after page. They understood most of the writing, but not how to use the book.

Zara shot out of the princess's bag. "No!" Kat hissed.

Evan looked up. "What's wrong?" he queried.

"Zara's loose." The illuminescent was nowhere to be seen, having hidden herself among the throngs of people.

Katarina headed toward the other side of the restaurant. She was pretty sure that was where the creature had headed. Suddenly her eyes landed on the clasped hands of a teenage boy and the reddish glow coming from them. "Hey!" she hollered to get her brother's attention from where he was searching nearby.

The teenager seemed nervous. Looking longingly at his food, he made a decision and bolted for the door. Kat pushed her way out of the restaurant to see the boy running down the road. "No! Stop!" she called after him, unwittingly allowing the desperation to come out in her voice.

Kat saw Evan race past her, pursuing the boy with a fervor she had never seen before. He was a faster runner than she. She hated to admit it, but it was true.

When Katarina finally caught up, Evan had a hand on the teen's shoulder. "Let me go!" the kidnapper was saying.

"Open your hands," she commanded.

The teen had short, black hair and his face was covered in freckles. He was not overly strong, but then again, neither was Evan. Katarina did not know who would win if there was a fight. Probably not her brother. He could wield a sword okay, but his street-fighting skills were lacking.

"Open them," she repeated louder. "Now!" she added with a boom.

"Why should I?" the teen yelled back, struggling to get away from Evan without using his hands. He stared at Katarina. How could someone so petite act so commanding?

Time to try another tactic, Katarina thought. The princess smiled at him and pushed her hair away from her face, then responded in her sweetest voice, "What you've got in them is really important to me..."

"You don't even know what I have in my hands," the boy countered. He was Kat's age and just as strong-willed.

"Oh, I think I do."

"Do you even know what it's called?" the boy asked. Evan had loosened his grasp.

Katarina continued to talk to the kidnapper, "Her name is Zara. My father gave her to me, and I haven't seen him in years, so she means a lot to me. Please give her back. You don't even know what she is."

The youth paused, as if struck by something she had said. "She's an illuminescent..."

"How did you know that?" Evan demanded.

The prince noticed that the teen had altered his stance. He was not searching for an escape route any longer. Evan released him. The kid questioned, "Who are you two?"

"Are you Seth?" the princess responded, trying to put the few pieces of the puzzle together.

"No," he laughed.

"Do you know Seth?"

"I know *a* Seth, but why are you asking these questions?"

"Because you stole our illuminescent."

"Where are you from?" his face was full of curiosity. There was something genuine about these two oddly dressed teens.

"Asandra."

His eyes flashed. Shaking Evan's hand and releasing the illuminescent, he told them, "Name's Max. Why don't you follow me?"

Chapter 3

Max had led Katarina and Evan to his family's apartment, not truly believing that they were from Asandra, but needing to know. He had spent the last six months dreaming about Xsardis, since he had returned from his adventure with Seth and Rachel on Issym.

The three had not spoken on the short journey to his home—there had been too many ears that might hear something they should not. The three were greeted upon coming into the apartment's crowded entryway by an eight-year-old boy. "Why are you here?" the kid asked Max, leaning on a stack of boxes.

"Meet Jesse, my brother," Max introduced to Kat and Evan with a perfected roll of his eyes.

The teen pushed past Jesse and led his guests into the kitchen. It was a small apartment, cluttered from the ceiling to the floor, with boxes and papers and dirty dishes. He cleared off two stools for Evan and Kat. "Sorry," he shrugged, embarrassed to bring the pretty Katarina to such a mess, "we just moved here."

Jesse stared at Kat. "Are you his girlfriend?" the little brother insisted on knowing.

Katarina raised an eyebrow.

"Get out of here Jesse!" Max directed, pushing his little brother towards the living room.

"Why should I?" Jesse responded manipulating his voice to make it as high pitched as possible.

"You can go into my room and play my new video game." He sighed, then snapped, "But don't touch anything else."

"Really?" The kid scurried away before his brother could change his mind.

Evan marveled at the difference between himself and his sister. He could see that she was impressed with how Max had commanded his brother. Evan did not know why there had had to be conflict. Certainly things could have been resolved more peaceably.

"So, who are you?" Max inquired, closing the door to the kitchen and planting himself onto the counter.

"I am Princess Katarina of Asandra. This is my brother, Prince Evan."

"What are you doing on Earth?" his question sounded more like an interrogation than an inquiry. Perhaps that was what he had meant it to sound like. He could not help being skeptical. Perhaps this was all a joke Seth was playing on him.

"Our world is in desperate trouble." Kat looked deeply into his eyes as she said it.

Max knew that he was getting played. Katarina was giving him too much attention, too much drama, too much of everything for it to be real. But what was her game? "I'll need some proof that you actually came from Asandra."

The illuminescent hovered in front of his eyes and zapped his shoulders. He quickly said, "Other proof—things that only a person who was really from Asandra could know. Name the continents of the world."

"Asandra and Issym," Katarina answered, hesitantly. She did not want to give too much information away to this stranger.

"How did they get named?" Max tried to dust off his Xsardis history. When he had been on Issym, he and a prisoner named Arvin had spent much time discussing the past. The man had used it to show Max why he needed to embrace the present and work for the future.

"Asandra was a princess whom Issym rescued," Katarina repeated the story that had been drilled into her mind. "After they were married for many years, she died and her people named one continent after her. Issym returned to his birth continent and became king of the land. When he died, his people named that continent after him.

"Now it's your turn," she told him. "Give us some proof. What is the name of our world?"

"Xsardis."

"Who created it?"

"God... but if you mean who imagined it that would be Seth and Rachel. They were friends when they were kids and spent their time pretending that there were talking frogs and mighty dragons. All of this came to life on Xsardis. Seth's creations and those he imagined with Rachel are on Issym. Hers are on Asandra."

"And how do you know Seth?" Katarina enjoyed pestering him for information.

"We go to the same school, same church—we've been friends for years."

"And he just decided to tell you about this world that he imagined?" Katarina scoffed. "I don't think so."

Evan kicked his sister. She was alienating their one ally.

"He didn't know that it existed until about six months ago. I was there when he stumbled into it."

"You couldn't have been to Asandra..." Katarina muttered.

"Issym."

Her face began to glow, "Oh, tell me about it! We've longed for news of that land for years. Everyone says that the food grows by itself, there is no sickness and no need for a government because the people are so noble."

Max wanted to laugh. From what he had heard and seen, food was one of the biggest concerns in Issym, Rachel had almost died from disease and the dragon Smolden had almost conquered the world for lack of government. "That's not exactly how things were. Seth was brought to Issym by Smolden. The dragon wanted his help in conquering the continent. Rachel was summoned by the airsprites." Max broke off as he saw a grimace on the teens' faces. What had he said? "The *airsprites*," he exaggerated the word and got a bigger reaction. What was so wrong about airsprites?

He went on as if he had not noticed, "They wanted her help to keep the continent away from Smolden. I tagged along because I was with Seth when he'd been brought. When Seth refused to help Smolden, he and Rachel were forced to race throughout the continent on their own, with the dragon's entire army chasing them." Max left out the part about how he had gone to Smolden's underground domain in order to help the dragon. He was not proud of that.

"Smolden himself wasn't even the biggest enemy. It was a shape shifter named Sasha." Max was looking at the floor, trying to bring back memories. If he had been facing Evan and Katarina, he would have seen their look of disgust and horror. "She... appeared to be weak, but I think she was a bigger problem than Smolden ever was. Anyway, they're both dead now and Issym is back to the way it should be. What's wrong with Asandra?"

Katarina's mind raced. If Max believed Sasha to be dead, he was not going to believe her when she said that the shape shifter was not. She tried to devise some lie, but when none presented itself she went for the truth: "About fifteen years ago, Sasha—the same Sasha you spoke of—began to terrorize us. She enslaved many of the people; built up a powerful fortress; and waged war with our family's kingdom."

"She was gone for some time," Evan put in. "Probably she went to Issym, where you fought with her."

"Her army continued to do her dirty work," Katarina went on. "People say she's back now, but we can't be sure. Maybe she did die. Either way, her army is still a very real threat."

"How strong a hold does she have?"

"It's bad. My father's been captured, my mother and brother and I are in hiding."

Evan went on, "None of our people dare speak of politics even in their own homes."

Katarina spoke over him, "Sasha has spies and a branch of her cult in every village; some towns are even occupied by her military. She has a fortress on the edge of the continent, full of slaves and her ever growing army. If anyone even audibly resists her, she takes their food, burns their houses and lands, then makes them prisoners in her fortress."

"Your family isn't strong enough to stop it?"

"We haven't been for as long as I can remember. We've been in hiding for six years."

Max shook his head and muttered, "We thought we had a tough job on Issym. I take it you want Seth and Rachel to swoop in and save the day?"

Evan nodded. He wished he could read this teen's freckled face. Could he trust him with the fate of his country? Would Seth and Rachel help if they could even find them?

Zara took the opportunity afforded by their pause in speech to shower Max with dust. Instinctively, he swatted the creature away, but as she began to speak in her language Max was amazed that he could understand her. "You have been touched by an illuminescent. That was why I flew to you. Who of my kind have you met? I was told I was one of the last two."

Max was glad to give her good news, "No. Many of your kind fled to Issym."

The illuminescent seemed to let off a happy purr and she glowed a deeper red.

Observing her, Max inquired, "What is your name?"

"They named me Zara."

Max marveled at how similar this illuminescent looked to Ruby, the one that had come to Earth with Rachel. If Zara had not been a little bigger than Ruby, Max would have sworn they were the same.

"Where's Seth?" Katarina asked. "We need to move quickly."

"He's in Maine right now, visiting Rachel."

"How do we get there?" Evan inquired.

"You can stay here tonight. I'm going by bus to join him tomorrow and you can come with me. Only, I don't know how we'll pay for your ticket."

Zara let off some sparks and they turned into gold coins. "Alright. You can stay here tonight and tomorrow we will go find Seth and Rachel."

Sword clashed against sword. The two teens were well matched. Their movements carried them across the yard and back again. Each was testing the other's skill, not yet using full strength. The girl's face was getting red with the exertion. It was hot summer day with no wind. The boy tried not to show that she was tiring him—they had barely begun their battle. He knew he was the better swordsman; he just had to wait her out—or distract her. "You're getting better, Rachel," he called to her.

"You're just getting worse, Seth," she answered back, with a smile. She did not mind talking while fighting; then again, she never minded talking with Seth.

"It's good to practice with someone other than Max. I can predict his every move."

"Stop trying to distract me. It won't work."

He came in with a low attack. She blocked and they stayed close for a moment. "Would it distract you if I told you that you are absolutely beautiful when you wield a sword?"

She knew she was blushing, but could not help it. She spun away from him and readied herself for another attack. "Only if you meant it."

"I do," he replied as he charged towards her.

Rachel had the home field advantage. She knew her yard well, aware of where every dip, every stone and every small hill was. She felt guilty even as she led Seth to a particularly rough spot, where he was sure to twist an ankle, but he deserved it. His tactics had been shameful. That was not to say she had minded.

Just as she predicted, he caught his foot on a rock and swung left. She waited just a moment, and then led with an attack, pushing him back. She cornered him between the siding of her house and the deck. "You've nowhere left to go. Do you surrender?" She smiled. She enjoyed his company. She enjoyed beating him even more. Keeping her blade towards him, she took a moment just to breathe.

"Surrender? To you? Hah!"

He swung his blade down; it collided with hers. He had the greater strength and he saw Rachel begin to inch lower and lower under his pressure. He waited till her balance was off, then jumped away from her, back to level, non-rocky ground.

She spun to face him once more and tried to block as he fought with his full strength. He came in with an attack to her stomach. She did not have time to parry. Seth tried to pull back. He felt the blade hit something. He dropped it instantly, afraid that he had hurt her. She looked down. "Thank goodness for my belt."

"We should stop."

"With you having gotten the last blow. No!"

He laughed. She might not be worried, but he would pull back a little. The last thing he needed was to make her parents feel like they could not trust him with their daughter. Picking up his sword, he waited for her to come towards him.

Rachel did not want to stop yet. She knew the battle would soon be over. She was breathing hard, wishing she had taken her inhaler.

Seth could tell she was panting. His mind flashed back to what seemed like a decade ago. He and Rachel had been sucked into a world patterned after the things they had imagined as children. Running for their lives, somehow Rachel had caught a disease called acena. It had attacked her lungs. He could still see her that day they had been fleeing from a band of minotaurs. She had tried so hard to keep going, but had collapsed before his very eyes. The fear he had felt came rushing back. He had been so sure she was going to die. He still wondered how they had made it. "Are you okay?"

She nodded. "Don't stop."

He was aware of the determination in her voice and eyes. Coming back to reality, he began to duel with her once more.

Seth scanned the area around them, not wanting to allow himself to fall into another trap. Across the street was a doctor's office. Children and nurses had lined up in the windows to watch their duel.

He tried to pay attention to his battle, but his eyes kept flicking back to the windows, wondering if he was scaring the kids.

Rachel took advantage of his distraction. She slipped a leg under his and he began to fall backwards. He grabbed onto her and they both tumbled to the ground, aware that their battle was over. "Cheater!" he laughed, spitting out a mouthful of dirt.

She shrugged, smelling the freshness of the deep green grass, "We said to treat it like a real battle."

They sat up and smiled at each other, dusting themselves off. Seth remarked, "I never expected you to be that much improved since Issym. I can practice with Max, but who do *you* practice with?"

"There is a group that meets at the Y." Rachel stood up and walked to the deck, grabbing her bottle of water and sitting down on a step. Seth joined her. He leaned back and closed his eyes. A slight wind blew across his face.

"Don't worry; the doctor's office is used to weird things going on in this yard," she told him. "I practice all the time and they always watch." She paused, then added, "I know you pulled back. You would have won."

He replied, "In archery, there would be no contest. You're the best."

Rachel, having no response to his compliment, just closed her eyes and thought about their heavenly past week. They had spent the time swinging at the park behind her house, swimming, walking together in the city forest, visiting the scenic places of Maine. It was not what they had done that made the time so wonderful, but that Seth had somehow brought the youth out in her. Even before Issym, she had always acted and felt three years older than she was—despite her imagination and creativity. The responsibilities and thought processes of an older child had always been hers and, before she knew it, youth was gone. When Issym brought on a whole new adulthood, she was sure she would never feel her own age again. But Seth had brought youth out. Not recklessness, but a joy and peace and warmth she was unused to. He made her feel alive.

She replayed the night they had taught her youth group a jig. They had learned it in Issym, at the bonfire after Smolden and his army had been defeated. Her normally 'I don't want to break a nail' fellow youth group attendees had actually gotten into it. It was Seth's presence, she knew. He naturally drew people to himself. Anyone who looked at him knew that he was confident, handsome, destined for bigger things...

She forced herself back into reality, wondering if they had lost track of time. Looking down at her watch, she bolted upright, "I'd better get in the shower. We'll have to leave soon to pick up Max and Tom."

She skipped inside and brushed out her hair. The sword practice had brought her memories back. She and Seth had been friends when they were kids, but he had moved away. When they first reconnected on Issym, he had been awful. Now, she could not imagine her life without him in it, even though he lived hours and hours away.

Their journey on Issym had been a whirlwind. With an evil dragon desperate to get his hands on them so that he could use them to conquer the continent, and his army searching for them at every corner, trust between the two teens had been necessary to develop. Sure, Issym was made up of things they had imagined, but that was when they were kids; they could not remember what they had pretended. They leaned on each other to navigate talking frogs, glowing illuminescents, a troll, a continent-wide earthquake and the like. Meanwhile, the creatures of Issym expected them to save the world. They were just teens. They had not thought they could do it. But they had learned that with God all things are possible.

When they had been on Issym, Rachel had been mad that God had allowed them to get stuck there. Now, she would not have traded that time for anything. Not only did the land and people change her, but what would she do without Seth?

When she got out of the shower, she could hear her friend playing his guitar and singing. She passed by her dad's office, alerted by his posture that he was intently listening to Seth's playing. Her dad had a hard time enjoying music; he spent most of his time critiquing it. But he was enjoying this. That made Rachel smile.

She joined Seth on the couch. He put down the guitar. "Don't you need to practice?" she asked. Seth was the lead singer in a band made up of his friend Max and his pastor's son, Tom. They had been growing in popularity and had come up to Maine to play for several events. Seth had wanted to come up early to spend some time with Rachel. She had not protested.

Her dad walked in, "We should get to the bus station."

She glanced at her watch, "You're right."

"Can I help you with that, Mr. Cottrun?" Seth asked as they walked out and saw him taking a large box from the back of the jeep.

Handing the box to Seth, Mr. Cottrun said, "It goes in the garage."

Rachel let Seth sit up front. As they pulled out of the driveway, Mr. Cottrun asked, "Grab me a pen from the glove box?"

As Seth opened it, a chaos of papers fell onto his lap. Stumbling to fit them back in, Seth saw a medal. "What's this?" he inquired, fingering it.

"She didn't tell you?" Mr. Cottrun answered.

"Tell me what?" he glanced back inquisitively.

"She's a hero!" Her dad was proud to boast. "She was babysitting a couple of girls when a lightning bolt started a fire in the house. She dragged them both out a window and a safe distance from the house before collapsing herself. It was a couple of days in ICU before she woke up. The mayor awarded her the medal for exceptional courage."

Seth put the medal back and pulled out the pen. He knew why Rachel kept it buried. "Pretty remarkable," he declared.

The proud father was not finished, "She tried to refuse it; said she did not remember rescuing them. But who else could have done it?"

Looking back at Rachel, he saw that she was shouting at him through her eyes. She had not rescued the children; at least, not that way. And the girl hated falsely accepting an award, hated lying to her parents, hated having to keep a big part of her life a secret. He said to her, "I know. But you *are* a hero."

Chapter 4

Bridget was seen by some as no better than the dwarves and the humans who worked for Sasha. Certainly she was not the typical prisoner kept in Maremoth, Sasha's fortress on Asandra. She worked, ate and slept with the others, but Bridget had a special rapport with the guards.

She had been captured by Sasha fifteen years ago, the longest living prisoner in captivity at Maremoth. She was ten years old at the time. Bridget had watched guards come and ago; helped build and tear down buildings; met Sasha face to face on more than one occasion; and seen the coming and passing of many prisoners. Because she had been around for so long, she had formed a friendly relationship with many of the guards. They said good morning to her, asked her how she was, told her about their families and often did favors for her. Her plate of food seemed always to have a piece of meat or bread on it, which she gladly shared with the other prisoners. If someone was sick, she could convince one of the guards to bring her medicines. And sometimes, she could get the guards' old clothes to keep them all from freezing through the winter months.

So she was a very helpful person to know, but some thought that she was *too* close to the guards. These were people who were bitter that they were stuck in Maremoth, like Josiah. He had been there for five years and he hated how content Bridget seemed to be. He knew that she was kind to the infirm, the old and the children. He knew that she gave of herself for others. Still, how could she smile in a place like Sasha's fortress?

Josiah knew it was foolish, but every kind word that came out of her mouth made him gag. Was it because he didn't believe she was genuinely that good a person? Or because he *knew* she was and he wasn't?

Josiah saw her walking his way with her plate of food that night. It had been a long day—the guards had been particularly harsh and he had been yelled at and whipped all day long. Why did Bridget have to bother him? Didn't she know that he hated her?

"Brooks was generous tonight," she informed him, speaking of one of the guards, a young man about their age. She brushed her long brown hair back with one hand and held her plate out with the other, "Take some."

"I don't need your charity," he spat. Surely his scowl and harsh tone would drive her away.

"No you do not. But wouldn't you like some extra food? You had it rough today."

So she had noticed. She seemed to notice everything. Even though she knew how cruel the guards were, she just smiled. "Take your happiness somewhere else."

"Is my smile that offensive?" she sat down.

"You're a traitor Bridget. You smile at me *and* the guards. Don't you get it? These people are our enemies and you're their friend. That makes you our enemy too!"

"Do you honestly think I want to be nice to the people who imprison us?"

"Then why do you do it?"

She gave the only answer she could, "The Bible says to love your enemies."

The Bible. Her God. The reason for that uncomfortable joy she always carried around with her.

If God really existed, why would Sasha be allowed to take over Asandra? If God really existed and loved the world, why would she be in captivity? And if God really took care of 'His people', then why would Bridget have been a prisoner for the longest of all the people in Maremoth? She kept His laws as closely as she could. Surely she was His most faithful follower. Why would God not rescue her?

Rachel saw Max step off the bus, with a younger teen who she guessed was Tom. Max said something to Tom and to the two oddly-dressed teens behind them. Then he alone approached Rachel, Seth and Mr. Cottrun.

Seth recognized impatient anticipation on Max's face. As soon as Mr. Cottrun went to put Max's bags in the back of the jeep, Max blurted out as quietly and quickly as he could, "Rachel, I've told Tom that those two teenagers, there, are friends of yours."

"I've never seen them before in my life…" Rachel protested.

"Of course not. Because they are not from *around* here…" Seth wondered if Rachel was as confused as he was. "They are from Asandra."

Rachel laughed, "Stop kidding around. You actually had me going for a second." His face did not have a hint of humor in it. Rachel's cheeks lost all color, and then it all came rushing back. "You're serious? What am I supposed to tell my dad?" She was talking more to herself than to Max.

"Their names are Katarina and Evan," Max answered as if that explained everything.

He waved to Tom, Kat and Evan and they walked over. Mr. Cottrun returned, only to be tugged by Rachel to the other side of the car. With a smirk on his face he asked, "Is this about Seth?"

"Dad!" she rolled her eyes, then turned serious. "I didn't know it, but Max brought along two extra people." She put her hand on his forearm and looked up at him, "Can they just stay the night?"

Her look reminded him of when she was a four-year-old, asking for an ice cream after a fishing trip. He was as helpless to refuse her now as he had been then. He replied, "I'll tell your mother. But we don't have room for everyone in the jeep."

"We'll walk," she answered holding back a sigh of relief.

As she moved back to her friends, a thousand thoughts and questions flooded her mind, but she waited to ask them until they were on the sidewalk of the busy road. Evan drew Tom to the back of the group so that Katarina and Max could talk with Seth and Rachel. Seth kept one ear tuned to Tom and Evan, wanting to be sure Tom did not feel forgotten.

Katarina filled them in, then added, "Max said that Sasha is dead. We need to know if that is true."

Seth allowed his mind go back to those few moments before Sasha had died. Exhausted and bloodied from defeating Smolden the dragon, he had gone to find Rachel. She was nowhere to be seen.

Just in time, he found her. He was surprised that he had no

fear when he saw the dagger aimed at Rachel's heart—at least not a fear he was familiar with. It was more like pain—sharp and deep in *his* chest. But when the woman holding the dagger moved towards him, the pain left. He would be glad to take the blow for Rachel, but he doubted he would have to. She was resourceful, a skilled fighter and a true friend. She would not run; she would figure something out.

And Rachel did. She reached for an artifact on the wall. Drawing the bow, she shot the woman who was mere inches from Seth. She fell to the ground, dead. Definitely dead. And definitely Sasha—Seth would have known the shifter's presence even if Rachel had not told him who it was. The weight of evil had filled the room.

He knew this memory like he knew no other. He would play it back in his mind over and over again when a nightmare came that Sasha lived: that she kidnapped his parents or killed Rachel and Max or conquered Issym. This was the memory that he *had* to believe was truth. He spoke: "She is dead."

"Are you sure?" Katarina pursued.

Rachel wanted to shut the whole subject up. Thoughts of Sasha always made her dizzy. "Whether she is alive or dead makes no difference. Asandra needs our help. Seth, you in?"

It felt nice to be asked if he wanted to go into a mystical world, unlike last time. He nodded, "When are we leaving?"

"As soon as possible," Katarina replied.

"How did you get here?"

"An illuminescent."

"They can do that?" Rachel asked.

Rachel skipped up the stairs to her bedroom. Asandra. They were really going to Asandra.

"Ruby," she buzzed in the illuminescent language as she entered her room. The little red creature flew from under the bed and rubbed up against Rachel's cheek. The teen had grown used to the static discharge she received. "I have a surprise for you," Rachel mused.

Zara flew from her hiding place behind Rachel. Ruby sent sparks flying with joy. She buzzed and purred, but Zara hovered completely still, simply saying, "It is true then. There are other illuminescents."

"Rachel!" her mom hollered her name up the stairs.

"Coming!" She left the two to get to know each other.

"What's up?" she asked coming half-way down the stairs.

"I see we have extra company," Rachel's mom inquired. "Tell me about them."

"They came with Max and Tom from New York…" Rachel hoped that answer would work again.

"Yes, but how do you know them?" her mom persisted.

"I haven't known them very long… They know Seth and I. They actually went to New York to look for him. When they heard that he was here, they hoped I wouldn't mind putting them up for the night. They'll be gone by tomorrow."

"You still haven't answered how you met them…"

Rachel knew that her mom was only asking the questions because she loved her; but the teen could not help getting annoyed at her insistence. Then again, maybe she should tell her mom about Xsardis, but she knew how insane she would sound. "The same way I know Max…"

"Because of Seth, who randomly sent you a letter one day… Rachel, if I did not know better, I would say that you are hiding something."

"Mom…" Rachel was mere seconds away from telling her the truth.

"Okay, okay. Backing off."

"Don't worry." *Don't worry, Mom, I'm only about to travel to an imaginary world and join in a war!* Rachel thought.

Her mother let her walk back to her room, figuring they would talk more later.

"Okay Ruby," Rachel declared, with much less enthusiasm. "You've got some stuff to explain."

"Like what?" Ruby asked.

"Zara brought Katarina and Evan to Earth. Could you have taken me back to Xsardis?"

"Yes! Can we go back now?"

"Probably. When we were brought to Issym because of Universe Girl's…" She flinched at the pathetic name she had given her, glad that the young woman had chosen to be called by her first name—Ethelwyn, "…orbs, our bodies stayed on Earth. Will it be the same when you take us?" Rachel asked the question, but barely listened to the answer.

She remembered walking into Universe Girl's castle after she and Seth had been running and fighting for their lives for what seemed like months. Ethelwyn had many orbs, each with a universe in it. The right orb could take them home. And then they had received terrible news that was almost too much to bear. The orb they needed had been stolen. They were stuck on Issym, perhaps forever.

"Nope!" Ruby exclaimed. "Not the same."

Zara's voice was monotonous, "Your bodies will disappear from Earth and reappear in Asandra."

But Rachel's mind was still on the memory. What if they got stuck on Xsardis again? Her parents would never know what had happened to her. She had to tell them what was going on. "Stay here," she ordered the illuminescents.

Rachel walked down the steps. She rounded the corner into the living room and bumped into Seth. "Sorry."

Seth moved them away from the living room and into the hallway, quietly saying, "Max and I think we should leave Tom here. We don't need more people knowing our secret."

"Seth, I really think we should tell our parents about Xsardis…"

"No way!" Max stepped into the hallway.

"I think we should go in the middle of the night. Time isn't the same here as it is there. We were on Issym for a long time, but only eight hours passed here," Seth had already moved on from Rachel's concerns. "That should minimize the risks of your parents finding out."

"It sounds like travel with the illuminescents will be different. More time may pass. We should tell my parents now."

"No," Max was adamant.

"We don't have time to deal with this right now. If they discover we are gone, when we return, we will explain." Seth was decisive. Rachel liked that about him. But she did not like that he was ignoring the fact that she *needed* to tell her parents. She remembered the way he had treated her before in order to please Max, and Rachel worried that he was going to shove her, her thoughts, and her needs aside again. But they had all changed since their adventure in Issym. She tried to swallow her fears.

"We'll go to bed around ten. It's early, considering it is summer, but we'll convince Tom that we need a good night's rest before our performance tomorrow. At eleven thirty we'll meet in the kitchen. Okay?"

"Great," Max liked the plan.

"Okay." Rachel hoped to get Seth alone and talk to him about her concerns later.

Max, Evan, Tom and Seth were 'sleeping' in the living room. Kat and Rachel were 'sleeping' in her room. Rachel hoped that she could ask Katarina some questions about Asandra.

Issym was made up of Rachel and Seth's creations, but mostly Seth's. Asandra was only her imagination. Her stomach flipped with the thrill of going to a place she loved so well, but had only ever seen in her mind's eye.

"So, what's Asandra like?" Rachel, sitting on her bed with her knees curled under her chin, inquired of Kat.

"Nothing like Earth!" The way she said the words, Katarina made it sound like Asandra was a palace and Earth was a dumpster. Rachel immediately got protective of her home world, but then again, Kat must have been praising her imagination.

Rachel waited for her to say more, but she did not. "How many people live there?"

"A lot."

"Just humans?"

"The dwarves abandoned us."

"What about other species?"

"There are some others," she answered with an edge to her voice.

Rachel decided not to press the issue. Kat's curt answers obviously were meant to end the conversation. No point in making enemies.

She pulled out a simple canvas bag and put in a few things she had wished she had had the last time she was on Xsardis—a toothbrush, toothpaste, a scrunchy, her inhaler... She changed into a pair of pants and a shirt. Her father had teased her that they made her looked like she belonged in a Renaissance Fair. Finally, she put on a necklace. Fingering the vial full of blue dust, she remembered being afraid as she woke up on Issym in a cave with a troll. But as he told her how the necklace he had given her contained the last tears of his beloved fairy as she died, she discovered that though the troll's appearance was fearsome, he was gentle and kind. The necklace of his love had saved Rachel from the acena virus.

It was 11:30 PM. They slipped out of her room, the two illuminescents following. Rachel hesitated by her parent's door. She could just go in, show them Ruby, tell them everything.

"Come on!" Kat hissed. Rachel walked on, disappointed in herself even as she did.

The boys were waiting in the kitchen. Tom was not with them. Good. They said nothing as Zara and Ruby showered them with dust.

Chapter 5

When the five teenagers emerged on Asandra, they were surrounded by complete darkness, except for the glowing of the illuminescents. In less than a moment's time, Rachel felt something in her hand. It lit up with fire and she saw that it was a torch. She looked at Ruby. The creature still had a few left-over sparks hovering around her from generating it. Evan also held a torch.

Max, Rachel and Seth felt their adrenaline pumping. This was the adventure they had spent their days and nights dreaming of since they had left Issym. Soon they would be seated before royalty, discussing how to save the world. They were determined to make this trip different from their previous one. They were not going to be hunted; they were not going to let fear move them. They were going to perform an amazing feat and go home heroes.

Rachel noticed that the illuminescents were flying lower than normal and their glowing was not quite as bright. "Are you alright?" she whispered, still unsure of their surroundings.

"Transportation takes a lot out of us," Ruby answered.

As their eyes grew used to the light, the group looked around them. The ceiling was low and muddy. It certainly looked like they were in an underground room. Max squirmed uncomfortably. His brain was telling him he was not supposed to be there. He needed to get out. It reminded him of the underground of Issym. He had learned a lot there, but nothing would make him go back. "Where are we?" he asked, reaching instinctively for the sword that was not there. Only Seth and Rachel carried their blades.

"Home." The word came softly out of Evan's mouth, as if glad, sad and worried all at the same time. Glad, because he was home; sad, because his home was a tunnel; and worried, because his home should not be this quiet or dark.

Katarina and Evan realized that they were standing next to the door in their mother's chambers. They were in the exact same place they were in when they left for Earth, but the room was barely recognizable. Papers, clothing, jewelry and other items were scattered about the room. The desk had been overturned. The bed's straw mattress had been ripped apart and the straw covered the floor. The color of Kat and Evan's faces drained. The princess broke the eerie stillness as she dashed out of the room, looking for someone, anyone. Evan did not move, but stared around him, studying every detail. His sister's voice could be heard shouting, "Mother! Anyone! Hello!" Her voice got louder and higher pitched with each call, terror seeping through her voice.

Katarina came running back into the room. "I can't find anyone!" she exclaimed to her brother—for a change, looking for someone else's guidance.

Evan stepped into her space. "Sasha found us out. Mother must have known this was coming. That was why she sent us to Earth."

"So now, Sasha," Katarina spit at the name, "has both the king and the queen!"

Tension was high. Seth tried to mask the danger, but he felt it keenly, "We should get out of here. It's not safe. The enemy could come back."

Rachel looked at Seth and Max, "You guys really need to change out of your modern clothes."

Sifting through the chaos, the teens pulled out the weapons and the clothes they could find and then hurried out into the woods. They did not have a direction; they only knew that they had to keep moving and that they *could not* get caught.

What were they to do? Where were they to go? The stronghold of resistance against Sasha had been defeated. The woman who had sent for them was gone. They were just five teenagers trying to save a continent. It was impossible.

Seth, Rachel and Max found that the adrenaline of being heroes on the run was fading as the fear that was their old companion came rushing back. They were alone. They were unfamiliar with the land. They were afraid. They were hunted.

For hours they stumbled through the woods, instinct driving their movements. They knew they had to put distance between themselves and Kat and Evan's home-turned-nightmare. Finally, they rested in a small clearing. The trees towered above them, admitting very little of the morning light.

"So." Max waited only a few moments before speaking. "What's next?" He was ready to prove himself.

"Next? Just like that? Those were our friends!" Katarina shouted at him.

Evan wanted the time to grieve and worry, but he came to Max's aid, "He's right. We can't just sit here."

"So, Heroes, what do you want from us?" Katarina mocked the three teens from Earth.

"You could start with giving us some more information," Rachel ignored Kat's tone.

"What do you need to know?" Evan answered, looking Rachel in the eye.

"What will they do with your mother?" Seth asked.

The prince sighed. "They will take her to Maremoth, Sasha's fortress. It is at the northern-most point of Asandra. We're about here," Evan drew a rough sketch of the continent in the dirt with his dagger. "In the middle. Sasha will make her execution public—it may be a few days or a few weeks from now."

"We have to go there now and try to save her," the princess was adamant.

"We just can't make an attack on the fortress," Max stated. "We need to raise your people's support first, like in Issym."

"You think we haven't tried that?" Katarina snapped back. "We didn't bring you guys here because we have absolutely no idea how to conduct a war."

"You didn't ask me to come at all," Max laughed, amused by how hotheaded this princess was.

"It's not as easy as you think," Evan replied. "Years ago, Sasha went to the island of Noric—where the dwarves live. She won over five hundred of them and had them build her fortress. She promised us peace, said that she was just 'coming home.' We did nothing to stop her. That was back when my father first became king."

Katarina shot him a warning glance, but let him go on, "He was a great dad, but not much of a king—in the people's eyes. He spent more time with us than he did ruling. And whoever came to him with a sad story received money. It depleted the treasury so he had to raise the taxes. It did not make him popular."

"What my brother is trying to say," Katarina could not keep silent, "is that Sasha started by taking over the towns that actually wanted her as their ruler. The very day my father had decided to fight back was the day our army captain took the troops and started working for Sasha." Her voice grew quieter, "That was the day we went into hiding."

Evan added, "After that, Sasha sent her army to the towns most loyal to us, captured our people and used them as forced labor in Maremoth. All the towns pay heavy taxes and if anyone disagrees with her, the townspeople offer them as slaves to Sasha."

"Is that what happened to your father?"

Katarina found her voice to say, "He was visiting an old friend when Sasha's soldiers arrested the entire household. Apparently the man had been a little too outspoken in his support of the king. Dad was wearing simple clothing. Sasha had no idea whom she had captured."

Evan solemnly declared, "We are not fighting to keep Asandra; we are fighting to get it back. And even if we succeed, the people may not want to live under us."

They were silent; everyone thinking. Rachel felt more pressure than anyone. This was her continent; she was supposed to have an answer. "We need to know Sasha's weak points. We need to know who is left that is loyal to your family. I remember imagining that there was a man who kept history and who gathered as much information as he could. Is he on Asandra, or does he have a descendant we could speak to?"

"There is a man named Joppa... a history keeper," Evan answered.

"Is he still loyal to your family?" Max asked.

"Joppa is an old fool. If you asked him that, he would say he is loyal to the truth," Katarina quipped.

"But because we are the lawful prince and princess he will support us," Evan added. "He is said to live in a great tree, about a two day journey from here."

Max was ready to stop talking and start doing. "Let's go."

Max looked skeptically at the tan blob on the stick in his hand and put it over the fire again. "You said this was edible?"

Rachel laughed. She was wondering the same thing, but forced herself to take a small nibble. Though it looked like alien batter, it tasted like normal bread. "Manna..." she muttered, remembering the day she had imagined it. She had just finished reading about how God gave the Israelites bread from Heaven when they were hungry in the desert. She put into an adventure that a goop-like substance grew on a reed by the water with no tending. It could be eaten raw or baked for bread. It was traveler's food.

"Be grateful," Katarina told Max. "If we were by a town, we would be starving right now. Manna doesn't last long."

"But it grows back so fast," Rachel pondered.

"Everybody's strapped for food. When they harvest it, they leave hardly enough for it to replenish itself."

"They have little choice," the prince spoke on behalf of his people. "They have to feed their families."

Max braced himself and took a bite. Then realizing that it tasted like slightly sweetened bread, he devoured his share. Trouble always made him hungry and after spending a day of hiking and hearing about all of Asandra's problems, he was keenly aware of just how much trouble they were in.

It was cold—either winter was passing or just arriving. He lay down as closely as he could to the fire; his screaming muscles not comforted by the tough ground. He'd gotten out of shape, relishing the more relaxing summer months.

Max heard Rachel sigh as she also tried to find a comfortable position. Her face looked weary. "Hey," he whispered, even though everyone else could hear him.

She opened her eyes and he said, "Xsardis is filled with such strange things. It makes me kind of wish that I had spent more time imagining."

She nodded, "Yeah; but it is pretty weird to have some of your imaginations hail you as a hero and the others try to kill you."

"You know, Seth and I aren't going to quit until Asandra's free."

Rachel smiled. Max—the once trouble-maker—was being a good friend. "I know."

Bridget dropped to the ground as darkness fell over the land. "Most people just try to survive here," an old man turned towards her with a smile, "but that's just not good enough for you."

The woman took a sip from her water and let him add, "You appeased the anger of scores of guards and saved many of our fellows today."

She shrugged, "Nicholas, the guards listen to me. If I did not use that to help others, what good would I be?"

Eating the food on her plate, she studied Nicholas. She could almost see a fuller face, a less crooked posture and a crown on his head—King Remar. She had had her suspicions about him since he had first arrived, but with every day she became more certain that this was her king. There was no doubt in her mind that this was no simple peasant. He would tell her the truth one day, when he was ready.

"How young were you when you came here?" he asked.

She paused. It was a strange change in the conversation. "Ten."

"Probably too young to have regrets about life before this dungeon?"

"No; not too young." She had plenty of regrets, but why did they matter? "Do you have regrets?"

He scratched at his long, brown and gray beard. "Plenty." He stopped, then found his voice to say, "Lately, those regrets have been about my children. I did not have enough time to fully train them. And I have a feeling that they are about to embark on a journey that will decide the fate of us all."

Chapter 6

There it was. Joppa's legendary tree. Even Rachel, its imaginer, could hardly believe the size of it. Then again, it made sense. As a child she had always loved to imagine bigger and bigger. When her mother had painted her room as a garden, Rachel had made her repaint the tree to be wide as her arm span. Only then had it satisfied her. Joppa's tree was the epitome of that creativity.

Looking at the tree whose leaves the cold had already stripped away, Max realized that winter was coming. They were going to do all this traveling in the dead of winter.

Seth surveyed the light-wooded tree, looking for an entrance. Even the lowest branch was well above what he could reach. He laughed and raised a curious eyebrow towards Rachel, "You made him live in an enormous tree?"

She shoved him, "Oh, like your creations were any cooler!"

Rachel reached up. The branch was just beyond her reach. She felt Seth give her a boost; her arms gripped around the branch. From there she began her climb. The others followed, scaling the different sides of the tree in an attempt to find an entrance.

"Are you sure we are in the right place?" Max asked Rachel, swatting at Ruby who had absentmindedly flown too close to his head. The illuminescent was getting on his nerves.

Rachel pushed on a slit in the wood. The bark fell inward. All she could see inside was darkness. Carefully putting her body in the ledge, she reached her feet down and touched a walkway of planks.

She could not help feeling like she was being swallowed by a monster as she lowered her frame. As her eyes adjusted to the darkness she distinguished the faint glow of torches. There was a slope to the planks that led up and down. Bookshelves filled the walls. Ruby and Zara's red bodies stood out in the darkness.

"Hello," her voice echoed as Seth and Katarina joined her. Evan and Max were not far behind.

Evan moved towards one of the shelves and pulled a thick book from it. Blowing off the dust, he began to read the carefully written script. "We are in the right place," he answered the question Max had asked outside—what seemed a different reality.

"Anyone home?" Seth called, touching the rope that was the only barrier between him and falling to the dark stillness below.

Max wandered down the planked-slope until he reached the bottom. Two straw mattresses—one bed made, the other not— lay on the dried-mud floor, with a desk that was cluttered with papers and books beside each one. A cooking area showed the remnants of the last meal. With a stick he poked at the ash, revealing a few leftover embers. "Whoever lives here has not been gone long," Seth remarked, as he joined Max. He rebuilt the fire to chase away the cold as the others took a seat on the beds and chairs.

"This place doesn't look ransacked," Max pulled off his too-small boot. "Joppa, or whoever, should be back, right?"

Katarina nodded, "I would think. You can be sure that Sasha does not know about this place."

"And how do we know that?" Max replaced his boot.

Evan replied, "Knowledge is one of evil's greatest fears. They would have destroyed the library."

A girl, about thirteen, landed gracefully before them. An empty rope swung overhead. Without hesitation, she questioned them, "Who are you?"

"Travelers," Seth told her—irritated that for safety's sake he could not tell her his name. "Come to seek Joppa the historian."

"You have come to the right place, but I am sorry, Joppa is not here," the girl responded as she turned her back from them and rearranged the books on the shelves.

"When will he be back?" Katarina asked.

"Joppa gave himself up to Sasha—sacrificing himself so that the shifter would give up the hunt for him and not find this tree or his beloved niece."

Her skin was fair and dark. She was a little shorter than five feet and very thin. Her black hair hung in front of her eyes.

"Do you live here alone?" Seth asked with concern, guessing

that this was Joppa's niece.

"Someone has to keep history. I am Reesthma. I have answered your questions. Now will you tell me who you are?"

She seemed trustworthy. They introduced themselves and her face lit up. "I am honored to meet you!" she exclaimed at least a dozen times.

"We are looking for any history that would be useful in our struggle against Sasha," said Rachel.

"I've read almost every scroll in this tree. I have lived here since I was two. I can help you find the information you seek!"

Seth pushed a few scrolls towards the back of the desk and revealed a map of Asandra. Rachel leaned beside him to look it over.

"Reesthma," Rachel started, still looking over the map. The girl, who had been sweeping around books and clothes and dishes in an effort to clean up, hastened to Rachel's side. "Why are some villages' names circled?"

"They are the ones who are still loyal to the royal family."

"The ones that are circled?" Reesthma nodded. Rachel and Seth stared in disbelief. "Only four?"

"So few?" Seth breathed in sharply.

Evan and Katarina shifted uncomfortably.

Reesthma went on, "You will find loyal people in every village, but in all the villages not marked, it is not safe to say who you are. People are looking to appease Sasha—nothing would make her happier than to have you. Seth, Rachel—Sasha cannot know that you are here! So far, no one in Asandra has been able to stand up to her, but you did!"

Max smirked as he saw Katarina glare at Reesthma. Seeing his expression, she moved towards him to whisper to him, "Some defeat; they thought she was dead!"

"We're not even sure she's alive," he retorted.

Reesthma pointed to a village on the west coast. "The queen is hiding here—in Illen."

"What?" The question squeaked out of Katarina in a tone of emotion she rarely used.

"Queen Juliet learned that Sasha knew where she was hiding. She fled to Illen," Reesthma repeated.

"Our first step has to be to get to her," Katarina decided.

"No," Rachel replied. "Illen is more than a week's ride away, and we'll be walking, so I can only imagine how long it will take us."

"We have to get to the queen," Kat was adamant, and indignant that anyone would dare to fight with her. "She summoned you here after all. Or did you forget that?"

"We'll make our way towards Illen, raising the villages support as we go."

Evan saw his sister's blood boiling and stepped in to stop her from making enemies of their only friends, "What she is trying to say is that my mother would not have brought you here unless she had a plan of what to do."

"I think they're right, Rachel," Seth put in. "*We* didn't even go to the villages of Issym—Flibbert did."

Reesthma spoke, "The people are submitting to Sasha. They think they are protecting their families. And she *is* gaining more power every day. They have a right to be scared."

"If that's true then we can't waste our time traveling to Illen," Rachel came back.

"You walk away from your messes! Who are you to tell us how to spend our time?" Katarina stared Rachel down.

We haven't known each other long enough to be quarreling, Seth thought. *This is what our enemy would want.* "Rach," he got her attention, "this is the right thing."

Rachel bit down hard on her tongue, tired of Katarina's attitude. When she was on Issym, she had played by everyone else's rules, but now they were on *her* Asandra. She wanted to protect it; she wanted to meet its people, feel its pulse and sets things right. But, sensing everyone else's will and Seth's certainty, she nodded her consent.

As Bridget washed the floor of the balcony overlooking Maremoth, she watched the dwarven chief of Maremoth—Malcon—torment the others. In the years Sasha had been gone, he had rarely been seen, living in the house the slaves had built for him a mile up the road. He had taken a few key prisoners there; Joppa, the historian, was the most important. Why he took them, she had no idea. His sudden, unexplained return to Maremoth, and the urgency with which he had them work, told Bridget one thing: Sasha was coming back.

Finishing the balcony, she returned to Sasha's living room and began to scrub out a stain Malcon had put in the carpet. The thud of his boots came up behind her but she did not turn. "Scrub harder," he commanded.

"If I scrub any harder I'll put a hole through it." Maybe that was what he wanted. Then the traces of the stain would be gone and he could blame Bridget for the problem.

His growl was animal-like. Malcon was spooked. For a year and a half they had believed Sasha to be dead. And because he thought she was dead, he had acted like king of Maremoth, doing things she would never have allowed him to do. One look between the dwarf and the servant and they both knew what the other was thinking: *if Sasha had lost a battle, her anger would be inconsolable.*

Bridget promised him, "I'll do my best."

For one moment the two creatures from opposite sides of the world stood together. But Bridget was unnerved by this and quickly asked, "How soon will she be here?"

"Any day now. You *will* have this ready."

By dinner, Bridget was done. She took food only to seem normal and headed straight for Nicholas. "What's wrong?" he asked seeing her face full of gloom.

"Sasha's alive and coming back."

"Malcon told you this?"

Nodding, she said, "I used to work in her palace. Malcon wants me to get everything back to the way she had left it."

"Well, now we know why Malcon worked us so hard today."

"Nicholas," she whispered urgently to get his wandering attention back. "If she really lost a battle on Issym, she will be anxious to prove that she should still rule Asandra. She knows the king is within these walls; she will search him out and kill him. It will be very hard for him to stay alive."

"I'm sure he knew that one day this was coming."

"The king, wherever he is, should try to make his escape now. Once she's back, there will be no chance."

"The guards are on high alert, expecting her return; there is no escape."

Chapter 7

Max gripped his horse's neck to stay on it. Riding was harder than it looked. He was sorry Reesthma had directed them to a farm that was selling their animals, even though he was tired of walking. No one else seemed to be struggling with their horse. Seth seemed so comfortable on his that he was, once again, lost in thought—probably about Reesthma who had refused to come with them. Seth never left people behind, but Reesthma had insisted that she belonged with history.

Max felt something rough hit his head and, turning to look, he saw the mischievous glint in Rachel's eyes. "Hey!" he shouted at her with a hidden smile.

She stuck her tongue out and threw another pine cone. Slowing his horse so that he could reach a twig, he chucked it at her. Rachel ducked, but the branch's moss scattered throughout her hair. Laughing, she picked the pieces out and threw some leaves towards him—most of them missed.

Max had turned his body from her, hiding something. By the time she realized what he was doing it was too late. Water splashed from his canteen onto her. "Oh! You are so dead!" She moved her horse closer to his and dumped the contents of her flask on him.

"You two are so juvenile," Seth mocked them.

Rachel and Max held each other's glances for a moment, then shot all their ammo in his direction. Seth laughed as he returned a volley of his own.

Katarina turned towards them on her horse and shouted, "Stop it! This isn't playtime. Don't you realize what's going on around you?"

All the joy was sucked out of the air.

"We came to get you; and our home was destroyed because we weren't there to defend it. This is your fault."

"You're blaming us again?" Rachel retorted.

"Why anyone would think you are a hero is a mystery to me. From what you've told me, you didn't even risk your precious life in the battle against Smolden."

That hit Rachel's nerve. She could feel herself grow suddenly cold while an ache covered her.

The princess continued, "And your stupidity left Sasha alive to terrorize us. You were on Xsardis before and you did nothing for *my* people!"

Evan rode up beside her, "Katarina, stop!"

Ruby rubbed against Rachel's cheek to offer a little comfort, while Seth informed Katarina, "When we asked her to stay behind, she chose to do the right thing. She helped stop Sasha from destroying the innocents we had left behind. Rachel risked everything for Issym; and now she risks it for Asandra, despite how you seem not to want us around."

Rachel was glad when the day was finally over and she could curl up on the ground. Ruby's bright figure landed on the teen's stomach, sending tingles across it. Rachel was unaware that Ruby was using her ability to induce sleep to help Rachel rest.

Seth took first watch. Zara and Ruby would guard over them the rest of the night.

The group rose early and continued their journey to Illen. "According to the map Reesthma gave me, there is a village about a mile away," Seth announced. "We'll have to get off the path to avoid it. We really should dodge any people we can."

'Getting off the path' made for slow walking and loud protests from the horses as they coaxed them through the thick brush. The late morning air was cold, but the effort it took to move through the ever deepening forest made both humans and animals sweat. With their swords they cut at the entwined bushes that blocked their path. Carefully they stepped over trees that lightning and decay had caused to fall to the ground.

Seth and Evan led. Rachel stayed a fair distance back with the illuminescents, finding the easiest way forward. Max and Katarina were almost out of eye sight. The princess told him, "If they had listened to me, we wouldn't be lost now."

Max, eager for her friendship, agreed. Katarina, pouncing on his understanding, kept complaining.

A shadow came over Rachel as her mind repeated Katarina's words: *You didn't even risk your precious life in the battle against Smolden. And your stupidity left Sasha alive to terrorize us. You were on Xsardis before and you did nothing for my people!*

A frustrated tear rolled down Rachel's cheek. Was that how Issym saw her? Was that how Asandra, her imaginations, saw her?

Seth and Evan passed the map back and forth. Having decided that they were past the village, they were looking to get back to the path. But after endless searching and the heavy tension that was radiating from Max, Katarina and Rachel, Evan said, "Let's stop."

Seth called back to the others, "We're going to take a break."

When Rachel and the illuminescents caught up, she looked at the map while Zara flew high into the air until she could not be seen. "Just how lost are we?" Max asked when he reached them.

Zara returned in time to save Seth and Evan from answering. "The path is that way."

The creature kept a grin hidden as it thudded out of the fortress. The people were scattering from its presence. It fed off their fear. It moved towards the palace, encountering mostly dwarves, who were less frightened but still significantly tense. They knew what it was.

It slowed down. One paw after the other it walked with authority, higher and higher up through the palace. Entering the throne room and seeing a fat dwarf on the throne, it let off a low growl. Instantly it pounced, knocking the dwarf to the ground. As the creature kept him pinned with the weight of its considerable mass, it snarled its vicious teeth and leaned in close for the kill.

But the creature disappeared and a woman dressed in expensive clothing sat on the throne, holding a sword and moving it through the air as if it belonged to her body. The dwarf jumped to his feet and scampered to the door, attempting to make an escape. "If you run, I will kill you," the woman said firmly.

The dwarf stopped. He swallowed hard, then turned with a bow and approached the woman. "Empress Sasha. I had been told to expect your coming and was checking to make sure that your chair was still strong," he excused himself. He had been savoring his last minute in the seat of power.

"Prove to me you deserve to live, Malcon," she responded, still gripping the sword and ready to strike. "You have always been a poor liar."

Malcon glanced around the room for some kind of help. He saw bare walls, the elevated throne and a balcony. His eyes lingered there, but dismissed the idea of jumping. "Only just this morning, my men sent word that they had captured Queen Juliet," he managed, his mind racing. The historian would have to die. He had sworn that Sasha was dead. She certainly was not.

His empress moved towards him, sword extended. He fell to his knees, closed his eyes and waited to feel the cold blade strike him down. Instead, he heard her voice say, "When will the elusive queen be here?"

"Tomorrow or the next day," the dwarf replied, forcing his eyes open.

"Are you lying to me, Malcon?" she asked, settling herself on her throne.

"N...no, Empress," he stammered, glancing once again towards the balcony. If he could make the jump, the darkness of the night might buy him enough time to...

"Then report to me where my army stands."

Malcon knew he was not out of trouble yet. Once she discovered exactly what he had been doing in her absence... "Things are going excellently. So many of the towns have given us their loyalty. Your army has been building."

"Very little; and the number of slaves seems the same."

"The villages support you; we did not need to take slaves."

"You have so much to learn, Malcon, and I have such little patience." She rose, walking towards him, the sword back in her hand. "A leader needs slaves. Do you doubt me as leader?" She tapped his stomach with the blade.

"We shall get you more slaves."

"Good. Now get out."

As she walked about her rooms, Sasha pondered her next steps. She had had three goals in Issym. The first was Smolden's death. The second was to have Issym under her control. And the third was eternal youth. Smolden was dead, but Issym was free. At least, she had contented herself, the dragon had given her youth. She had gone to the island of Noric, as he had said, but she had not found the secret. Even in death the dragon had mocked her. And yet, she knew there must be a way. She could feel it. A powerful source of some kind, somewhere in the world. She had to find it. She would.

Asandra 58

Chapter 8

"Are we in the right place?" Rachel looked over the clay houses that were supposed to have withstood Sasha's grasp. Where was the fortress? Where were the lookouts? Where were the armed guards to stop them as they walked into the bustling city center? This was one of the few towns that were safe from Sasha—safe enough that Queen Juliet would choose to hide here?

Evan nodded, "Yes."

They hoped to go unnoticed. Five dirty, out of town teenagers, however, drew the eyes of many villagers. They moved quickly towards the inn and tethered their horses outside. Sitting at a table between the door and the bar, Seth could not help feeling like they were walking into a trap. He surveyed the room for any signs of danger, but the only other people in the dimly lit area were the owner, and a weary patron who was more interested in his mug than the strangers.

Katarina checked her bag to make sure the illuminescents that hid within were safely concealed as the owner walked over. "What can I get you?"

They ordered bread and meat and said nothing else until he left. "What are we going to do?" Max leaned in to whisper. "Go to each house and ask where she is?"

"She'll find us," Evan said with certainty.

"But how long will it take?" Rachel looked instinctively for a watch that she had left back on Earth.

Almost as soon as the food was on the table it was gone. When the owner came back to take the plates, Rachel asked, "Have any strangers come to town lately?"

He looked them over, "Perhaps; why do you want to know?"

"We are looking for a friend of ours," Seth answered.

"I know everyone who comes to town. Give me a name and I might be able to help."

"She's about forty. You would know her if you had seen her," Katarina answered.

The man thought for a moment, then walked straight to the door and called the guards.

Seth jumped to his feet, his chair clattering behind him, and drew his sword. "That's just great," Max sighed, standing more slowly.

The other patron was motioning to them. They had less than a second to decide what to do. The man did not look reputable. He was scruffy as if he had not shaved in many days; he wore plain clothing and a tattered cloak. But armed guards were probably heading their way as they thought and their server blocked the only entrance.

"Behind the bar," he murmured as Seth moved towards him. "Small door." The teen stared at him before realizing that it did not matter whether or not he trusted this man; he had no choice. "Go!"

Seth glanced at the owner, whose form filled the doorway. His focus was outside. "Come on," he mouthed to his companions and hurried behind the bar. It was cluttered and, from the looks of things, far from sanitary, but Seth could not have cared less. He was desperate to find a way out as he ran his fingers along the wall. Only a few seconds had passed in reality, but it had seemed like an eternity.

He sensed Rachel crawl beside him. She felt along the floor. "Beneath you," she breathed.

Moving back, Seth saw a hatch. He pried it open and jumped down. If it was some kind of trap, he would be the one to find out.

He could literally see nothing, but he could smell the stale air and feel the ground surround him. He barely had the space to crawl, but somehow he moved quickly and heard the others follow behind him.

Was it seconds or minutes later when his head smacked into wood? "Ow," he let out. He pushed against it with one hand and it fell before him. He gratefully stumbled out into the crisp air.

He offered a hand to help Rachel, then Katarina out. Max and Evan followed and... the patron from the inn. As soon as he was out of the tunnel he was pushing them into the woods before them. "They are right behind us." He blocked the exit with a heavy barrel.

"What happened to Illen being a safe town?" Max asked no one in particular as they put distance between themselves and the tunnel.

"Nothing is really safe anymore," the man answered as he led them down a mossy slope.

As they passed under the cover of an outcropping, Katarina pulled on her brother's arm, "Wait."

They all stopped, the sounds of the stream beside them covering their heavy breathing and conversation. "Who is he?" Ruby flew out of Katarina's bag and into the man's face.

"Whoa!" he backed up to the rock wall. "What are you?"

Zara emerged as Rachel answered, "They're illuminescents. They want to know who you are."

"Name's Drainan," he addressed the humans as he knelt and took a drink.

"The queen..." Evan started.

"She came to Illen, thinking it was safe. Sasha's men captured her—as they would have captured you, if I had not helped."

"Why did you help us and not the queen?" Katarina demanded.

"I tried, but there was nothing I could do for her," Drainan answered.

They sat in the safety of the outcropping, trusting that their pursuers could not find them there. Would anything go right for them?

The girl pressed herself into the house wall, knowing that if she could just remain still her black clothing and cloak would keep her hidden. She held her breath and angled her sword to keep it from reflecting the pale moon light.

She listened as the dwarf who had been chasing her tried to pinpoint her location. It was not difficult for her trained ears to follow his movements as he walked away, even over the shouts the town was making. Lucky for him that he chose to move on.

Why had Sasha's men come to the town of Mordel? It was loyal to the empress; yet she had counted fifteen, perhaps twenty young men and women being dragged from their homes. It was the middle of night; the people were unprepared. She had heard the noises from the cave overlooking the town. She and the cave's leader had snuck down to find out what was going on.

As she leaned around the corner of the house, the evening

light illuminated the youthful curves of her face. She scanned the area and saw no one between her and the next building. Darting across to the nearest house, she made her decision. She had no love for Mordel—the people were cowards—but she could allow Sasha to gain no more power.

Another figure emerged from the shadows and worked his way towards her. "Vaylynne," he whispered, his voice deeper than the average person she worked with. "What do you want to do?" He was ready and willing to follow whatever command she gave.

"How many are there?"

"Around thirty throughout the town."

Thirty against two. "Get into position."

They silently moved to opposite places on either side of a cart that held over a dozen prisoners to be taken to Maremoth. She gave the area one more look to make sure she was missing nothing, then pulled her bow and notched an arrow. She let two fly before dropping the weapon. Then she drew her sword and charged. Two other men were down to her partner's arrows. With him, she knocked the remaining five guards unconscious.

"They what?" Sasha's voice penetrated the floor of the palace. "How could thirty of your men have failed in such an insignificant town as Mordel?"

Though Sasha did not move, the commander who had been sent to Mordel felt her presence closing in on him. He stepped back without looking, knocking a heavy iron candle stand onto himself. A nasty gash on his face gave him leave to escape the room with his life.

Malcon, who was hiding in the doorway, tried to run before his empress saw him, but she called firmly, "Malcon!"

He entered with a low bow.

"Tell me how this happened."

Her mind was calculating and that always sacred the dwarf, "According to the commander there was a…" he paused, "a warrior maiden."

"That was the best he could come up with?"

Malcon shrugged, "In your absence, Empress, there have been increasing reports of this girl."

"She fights for the royal family?"

"For independence."

"Independence? In Asandra?" Sasha laughed.

"She has an increasing following; her army lives in caves."

Sasha's eyes narrowed on Malcon like a hawk on its prey. "You let her get an army?"

"How was I supposed to stop her?" as soon as the words slipped off his tongue he realized how daft he sounded.

"You should have hunted her down and killed her, the instant she became a problem. Or were you too busy for that?"

"What should be done with the commander?" Malcon distracted her with punishing someone else.

"Demote him, for now. I'll deal with him later."

"Empress," exclaimed a man who was more excited to come in than he should have been given Sasha's mood.

"What is it?"

"I have brought you their queen."

Sasha felt her whole body relax. Finally, after decades of planning, she had complete control. Surely Juliet knew this, but as she was led in she did not look like the defeated queen she was. Sasha remained seated, towering above the once-queen and gestured towards the balcony, "Do you like my kingdom?"

"You think you have caused all this, but you are just a pawn."

Juliet's words rang through Sasha's head, but the shifter spoke as if she were unfazed, "It is said that you would do anything for your people. Is this true?"

Juliet affirmed, "Anything."

"Then there is no reason to cause a war. I have you and your husband. I have a fortress full of slaves and soldiers. I can become hundreds of monsters at my will. I have spies and soldiers in every village. I could make the lives of the people very miserable. But I do not have to."

"You already have."

"I will release the slaves. You and your family can go to Issym," Sasha continued as if never interrupted.

"What do you want?"

"Tell your people and the slaves here, not to fight me. Tell them that you are giving up rule to me. Issue a decree and send it out. Make a special proclamation to your children, ordering them not to resist me. There will be no bloodshed."

Juliet shook her head, allowing her wavy locks to fall over her shoulders, "No."

"You have no love for your people then!"

"You will release the slaves, only to make all of Asandra slaves! And I am not so much of an idiot as to believe that you will really let me and my family go. Besides, if you really had as much control over Asandra as you say, you would not need to barter with me."

"You foolish woman," Sasha spat. "Are you so proud, that you will not give the people the ruler that they desire? Would you really cause a war just to keep your power?"

"I will not bargain with you."

"I don't need to bargain with you. I was just giving you a chance to make your people's lives easier. Now, you will most certainly die and they will most certainly suffer."

Chapter 9

Having decided to spend the night underneath the outcropping, the group should have relaxed. They would be safe here, but for how long? "Well that was a waste of time," Max quipped.

"Like Rachel's plan would have been any better," Katarina defended. She honestly believed they had done the right thing.

Drainan, having figured out who these teens were, was beginning to think he should not have followed them. He was getting sucked into this war.

"Your plan almost got us captured, and you're still blaming me?" Rachel stood up, no longer willing to take the princess' sourceless blows.

Katarina rose to her own feet, "We would have gotten caught no matter which village we were in!"

"Look around you, Katarina. We don't have the privilege of fighting."

"You think we need you that badly? We were doing better before we sent for you."

"This is not about you!" Rachel shouted in an attempt to break through.

Evan gripped his sister's shoulder, but she ripped away.

Seth sighed. *We are so far from being the tightly-knit last defense of Asandra.* "Come on Kat; this isn't worth fighting over."

"And so from now on we have to follow Rachel because the rest of us were wrong—once!"

"How can you distort everything I say?" Rachel demanded.

Katarina charged over Max in an attempt to get to Rachel, but he pushed her back. Evan quickly held her arms back.

Seth moved to stand next to Rachel as Drainan's voice brought order, "Get a grip you guys. Whether or not you are or want to be, it is time to act like adults."

"Who even are you?" Max asked, his breath showing in the air.

"A friend and that should be enough these days. The queen was alerted that Sasha was coming to her hiding place. They ran to Illen. I recognized her and helped her to hide—for a little while at least."

Katarina recognized that the group's support had shifted to Rachel and forced herself to calm down. Evan let go of her as he questioned, "*They?*"

"Many of your followers escaped. A few stayed behind to delay Sasha's men."

"You walked into her trap just like the queen did," Drainan went on. "Sasha made it look like there were a few safe towns so that you would run there."

It made sense, Rachel realized. That was why Illen had no fortress. It needed none. It served Sasha in a way that offered total protection. She paced back and forth.

Evan touched her arm to get her attention. "I'm sorry about my sist..." The color drained from his face and he drew his sword, putting himself in front of Rachel.

"Evan?" Rachel followed his focus and saw a man where none had been before.

"Shape shifter. Get out of here," Evan commanded the form.

Everyone had their weapons drawn before Rachel had a chance to recognize the shifter, "Stop! It's Edmund."

Seth lowered his blade, but kept it ready. He saw no reason for Sasha to deceive them by pretending to be Edmund, but he could not be sure. "What are you doing here?"

"Same as you; trying to stop my sister."

"Sister," Drainan repeated. "Sasha."

"Edmund worked for Sasha once," Seth began.

"I learned my lesson," he cut in.

"He defied her and let Rachel and I go with the one thing that could stop our enemy Smolden."

Drainan stared the shape shifter down, ready to do something if there was anything that could be done. Seth repeated the man's own words, "'A friend and that's enough.'"

"I left Issym before the battle; I've been scouting out Asandra and its island of Noric since then," Edmund informed them.

"How did you find us?" Seth motioned for the others to sheath their weapons.

"Pretty easy when you can soar as an eagle, run like a bear and be the fly on the wall," he gloated.

As he sat down and Seth sat with him, Max refused to put away his sword. He had this overwhelming sense that they should not trust this shape shifter.

"How much do you know?" Edmund questioned Seth.

"Not enough."

"Before Sasha came back from Issym, I took on the form of a dwarf and went to Maremoth. The fortress is impenetrable; the slaves are locked up in three or four buildings each night; during the day they produce weapons to make her army ever stronger—an army she doesn't even need. Her powers alone could defeat us right now. An open attack would be an utter failure."

Edmund stopped speaking to take a drink. Seth noticed that Max still had his sword out. "Put it away," he mouthed.

Max shook his head.

Seth was forced to look back at Edmund when he began again, "She came to Maremoth and sensed my presence so I fled to Noric. Most of the dwarves there don't care what happens to Asandra, but some of them would help us if they thought there was a chance of winning."

"Why do we care about dwarves, who don't care about us?" Katarina asked.

"Because the only dwarves on Asandra work for Sasha, so dwarves are admitted into her fortress, no questions asked. Imagine, if we could get our dwarves on the inside, armed with her weapons and ready for battle. They release the slaves, open the gates, fight themselves. Just think about it..."

"So how do we convince them to fight?" Seth probed.

"You remember how impressed Issym was with meeting Xsardis' imaginers? The dwarves will be impressed too. If Seth or Rachel comes, we might get their help."

The way the shifter commanded the situation made Rachel shudder. He had acted the same way when he had captured her. She could still feel the coolness of the blade he had held to her throat to keep Seth from fighting. The helplessness she had experienced when Edmund had forced Seth and Rachel away from their rescuing friends and had left shifter duplicates behind as a trap... Edmund was devious;

he was intelligent; he was evil. She suddenly realized that she could never trust him. He had to go.

"Seth," Edmund said, knowing what Rachel's pale face meant, "are you coming?"

Ruby flew over to Edmund. "I have to go with you! I was born on Noric and must go back."

Seth stared at Rachel. How had things gone so rapidly wrong? They were supposed to stick together—to be the unstoppable duo, just like they had imagined as kids, just like on Issym. Now they were going to have to separate and he was leaving her with trusted Max, unknown Drainan, quiet Evan and antagonistic Katarina. If Asandra was to be saved, it would take months, maybe years. If he and Rachel started going in opposite directions now, things would get a lot harder. And Max? He belonged in modern day New York, not Renaissance Fair Xsardis. But they needed the dwarves' help, so he said, "I'll go with Edmund."

"That's it!" Rachel burst. "You can't go with him. So Edmund, Sasha's brother from *Issym,* just happens to show up on *Asandra,* in our hiding place? He wants to take one of us with him to 'Noric'. He has intimate knowledge of his sister's fortress. He has helped her in the past. And you just want to waltz off with him?"

"Rachel," he spoke softly but firmly. Her sweeping movements and loud voice showed that she was almost beyond reasoning with, but he was going to try. "He helped us on Issym. Remember."

"If I wanted to harm you," Edmund put in, "I wouldn't need to take you off one at a time. There are no stones of the frogs here. I can't be killed."

That only made Rachel more nervous. Max piped up, "Seth, I think she's right."

Seth rolled his eyes. Rachel and Max united against *him*?

Rachel took Seth's elbow and led them to where they could have some privacy. "Please, don't do this."

"I don't want to," he hoped that she could see that.

"Why won't you listen to me? When you left me behind and went to battle Smolden, I listened. Seth on Issym, *you* led and people followed. And that was okay because Issym was mostly your imagination. But Asandra is mine and I need to lead."

He looked her deeply in the eye. She needed to understand this. "I'm leaving so you can. You need to be here. I can handle some dwarves on Noric and you can lead Asandra."

"You're my best friend, Seth, and we were supposed to do this together. I need you to stay." Rachel felt idiotic as her eyes grew wet. It was just so much pressure. "We went from being teenagers on Earth to adults on Issym, to teenagers again, to adults once more. We're doing things that would make normal people shake. This is crazy. Shape shifters, illuminescents, dwarves, fighting a renaissance war. Tell me it's all a dream! But don't tell me you're going to leave me to face it alone while you go with the brother of our arch-enemy, who will probably kill you, because he has already tried!"

He sighed a heavier sigh than she had ever heard before and pulled her close. "Rachel, I wish we could have done this together, but I have to follow where God leads, just like you."

She stepped back and gave him a smile, "That's why you're the man I have grown to respect."

"Just like that, you accept my decision?"

"You're right, Seth. What can I do but trust you?"

He took her hand for a second as if to say something, but he swallowed the words. In the stillness, she watched as Seth, Edmund and Ruby departed.

Even as Bridget rose from her bed she had no idea what she was doing. She had even less of a clue as she walked towards the building's door. Judging by the coolness of the night and the brightness of the stars shining through the barred windows, it was at least two in the morning. She knew that there would be a guard standing just outside, waiting for an opportunity to lash out at some prisoner.

Bridget moved silently, confident that the mud floors would not make a sound. The wooden door she was approaching probably would. She swung it open—not even a squeak.

As Bridget gazed out at the barren land before her, she was reminded how much she missed the mighty trees that had once grown there. Her bare feet stood on the threshold of the door, no longer compelled to go any farther. Then came the words she had been expecting to hear, "What are you doing?" But the tone was soft—not dwarven and not about to punish.

She looked down. Brooks, the new guard her age, was sitting beside the door. "Not trying to escape," she answered, sitting beside him. He looked like a defeated man. "Are you okay?"

Genuine concern. It had been so long since he had heard that, but he gave her no answer.

"My dad used to wake me up in the middle of the night and take me to a hill where we would sit and look at the stars," she said, smiling at the memory. "Those were the best parts of my life."

"You must miss him very much." His look became even more distant.

"He's dead, along with the rest of my family. We had never been very good at submitting to Sasha."

Everything stopped for Brooks. "Sasha killed them…"

She cut in, "Her army did."

"And you're still polite to the guards. How do you manage that?"

She looked him straight in the eye, "It's not easy."

"Then why are you sitting beside me?"

"I thought you might need a listening ear; but I caution you, I like to speak my mind."

"I figured that out the first day I was stationed here."

The corners of her lips curved in a laugh, but she simply asked, "Why did you start working for Sasha?"

His voice slowed as he turned to storytelling mode, "When Sasha burns a village fully, and she has burned only a very few this way, she destroys all the homes, all the farms and all the manna for miles."

"For generations my family had lived on a farm, providing for ourselves and staying as far away from the village as we could—we had always been loners. We were enough distanced from the town that Sasha's army didn't reach us when she burned it. Almost all the manna near us was destroyed and our crops were doing poorly that year. We had enough for ourselves, but not for anyone else.

"But my parents couldn't just leave all those villagers homeless and helpless. We put as many as we could in our house and barn. As we quickly ran out of food, I was angry and I ran to find my own fortune."

"That didn't go so well, I take it."

"No. Working for Sasha or going home were my only ways to survive." He was silent for a moment. "I chose Sasha; foolish decision."

She glanced around them, "Someone might hear you."

"You're not afraid; why should I be?"

"I have God on my side, Brooks."

"Oh; you're one of them."

"*Them?*"

He made sure she heard every word of what he said next, "God has forgotten us. He has forgotten Asandra."

She was just as firm, "No."

"How can you believe that?"

"I thought my life was over when I came here, but God found me. He told me that He had not forgotten me, and that if I wanted, He could do incredible things through me here in Maremoth. I accepted. Everything changed that day. He forgave my past and I was determined to tell everyone—prisoners and guards. I stopped trying to escape and starting *living* here."

"Guards? You think God is going to save the people who are enslaving Asandra?" he laughed.

"There was this guy—Saul—he killed Christians, persecuted the church. God saved him and used him to change the world. God's reaching for you Brooks. All you have to do is accept Him."

Josiah had watched from his window as Bridget had slipped out of her building and talked with a guard. And then he understood. All that talk about her having God-given strength was just a tool to make everyone like her, especially the guards. She had been waiting for the right guard to come along, one who would help her escape, and now she had found him.

The bitter man did not know the name of this guard she was manipulating, but he would find out. And then he would turn them both in to Malcon.

Chapter 10

"Do you think we should wake him?" Max asked when everyone but Drainan was up and ready to go. They had spent far too long in the outcropping already. Max bent over and shook the man's shoulder. In one swift motion Drainan had the teen's collar in one hand and a dagger he had pulled from his boot in the other. The blade was mere inches from Max's throat as he fixed his eyes on the freckled face, as if trying to figure out who Max was. "Drainan, what are you doing?" Katarina shrieked.

Recognition finally dawned in Drainan's eyes, much to the teen's relief. He dropped Max, who scampered away before the man had a chance to change his mind. "Sorry," the stranger muttered, putting away the dagger.

The teens stared at him, unsure of what had just happened. "We should go," Drainan declared, standing up.

They began their cautious walk through the forest. Sasha's men could be around any bend. They did not yet know where they were going or what they were going to do. They were just moving away from Illen.

"I know the towns along this coast. If you want, I can get you in and out with relative safety so you can raise your army."

"What's the closest town?" Max inquired.

"Adlem. We might get there tonight; or early tomorrow morning. Is that where we're going?" Drainan turned to Rachel and Katarina.

The princess nodded, so Rachel said, "Yes."

As darkness, and the bitter cold that came with it, fell, the band was relieved to see the town's fortress come into view. Zara was snuggled comfortably in Katarina's bag, where she had spent the day. The cold was especially hard on illuminescents.

"What are you doing?" Drainan hissed as the teens headed towards the main gate. "Get back here." They did as they were told.

"Are you crazy? You can't just go in through the front door. Haven't you learned anything?" He led them through the woods, around the fort, and finally showed them a narrow door.

After Drainan had knocked, a middle-aged woman opened the door. "Drainan," the way she said the word made them feel suddenly very small. "Why do you come to my back door in the middle of the night?" she demanded.

"Have any visitors come to Adlem?" he replied, not answering her question.

"No."

"No one from Illen?" The important matters had to be dealt with before he would bother acknowledging the woman's questions.

"No." Her voice was layered with impatience. "What are you up to Drainan?"

"I've run into a little trouble."

"Not surprising. But you won't find this house open to a law breaker."

She moved to shut the door, but he put his foot in the way, "It depends on whose laws I break, doesn't it?"

The woman stopped, but did not admit them. As far as Rachel could tell, she had not noticed the four teens behind Drainan. He stepped aside to reveal them. As her eyes widened, he quickly told her, "I helped these Juliet supporters escape Illen."

"And you brought them with you? Here?"

"Annie, what would you have me do with the prince and princess and Asandra's imaginer?" Remembering, he added, "And their friend Max."

Max rolled his eyes. He would always be in Seth, now Rachel's shadow—be it on Earth or Xsardis.

Annie led them through the kitchen and into an area full of chairs and tables holding scant meals, which filled the room with aromas that caused Max's stomach to cry out for food. Katarina willingly accepted a seat on one of the rickety chairs, and let out a breath she felt like she had been holding ever since her mother had smashed her amulet and Zara had taken them to Earth.

Annie went back into kitchen to prepare some food for the

weary heroes. Drainan followed and poured himself a cup of hot cider as he watched her move about the small space. "Listen," she began, "I'm risking a lot by having them here."

"And you doubt my story," he interrupted.

"It's not your story I doubt."

"It's me." He felt himself getting angry. "Why? Because of my stupid seventeen-year-old cousin! Don't you have a relative you're not proud of?"

"I didn't help mine start a rebellion!"

"A rebellion? That's what you call it..."

"Vaylynne is waging a war. She is disrupting everything. And you helped her."

"For half a year. Now I'm helping the rightful rulers—doesn't that prove something?"

"Proves that your loyalty jumps pretty quickly. When you turn to Sasha, will you tell her that I housed these 'heroes'?" She put a ladle in the pot, then stuck her hand to her hip, "Look Drainan, you're a danger to these people. Your cousin will do anything to get to Rachel or the prince and princess. She knows you and she'll exploit that to find them. They would be better off if you stayed away."

"They need my help and they are going to get it."

"Then you'll be the death of them."

As Seth sat on lookout, he watched the fire—that he and Edmund had risked—peter out. "We're in a remote place," Edmund had said. "No one will be looking for us here."

Edmund, in lion's form, was in deep enough sleep to be purring and it irritated Seth. The shape shifter was comfortable in his warm skin, while Seth's body was stiffened with the cold.

Perhaps it was just Seth's imagination, but he thought he heard a branch snap. When another branch broke, he was sure of it—someone or something was out there.

To his side he heard new noises. They were barely audible, yet Seth was sure that they were footsteps. He woke Edmund, who quickly resumed human form.

Behind him the noises were obviously of many men. The footsteps to his side belonged to one person. Seth could distinguish a figure covered in a dark cloak. The shadow moved swiftly with a sword drawn, but not pointed at them.

Edmund and Seth stared onwards until the figure finally came clear enough for them to see that it was a young woman. She kept her face hidden in the hood of her cloak as she beckoned with her hand for them to follow.

The noises behind Seth were getting closer. Was this girl trying to rescue them from whatever was behind? He and Edmund decided to follow.

She moved quickly—now hardly bothering to quiet her steps. Edmund and Seth hurried to keep up. Even in the darkness, she knew where to put each step.

Finally the thicket gave way to a path that ran along a sheer rock face. Its height was masked by the darkness of the night. At the sound of her whistle a rope slid down the wall. "Move," she commanded Seth.

Was she the enemy, or were the footsteps behind them? Seth began his climb. With no footholds it was grueling work. His arms were shaking as he reached the top and a hand extended to help pull him up the rest of the way. He fell gratefully to the ground.

Seconds later a bird flew up and turned into Edmund's human shape. He looked smugly at Seth, who was panting for breath.

In a moment, their guide had climbed. The rope was quickly pulled up and everyone was silent as a troop of footsteps came to the wall. With grunts and moans, the footsteps dispersed in both directions of the path.

Seth sat up and looked around him. They were on the edge of a cliff, with a cave bearing no light behind them. An arm pulled him to his feet and silently pushed him and Edmund into the cave. There was no point in protesting. This was not a request.

The cave immediately bent and they entered a well-lit oval cavern. Men and women, all under thirty—some no more than ten years old—sat or stood, cooking, sleeping, whispering or cleaning weapons. The presence of the place breathed that it was a military camp.

The girl threw her cloak aside. Black hair cut carelessly short, thin body and nothing special adorning her, she somehow possessed a fearsome beauty. Their rescuer—or captor—commanded the space as she ordered, "Names."

"We appreciate your help, but we had better be going," Edmund tried to pass the question off.

"No. Those men were Sasha's and you would have been overpowered. You owe me your lives and all I ask is for your names."

"I just can't figure out how she found us so quickly," Seth murmured as he thought to himself, *I hope she hasn't found the others as easily.*

"You obviously stand against her. Who do you support?" No relaxation or joking could be seen in her or any of the others, who were acting like they were not paying attention but clearly were.

Seth knew he could not remain silent, "Queen Juliet and King Remar are the lawful rulers."

"Then you fight Sasha on their behalf?"

"Yes."

"Get out," she snapped and turned away.

Seth saw guards moving towards him, but he called out, "Who do you support then?"

She turned and walked defiantly to him, "We fight for our independence!" She paused to study his face before continuing, "We might never get a chance like this again. While Sasha and Juliet battle it out, the common man is forgotten. But we have not forgotten them. We will win our independence while the two fight with each other and ignore us."

Edmund rolled his eyes, "You're Vaylynne, aren't you?"

"Heard of me?" At that she smiled. "Good."

"We won't bother you any longer," Edmund was quick to head for the exit.

"We appreciate the help," Seth made his thanks known.

Her face went cold, "It won't happen again. We try to keep the balance between the two factions, but we don't save the lives of the soldiers of Juliet or Sasha."

Again Edmund moved away, but Seth could not contain himself, "Don't you know what Sasha is? She will destroy Asandra from the smallest piece of manna to the largest animal; from the youngest child, to the oldest man. She'll spare no one and nothing and keep no bargains she makes."

"And Remar and his taxes? He starved my family. Some of them died!"

Edmund put a hand on Seth's shoulder and pulled him towards the way out.

"That's right," Vaylynne laughed. "Run away when you don't have an answer. How like Remar!"

Seth wrenched away from Edmund, "You don't know what's going on here."

Vaylynne moved her face to mere inches from his own as she told him, "We will give up everything we have—fighting to the last breath of ourselves and our children—before we submit to Remar's careless power."

Edmund forced Seth towards the door, but at the click of Vaylynne's tongue, two guards blocked the entrance. One was only thirteen years old.

Seth and Edmund turned. The shape shifter was fuming. If only Seth would have left when they had had the chance! Now they were going to have to fight their way out.

"I believe I asked for your names," Vaylynne demanded. "If I may offer a word of advice: don't lie to me."

Seth told the truth, "My name is Seth."

"Where were you born?"

"Maine."

She stopped a dagger just short from his neck, "I said not to lie to me."

"It's on Earth," he leaned away from her, flicking his eyes to his traveling partner. Would the shape shifter intervene if things got any worse?

She did not move the weapon, but looked towards Edmund. "And him?"

"Edmund."

The shifter rolled his eyes. Why did Seth have to tell the truth?

"Sasha's brother." Vaylynne addressed the room as she took the dagger away from Seth's throat. By now every eye had already been fixed upon them. "Indeed we do have a find! The Seth who imagined Issym and Sasha's brother." She looked towards Edmund, "Interesting that you work against your own sister."

"I once worked for her. Believe me, you don't want her as your ruler."

Something about the way he said it, made Vaylynne pause.

"And you, Seth," she declared, "you want to help the king and queen. You won't have to live under them."

"I would not risk my life in another world unless I was committed to the cause. I know it is the right thing," he answered.

"You're a foreigner to this world. You can't understand the way things work. Go home."

"Not until I have finished what I came to do."

"You will find here that imagination is not a safe plaything. You can't discard us whenever you fancy something else."

Feeling the sharp truth in her words, he could find nothing to say.

Seeing his face, she let up, "Where are you heading?"

"I think it's better if we don't say," Edmund spoke.
"You won't leave unless you say."
"Noric. We're going to Noric."
"To raise the support of the dwarves. How clever!" She toyed with her dagger for a few moments. "Power is far greater on Sasha's side; she could use a little competition. You're free to leave, but pray that you don't cross paths with me again. I won't be able to release you."

Chapter 11

"Can I help you with breakfast?" Evan asked, slipping into the inn's kitchen in early morning.

"Much appreciated," Annie grinned, but it fell short of a true smile. "A prince helping me cook."

He took a little of the grain from the cup beside him and popped it in his mouth. Sasha's bread. It had no flavor and offered little nutrition, but it filled one's stomach. He readied the cider as they spoke. "How do you know Drainan?"

"He and I grew up in the same town. It was ravaged by Sasha. We threw our backs into fighting for you, but every time we gained something, Sasha came in and wiped us out. That was when Drainan's cousin gave up and started the independence movement."

"His cousin is Vaylynne?"

"Drainan worked with her for a while. Now he's working with you. Soon he'll be working for Sasha."

That was harsh. "What about you?"

"I work for myself. You don't understand, Prince," she kneaded the dough furiously. "Your life has never let you see our troubles. Once, we fought for you. But while Sasha destroyed us, you did nothing. My husband—Jacob—and I have given everything to build this inn. If you have to ask for our support, we will give you as much as you gave us."

A groggy Drainan stumbled into the kitchen. "Morning," Annie greeted.

Footsteps could be heard coming to the back door. Drainan

pulled out his sword and stepped behind the door. Evan made ready to do the same, but Annie pushed him out of the way, "It could be a customer!"

But the heaviness of the boots was a noise Evan knew too well. How many times had he and Katarina barely escaped them?

The bang on the door resounded through the kitchen. Having no time to hide, Evan pressed himself into the wall and watched helplessly as Annie opened the door.

"Move aside," came the gruff voice.

Annie was instantly indignant, "Only if I want to. This is the entrance for family only and you are not family."

"Listen, Woman!" came another, older sounding voice. "In the name of the empress, move!"

"What has you in such an uproar?"

"You are suspected of harboring fugitives. Now, move!"

Annie was flattened into the counter as the soldiers pushed past her. The first one did not see the blow Drainan landed on his head. The second did not expect Annie's frying pan. Both were down before they could make a sound.

Drainan swiftly pushed the door shut. Annie knelt down to feel for their pulses; both were alive. Evan found himself reaching for the rope beside him. In moments they were bound and stuffed in one of the guest rooms. "I can't keep them here forever," Annie protested. "You need to move them."

"Not until we have spoken with some of the townspeople," Drainan insisted.

"Haven't you caused enough trouble?" she demanded.

"Annie," he grasped her arm, "this is important."

Evan looked to Drainan, "You get the people you think we should talk to. I'll take care of the soldiers."

"How?" Drainan questioned.

"Everyone is always complaining that my dad did not take care of things. Let me do this and you'll see that my family and I will do what needs to be done."

Evan ran to his sister's room, waking both her and the illuminescent Zara and telling them what had happened. They hurried back to where Annie stood anxiously by the unconscious guards. She grew all the more nervous when she saw Zara. "What is that thing?"

"Zara, can you put them into a deep sleep for a couple of days?" Katarina buzzed, knowing from Max's stories that she could.

When Zara had showered the guards with dust, their breathing began to slow and their skin grew whiter. "What did she do to them?"

Annie asked.

"They'll wake up in a couple of days," Kat assured.

"But what am I going to tell the soldiers who come looking for them?"

Katarina smiled. This was her area of expertise. "I'm sure we can think of something."

As she told her plan, Annie's face grew more relaxed.

"What is this all about, Drainan?" a man grumbled as he lazily took the last open seat at the table, noticing that Annie was nowhere to be seen.

Drainan nodded to the teens and Rachel began by telling them who they were and why they were here.

"You want us to fight, then?" a man in his fifties, who looked like he was no stranger to war, introduced himself into the conversation. "I served in the king's army and I am not afraid of a battle, but I won't help under these conditions."

Max asked, "What do you mean 'under these conditions'?"

A woman glanced uncomfortably at Evan and Katarina before answering, "Gulbraith is right. And I think I speak for everyone when I say, we're willing to risk our lives and fight Sasha, but not just to put King Remar back into power. We want someone who can protect us and rule us well. We...Rachel, we want you as our queen."

Rachel's brain stumbled to comprehend what she had just heard. Never had the thought entered her mind. She did not dare to look at Katarina, whose face was quickly turning purple with fury.

A man saw the look on the princess' face and added, "We are willing to rescue the king and queen. Just not to have them rule us."

"After all they've done for you?" Max inquired.

One of the women could not contain herself, "Done for us? They've been in hiding for six years and now they bring in someone else to do their job for them. They didn't protect us. They can't even protect themselves. Why would we put them back in power?"

Rachel lowered her voice, "I cannot, I will not usurp the power of King Remar and Queen Juliet."

Gulbraith looked into her eyes, "We need your help. Please, we beg you."

Rachel hated the position she was in. She wanted to restore this land but she could not just turn on the king and queen. Why not? She had never even met them. If Katarina and Evan represented who their parents were, who was she putting on the throne?

Katarina's infuriated voice broke her train of thought, "None of you know what you are talking about!" She hurried up the stairs.

Gulbraith pulled Rachel outside, and said, "I don't know whether you don't understand just who the king and queen are, or if you don't want to stay because you have a life on Earth. And I don't blame you for either one, but we…"

"Gulbraith," the teen interrupted. "I would do anything for Xsardis—I love it. I'm here, aren't I? I love home too, but if I was meant to be queen, I would stay," she made sure he understood her every word. "But this is not right. I'm sorry."

Rachel went upstairs with a heavy heart, where she heard Katarina telling Evan, "I will not travel with that self-righteous Rachel!"

"Katarina," her brother tried to reason, "she said that she would not be queen. You should be grateful."

"Grateful? Grateful! Maybe if she wasn't here, those people would have helped us!"

Rachel could handle this no more. Max, who had been drawn in by the shouting, understood the look on her face. "Don't," he mouthed, but Rachel had already made up her mind.

Opening the door, she spoke with finality, "Then why don't we go our separate ways."

"That's probably safer anyway," Drainan stepped beside her.

Max knew that the decision had been made. He resigned himself to it and voiced a plan, "Has everyone forgotten that Sasha cannot be stopped unless we get the stones of the frogs? Somebody needs to go to Issym."

Katarina's eyes lit up. Evan saw some kind of plan hatching in her mind, but what was it? "I will go!" she exclaimed.

Evan unhappily spoke his own thoughts, "It seems to me that someone who has been to Issym should go as well," he responded. "To convince them that we really are who we say we are."

"Then I'll go with her," Max readily agreed to the trip. "Zara, can you get us enough coins so that we can hire a boat?"

"Of course."

"Then it's decided," Drainan nodded. "Rachel, Evan and myself will raise an army here. And Max and Katarina—to Issym."

Chapter 12

"It was the prince and princess who knocked you out. They forced me to house them and when you came to save me, they attacked you. I've been taking care of you ever since," Annie explained to the newly-awakened guards—whose color was returning—and the soldiers who had come looking for them. She turned to the captain and added, "You know that I have always housed the empress' soldiers whenever they come into town. I would not willingly have sheltered Juliet supporters."

"Is that how it happened?" the captain asked his men.

Groggily rubbing his bandaged head, one of the guards answered, "All I remember is seeing Annie as I walked through the door and then getting hit with something hard. But she's been very hospitable ever since."

"Who else was with them?" the captain turned back to Annie, still not trusting her story.

Annie knew that she should not say. If Sasha found out that Rachel was on Xsardis, she would stop at nothing to find and kill her. But Jacob loved this inn. If she lied and anyone found out, he could say goodbye to it, to everything they had worked so hard for. "Rachel was with them," she spat it out before she could change her mind. "I heard them saying that Seth was on Xsardis too."

Max's ears were filled with the sounds of his own labored breathing and his rustling footsteps. How did the princess expect him to keep this pace? If it had been on a track field, yes. In an area so wooded he was sure a path did not exist, no. And besides, his movements were slowed down by the intense cold.

She turned and smiled at him. The princess thought he was a genius—maybe that was because he agreed with everything she said. Still, it was nice to have someone take an interest in him. When he had gone to Issym, Seth and Rachel were the ones who were seen as special. Now, to be the one who had something important to say was a nice change.

A flash of red swept across his vision and slowed before Katarina. "There are a few cottages ahead," Zara informed the princess and then returned to the comfort and warmth of her bag.

Zara rarely came out. When she did it was only to scout ahead and report what she saw. It was almost like the illuminescent was not even with them.

Katarina glanced at Max, "We'll have to get off the path."

He followed her, watching her careful movements as she tried to keep going the right direction for the right amount of time. He quickly realized that they were completely lost.

Max listened as Katarina talked on and on. He was beginning to think that she was just talking to keep him distracted. Distracted from what?

"Is this winter?" Rachel's breath showed as she asked the question. She lived in Maine so she was used to cold from September to May, but it was summer at home. Her body expected it to be in the high sixties.

"Mm-hmm," Drainan grunted, not interested in conversation. His eyes were constantly darting around—watching for danger or for something else?

She wondered how Asandra was really made up of her thoughts. She had imagined things full of life and hope and wonder. This continent seemed cold and dead. So far she had seen no creatures other than humans, a shape shifter and a couple of illuminescents. Where were the frogs, mushnicks, illuminescents and fairies? If all those creatures were in Issym, certainly some of her ideas were in Asandra.

"Do you hear that?" Drainan asked.

Rachel pulled herself away from her thoughts and listened. Someone was talking in the woods to their left. Evan made the decision to move towards the noise. Sasha's men would have no need to hide in the woods.

As the three approached an open knoll, they saw a large group standing around a brawny man. He was saying, "And we all know what kind of a ruler Sasha will be. So I'm asking you to join with me." He appeared to have finished. The group seemed persuaded.

Rachel looked to Evan as they hid behind some bushes. They both knew they needed to speak to these people but after the conversation in Adlem they were not expecting much. Standing at the same time, the teens entered the middle of the circle. Drainan stayed on the edges.

"Who are you?" the man looked down at them.

"I am Rachel, imaginer of Asandra."

He stared into her face to discern the truth. After a few moments he warmly told her, "Then welcome! We could use your help."

"And we could use yours."

"Then speak to us."

Rachel once again repeated that they were gathering an army to take down Sasha and put the lawful king and queen back in power. She kept Evan out of the conversation. These people looked like a mob. If they were against the royal family as Adlem was, then Prince Evan could be in a lot of trouble.

"No!" the man shouted, interrupting her. His welcoming attitude had disappeared as quickly as it had appeared, "We will not help that King Remar. Go! We don't want you here."

Rachel and Evan walked out of the crowd and back to the path, Drainan catching up. "This is impossible!" Rachel let out. "No one will help us. What are we supposed to do?"

Evan took her shoulder and stopped her, "Then maybe we should grant their demands."

Rachel looked into his eyes and saw that he was sincere. He

would give up his throne to protect Asandra.

"Right now," he continued, taking his hand away from her shoulder, "all that matters is that we stop Sasha."

Rachel took a second to think. "We do need to stop her, but we're putting your family back on the throne."

"Wait!" a voice came from behind them. They stopped. A thin, tall, blond man in his early twenties was running towards them. "You really are the Rachel who imagined Asandra?" he asked. At 6'5 he towered over them.

Rachel nodded.

"Then let me come with you. I want to help."

"We'd appreciate it," Rachel answered.

He extended a hand, "Name's Zachary."

"Rachel and Seth are on Xsardis!" a breathless soldier panted the words as he ran into Sasha's throne room and slid into a bow.

Sasha gripped the edges of her throne as she let the words sink in. "Where are they?"

"Rachel was in Adlem, with Evan, Katarina, Vaylynne's cousin and some kid named Max."

"And Seth?"

"We have not seen him."

Rachel and Seth were back to wreck another dark plan—only this time it was hers, not a thick-headed dragon's. *It is fine,* she assured herself. *They can do nothing to stop me now.* Still, it wouldn't hurt to make sure that they stayed out of the way.

"Malcon!" she called. He entered as she stood and descended the steps. "I am leaving for a short time. See that things are kept in order."

"Where are you going Empress?"

"To see Vaylynne. We have things to discuss."

Chapter 13

"I was the younger of two brothers," the man said to Rachel, Evan and Drainan as they continued their brisk walk. "My family ran a farm, but I was dreaming of becoming a pastor. We saved up everything we could to send me to school and I went for one year. When I received word that a fever had taken my brother's life and that my father was also sick, I returned home and helped with the farm. Both my parents died not long after that. I figured all that was left was to sell the farm and go back to school."

"Why didn't you?" Rachel asked.

"While I was away, 'bandits' attacked the school—probably Sasha's men. It was destroyed. I can only hope that some escaped."

Drainan pulled out his sword with a sly smile, "Let's see how you heroes can fight."

Rachel slid her own weapon from its sheath and offered, "I prefer a bow."

Zachary and Evan turned to each other. Rachel moved to defend a heavy blow from Drainan. He was quick to come at her with another. She forced herself to slow her breathing and find the instinct she had imagined herself to have.

She went on the offense and pinned Drainan to a tree. "Surrender?"

He nodded and they both turned their attention to Evan and Zachary. Evan clearly had the upper hand. His movements were precise. He was aware of his environment. He was studying his opponent. When he was confident that he understood all the variables,

he attacked in Zachary's weak spot—the man never protected his legs.
"Okay, okay!" the young pastor called.

Evan sheathed his sword and walked to Drainan, "Satisfied?"

"Beginning to be."

"Kat, come on; slow down!" Max hollered. The princess was almost out of sight.

His legs were cramping; his lungs were burning; he felt like he could have fallen over from exhaustion. For days he had been keeping up Katarina, but she seemed to be getting faster and he seemed to be getting slower. He stopped walking. Kat would turn around when she realized he was not following.

The princess did turn back but only to tease him. She sprinted to his side, "We've already stopped three times this morning. We have to keep going."

"Maybe if you would walk slower, I could walk longer," he retorted, now sitting on the hard land.

She grabbed his arm and tried to pull him up. When he would not budge, she plopped to the ground in frustration.

Max knew they had to keep going. Every second counted and Sasha's men could be around the bend or just behind them. Of all the missions, theirs might be the most important. If they failed, Sasha could not be stopped. No pressure, Max laughed.

Vaylynne kept her sword ready as she felt the thrill. She was going face to face with Sasha—alone in the woods. She had become a big enough power to capture the shifter's eye.

In her simple clothing, Sasha moved to the girl's side. She was surprised at Vaylynne's features. Young, fierce, determined... if only she could be converted to her plans. "I wish you no harm," Sasha proclaimed.

"What do you want, Shifter?" Vaylynne countered.

"I have information for you."

"I don't need your information. I gather my own."

"Then you know that your cousin is traveling with Rachel, Evan and Katarina."

Vaylynne managed a convincing lie, "Of course."

"Then you also know that I am about to intercept them. I have no use for your kin—I will kill him."

"Why would you tell me this?" Vaylynne knew she was becoming distracted.

"In the interest of good will between us. I give you a favor and later you give me one."

"I owe you nothing, Shifter! I did not ask for this information."

"Then let us say that I am impatient. It will take me weeks to hatch my plan for their capture and I know that you can predict your cousin's moves. You tell me where they are, after you have gotten Drainan away."

Vaylynne considered it for a moment. She could rescue Drainan without telling Sasha where he was. But sooner or later, Sasha would find them anyway. And if she did not help, she would jeopardize the little peace she had with the woman. Vaylynne knew that her army was not yet ready for battle. She had no choice. "Okay."

Edmund stopped by the water's edge. Grateful for the break, Seth got off his back. The shape shifter morphed from a lion to a human as Ruby flew out of Seth's pocket. "How do we go from here?" the teen asked.

"I'm thinking a really, really big bird..." Edmund replied.

"Big enough to ride?"

"Claws large enough for you to be held in."

"You've got to be kidding."

Edmund shrugged. "Being ridden is harder than you think. And I am not as skilled as some of the other shifters—I can only morph into so many forms."

"I could use some food," Seth changed the subject. Anything to ignore the unwelcome concept of riding in Edmund's claws.

They did not have to search long to find some manna—it grew

wildly around water. As sparks fell from Ruby they turned into spices. Seth liberally applied them to his food.

"What's the plan when we get to Noric?" Seth asked.

"The island is big. It has about four, maybe five hundred dwarves on it now, and that's after Sasha took a large part of Noric's population. When we land, we'll ease them into the idea of helping us in a war. I'll tell them who you are. We'll let them get to know you. Then, we'll tell them what we want."

"So it will take a while," Seth sighed. How long would he be away from Max and Rachel? How long would they be on Xsardis? Was Edmund even trustworthy? It seemed like the question list kept increasing and no answers were supplying themselves.

Chapter 14

Three villages had already refused to help. Rachel wondered why she was compelling her body forward. Zachary's conversation was at least a distraction, "Ulis, the Bible school I went to, had three leaders—stubborn men who refused to close the school despite the dangers. Everyone knew the risks when they came."

"Orune, Peter and Jamine—those were their names," he continued. "Orune must have been eighty years old. He was the wisest of three, but you never would have guessed it from his humble appearance. I was there when his wife died."

The pain marked Zachary's face, "Orune suffered so much sorrow. I wish I had been at the school when it was attacked. I was one of the few who knew how to fight."

"They would have targeted you first. You would have died," Evan told him, eyeing the heavily-clouded sky.

"But at least I would have been there for Orune and the others."

"Some must have escaped," Rachel could never accept unhappy endings.

"I pray so." He took a drink from his flask. "Orune, Jamine and Peter wrote books on the Bible. Their manuscripts are now in Joppa's tree under the care of a girl named Reesthma."

"Joppa's niece. We met her." Rachel wondered how the girl was faring. "How long has she been on her own?"

"A little over a year. She's pretty smart. She's probably doing better than most adults would in her situation—suddenly alone in a tree that Sasha is determined to destroy."

Drainan grew tired of all the story-telling. "Can we think about our mission? We're going to the biggest, meanest, least-trustworthy city outside of Maremoth itself. And we haven't had the greatest luck so far."

"Cremar," Zachary paled. "I really think we should skip this town. It loves Sasha."

"Does part of her army live here?" Rachel asked.

"A big part of it," Drainan nodded.

"Then maybe they'll know what Sasha is really like and be tired of her."

"Maybe," Evan was doubtful as he continued to stare into the darkening sky. "Regardless, we have to get inside before this storm hits."

Rachel had tried to ignore the blue-gray clouds, but they covered the sky as far as she could see. The group would probably be stuck in Cremar for several days.

Cremar. It stretched out before them with its black walls and towering gates. Maybe it was just the weather that radiated shadows and darkness, or maybe this place really was evil.

"Just don't say anything," Drainan ordered grumpily. "We can't take risks here. I'll do the talking."

Drainan led them past the gate and through the town, his cloak billowing out behind him as heavy winds set in. Their cheeks burned with the cold.

Drainan took them to the inn—it was triple the size of the one run by Annie. Inside, with the fire and the people and the warm although tasteless food, it was easy to forget about the cold. After dinner, Rachel found her room and fell into the warm blankets.

A fast and hard knock at the door woke her. How long had she been asleep? The second knock was louder, more determined. She threw her cloak around her and opened the door.

Evan had never looked so scared.

"What's going on?" she panted, reaching for her bag.

"We have to go. They know who we are."

Rachel slipped her boots on and hastily followed him down the backstairs and to a seldom-used door, forcing her brain to wake up. "Where's Zach?"

"They already got him," he said, opening the door to the storm. Snow poured from the sky and the wind twirled it around. They were going into a blizzard.

"What? We have to help him! What about Drainan?"

"It is his fault."

The words did not seem to make sense. "We can't go out in this and we have to help them!"

"It's too late," his eyes bored into hers and somehow she knew, he was right.

Rachel stepped ahead of him into the windstorm and snow, running for the forest she knew was before them. They were outside the town, on their own and on the run. Rachel turned to make sure Evan was still following and could barely discern his form through the weather. "Where are we going?" she called, hoping that the plan was not to run through the night. They would never survive in this cold.

Closing the gap between them he motioned for her to go forward as they pushed through the pucker brush and heavy trees. The snow had already built up on the ground, forcing them to guess at where to put their feet. They kept catching their ankles and tripping. "Evan, what is going on?" Rachel begged for information, but the wind was getting stronger and it snatched her voice away.

The prince had already turned numb in the intense cold, which slowed his movements. They would not survive this night if they did not receive a miracle. The adults were gone and he had no idea what to do. *God, help.* He would have opened his mouth to pray, but he would not let anymore cold in.

Rachel fell to the ground, getting a face full of snow. She did not rise. He knelt beside her, wondering if he would be able to get up. Evan managed to get her head against his chest so that the wind would not take away the sound of his words. "They might be right behind us," he tried to explain. "We just have to keep moving."

"Until when?" she gasped.

Evan's eyes once again bore into hers. Her brain tried to figure out what she saw there. He was scared but he was determined. He was weak but he would be strong for her and Asandra. He was tired but he was alert. He was trustworthy. She nodded and they rose to their feet. Huddling together for warmth and support, they pressed through the blizzard.

Minutes felt like hours and now Evan was lurching forward. "If we stop for long, we'll freeze," Rachel reminded him.

A fire was out of the question. Not only were Sasha's men behind them, but it would be impossible to build one in this weather.

Rachel could not help a tear running down her face. She had come all the way from Earth to die in a blizzard! "God, please!" she implored. The storm just grew worse.

Evan crumpled to his knees. Rachel sank to her own beside

him. He moaned to show that he was still awake, for now.

Rachel looked around them for any hope. In the distance a fire sprang up, shooting high into the air. She had heard of mirages in the desert, but never in a blizzard. Sasha's men had probably turned back. They could not survive the weather either. Maybe she and Evan could sit in the fire's warmth and not be found. "Just another minute, Evan, come on," Rachel's voice forced him to his feet.

His eyes locked on the fire, "We need to get away from that."

Rachel wondered if hypothermia was affecting his mind, "Away?"

"It's probably..." he tried to say but the wind snatched away his warning.

In the darkness of the night, Katarina watched the light snow fall and refused to allow her body to shiver. Max leaned against a tree beside her. She did not tell him to try to rest, for it was not the cold that made her blood chill. Katarina could feel that the soldiers who had been trailing them all day had not camped for the night. They were still coming.

It had just been wrong timing. Three soldiers had been walking along the path. She and Max had not seen them until it was too late. They had tried to get into the cover of the woods, but the men had seen them. Their suspicious behavior and their young age made the soldiers guess that they were Evan and Katarina. Half true.

Katarina and Max did not move or make a sound. Her sharp ears listened and she realized that if the soldiers did not change course, they would walk right over them. Silently, she stood up and directed Max to move. There was not time to get away, so she positioned herself and Max in the shadow of a few tall trees and waited.

The princess weighed her options. She could let the men walk right past, but the news would get to Sasha and the area would be heavily patrolled for weeks. They would not be able to travel safely or quickly. She made her decision.

Allowing the first man to walk by, she jammed the butt of her sword into the second's forehead.

What is she doing? screamed Max's mind. *You should help her.* Max lunged for the first man, who had doubled back, but Katarina did not need his help.

She kicked the third man in the stomach, sending him backwards. The first man was the unlucky recipient of a punch to the throat. He fell gasping to the ground. The third man gripped Katarina's shoulders from behind. She flipped him over and told him, "Don't mess with Vaylynne." Her sword's hilt to his temple knocked him out.

She had told him she was Vaylynne. Effective, if untrue.

Katarina sheathed her weapon and scowled at his look. "I didn't kill them."

"I know. It was impressive."

"You mean reckless."

"No. Impressive."

She softened. "Oh. Evan doesn't…"

"Appreciate your bravery?"

"I was going to say rashness, but I like your way better."

Zara flew out of the bag, her red light illuminating Kat's genuine smile which made Max smile. "Next time you are going to wrestle with three brutes, make sure I am not in a bag around your waist."

Katarina and Max just laughed the tension right out of their bodies.

As Seth lay in Edmund's giant bird talons, the wind raked across his body. Seth had nothing to do but think. Think about how if Edmund opened his claws, Seth would plummet to a painful death. *I didn't know I was scared of heights,* he pondered before forcing his mind onto something else, but he did not like where his mind went.

You would want to help the rightful king and queen. You won't have to live under them, Vaylynne's words echoed in his mind. Did he have any business interfering in this war? He would not have to live under the king and queen. He had not met them. Asandra was not even his imagination!

Issym had been so beautiful, so inspiring, so ready to do the right thing—and that had forced him to wake up. But Asandra was destitute and broken, as if fear and pain had truly conquered it. How could he fight that?

You don't have to, God's voice reminded him.

Seth tried to believe it, but it was a lot easier to accept when he was not staring in the face of so much pain with so much more to come. If he stayed on the continent too long, would he become just as broken?

Smolden. Sasha still shook with rage when she thought of the beast. With their combined talents, it should have been simple to conquer Issym, but now she had lost all those years, her shape shifter following and the people's fear—a powerful weapon.

Still, she reasoned, she had a strong enough hold on Asandra. But now that Seth and Rachel were back... "They can do nothing to stop you, Empress," Malcon tried to reassure her, but she knew the truth.

"Nothing?" she questioned, watching a young woman tremble as she swept her floors.

Malcon should have realized that the conversation was dangerous, but he did not. "Nothing. You are far too powerful."

Sasha shook her head. She dealt with imbeciles. "Tell me again why you have not rid my kingdom of this slave you were telling me about—the one who receives favors from the guards..."

"Ah yes..." he interrupted. "She is just one person."

"One?" The shifter laughed, clenching the sides of her throne. "Do you realize what one person can do?"

He thought about it, but shook his head.

"One," she whispered for emphasis. "One was all that it took to give the world salvation."

"Empress?" Malcon was not following.

"The world was in darkness, Dwarf. Wonderful darkness. And then the Christ was born. One heart at a time, He changed the world. Satan thought he had succeeded by killing Him, but Christ's death brought God's greatest gift." Sasha thudded her scepter on the ground, cracking several tiles.

The dwarf had never heard Sasha speak of Satan and God so clearly. This woman, his empress, believed in God? It did not sound right for her.

"Think of Esther—one woman saved her people from destruction. Think of Jonah. He did not even want to help. Gideon,

David, Joshua, Paul, Daniel. Must I go on?"

He shook his head. He did not know who those people were, but it was better just to agree.

"So you see, Malcon," Sasha finished, gripping his shoulder, "never underestimate the power of one if they have God on their side."

"Yes, Empress." He did not really understand, but the yes answer had worked once before.

"You should have gotten rid of her. Does she hold to a faith in God?"

Malcon's eyes flicked to young woman sweeping around them. She avoided his gaze. "Yes."

"Then she is dangerous. I want her gone."

Malcon bowed, but protested, "She holds the slaves' spirits together, helps them work and listen to us. She is invaluable."

Sasha came in close to the fat dwarf's face. "No one is invaluable. And she obviously knows how to manipulate. Get rid of her! That's an order."

"Yes, Empress."

Sasha called to the sweeper. She came forward, head low.

The shape shifter looked over her. "Have you changed anything Malcon? This is the same girl that worked here when I was last in this palace."

"She does her work well."

The girl tried to keep her knees from knocking together. All color was gone from her face.

"What is your name?" Sasha asked, with a hand motion ordering her to rise.

The girl answered with a brave tone that did not match her appearance, "Bridget."

"Take Bridget as an example, Malcon. She looks in fair enough health. Have you even worked her hard?"

Malcon was speechless, until he finally decided that this prisoner was not worth protecting. "This is the woman you ordered me to dispatch."

"Then lock her up until I am ready for her. Now."

Malcon summoned another dwarf, who led Bridget away.

Sasha moved on quickly, "And what about my fortifications? Why have they not been expanded? And you have brought me no more slaves."

"How am I to get you more slaves? You have no enemies."

"Seth and Rachel are gathering support."

"Empress, no one will support them."

"I don't believe that."

"And well you shouldn't, Empress Sasha." It was a human voice.

The twenty-five year old man was leaning against the door, looking very cocky. Malcon's eyes sent daggers in his direction, but Sasha seemed amused. "Go on," she decided.

"I only enter to inform you of what your dwarves have been doing. Ask Malcon where he lives."

"Get out of here, Stewart," Malcon spat. "You have no right to address the Empress."

"You're correct," he responded. "You dwarves won't allow qualified men to take your positions. While we work all day and all night and sleep in huts, you and your dwarves live in..." Stewart gave a dramatic pause, "palaces."

"Palaces?" Sasha pretended to be indignant, but she was enjoying this. It was so much fun to watch lesser deceivers get caught by greater ones. She might have to get rid of a few dwarves to set an example—but causing fear was her specialty. She enjoyed it.

"How regrettable that I have to tell you this," the man went on, "but Malcon and the other dwarves have been using the slaves to build houses for themselves outside the fortress."

"*Outside* the fortress." Now Sasha was angry. She never allowed prisoners outside the fortress—the risks were too great if they escaped. Sasha had made the people think that Maremoth was not all that bad. If the truth were told, she feared that she might lose her grip over Asandra.

Seeing the cold look in her eyes, Malcon fell at her feet. "Empress, I beg you, don't listen to this imbecile," he groped to say anything that would save his own life.

"You are the imbecile, Malcon, to think that I would not discover what you have done. Guards!"

Two dwarves came in. "Will you question my orders?" she demanded.

They were not overly intelligent but they knew how to answer that question, "Never."

"Then take him," she extended a pointed finger, "to the deepest hole in my dungeon and leave him there."

They moved towards the human. *Idiots*, she grimaced. *All I have to work with is idiots.* "The dwarf! Can't you see where I am pointing?"

But they were not looking in the direction of her finger; they were looking at the finger itself. It was a talon; long, sharp and scary.

Her whole hand was soon that of a terrible bird—one that she was becoming as wings shot out of her back. In fear, the guards dragged Malcon from the room—he did not protest. In his own terror, he would gladly face the dungeons as long as he could get away from Sasha.

  Stewart just nodded, observing everything and realizing the truth. Sasha was not changing because she wanted to. She was losing control of her powers.

Chapter 15

As Rachel neared the billowing fire she dropped to the ground. The heat burned against her skin and brought back feeling—painful feeling. *Thank you God!* she prayed, believing that she was now safe. She spent no energy trying to figure out what could have caused such a strange fire, which grew higher but not wider.

What had Evan said? He had sounded like he wanted her to go away from the fire. Away? She must have misunderstood. As he came up behind her, he muttered, "Great."

She glanced at him as her front was boiling and her back froze. "What's wrong?"

"Look in that fire. Sprites."

Rachel stared into the tornado of fire. Four creatures the length of her forearm were spinning up and up, causing the fire to expand as they went. They looked like the fairies on Issym, expect much smaller and lacking the sparkles that decorated their eyes and wings. These creatures' wings protruded from their backs and were deep red. Rachel smiled. Finally she was seeing the creations of her imagination. "They are fire sprites," she told Evan, still on her knees in the snow covered forest. "They built a fire and we're in a blizzard. What's the problem?"

"Perhaps you have forgotten. Sprites are trouble makers."

"A little trouble right now is the least of our worries." The heat was bringing back logical thought. Rachel forced her brain to process the events of the past hour. Drainan and Zachary were captured. As soon as they were safe, they would have to rescue them—perhaps ambush the soldiers as they took them to Maremoth.

As the sprites came away from their fire, they moved towards

Evan and Rachel. On the night she had first been taken to Issym, Rachel had entertained two children with a story of water sprites—they had been noble and beautiful and fun. Finally, some decent people to recruit. But as Rachel looked them over she became aware that something was very wrong. Sure the sprites' pupils were red, their shoes were red, their clothing was red—all as it should have been—but their faces were filled with spite. It hit her then that the prince had been right. They needed to go. She forced herself to her feet and started to move back. A wall of fire sprung up behind them.

"This is ridiculous!" Rachel shouted over the roar of the fire. "We can't get even a little break, can we?"

"No one who falls into the hands of sprites survives," Evan droned in a creepy tone.

"Why are they so evil?" The sprites were closing in.

"They start off scrawny and with wings, but when they mature, they grow not only slightly taller and fatter, but they lose their wings and a lot of the abilities they had before. That transformation only takes place when they are deemed adults. So one girl decided to cause so much trouble no one would ever think she had grown up. It worked and hundreds of sprites followed. They are now so out of control that not even Sasha's army dares to deal with them. At first it was cruel jokes, but now houses are burned down, people are injured, some even die..." he finished in a low voice as four sprites hovered before them.

Rachel's body was burning. They had to get away quickly. A memory flashed in her mind. The illuminescents on Issym had been viewed as murderers before Rachel had helped the race become understood. The creatures had joined in the battle against Smolden. Maybe she could do it again. "Thank you for sharing your fire," she offered.

They laughed. "Sharing? We do not share. We sell our fire."

"What could you possibly want from us?"

"What do you have?"

"Nothing! We have nothing! I have never had anything," Evan shouted at them. Sprites really ticked him off. He had been forced to grow up at an early age—the sprites absolutely refused to. So why had he, who had done the right thing, lost so much, while the sprites seemed only to gain?

Four adult sprites walked through the fire behind them and stood between the young sprites and the teens. They came up to Evan's knee and wore shirts of red and pants of black. "What are you doing?" one demanded of the children.

"What business is that of yours?" retorted a young female sprite.

"What did they do to you?"

"They used our fire. Should we not charge a price? You always knew how to extort people."

Father and daughter locked in a timeless struggle. "That is enough, Iva."

"No. They will die just to prove to you…"

Now Rachel shouted into the sky, "Will my imaginations never stop trying to kill me?"

Evan slumped into the snow. His body was succumbing to the intense heat.

"Who are you?" the father demanded of the teens.

Rachel, trying to convince them to help, gave her name as she dropped to the ground.

The men looked very sad, none more than Iva's father. The children began to snicker, realizing their catch and believing that the adults would do nothing. But with a heavy sigh, the father turned back to his daughter and implored, "Iva, please. Let them go. Daughter…"

"Don't call me that!" Iva shrieked. Her hands shone brightly seconds before she engulfed her father with flames. When the fire dissipated, he was unharmed. Iva's hands glowed even hotter as she turned on Rachel and Evan. The sprites behind her shifted nervously as the father and the other adults showed a grim determination. "Iva, I give you one last chance. I will stop you, if I must. Come back to the community, to your mother and I. Don't you know how we love you?"

"No!" the words echoed around them. Rachel and Evan were barely sitting upright, the weight of the heat sapping their strength, making it impossible to breathe. Iva swooped in to attack her father and he gripped her wing. "It is time for you to grow up," he whispered into her ear.

"No!" she wept. "I am not grown up."

"But you need to be."

Convulsions shook her body. The other sprites flew away and the fire rescinded. Iva was sobbing, not in pain but in anguish of heart. "Please, go now," the father said to Rachel and Evan. "Just a few minutes east you will find a cabin."

Noric was a barren island. It had a sandy shore and a dirt and rocky terrain for the length of the land. Seth wondered as they walked inland why anyone would want to live there. But he himself would gladly have lived on the island if it meant getting out of Edmund's bird claws. His body was stiff and sore.

Seth glanced up at the sky from which he had just descended. It would snow soon. He could not help but notice the contrast between the cold atmosphere he had just occupied and the warmer earth where he now stood. "Where is everyone?" he asked. All he could see were rocks.

"They live in tunnels underground. In the summer, it keeps out the heat; in the winter, it keeps it in," Edmund replied. Somehow his human shoulders were still sore from flapping his bird wings. And already he wanted to take to the air again. There was nothing like it—flying.

Ruby flew out of Seth's pocket. "I have to go!" she shouted and flew away before he could protest.

"Hey! Guys! Hello!" the voice was small but trying to be loud. Where was it coming from? "Oh..." the voice became frustrated.

"Who is that?" Seth looked around him and then to Edmund.

"Keep walking." Edmund's face betrayed his irritation.

"Who's talking?" Seth looked again, seeing only a small river, rocks, dirt and large mushrooms—mushrooms that were not there a few seconds ago.

"Yeah; it's the mushrooms," Edmund confirmed. "But you don't want to strike up a conversation with them. Believe me."

"The mushrooms can talk?"

Edmund simply shook his head and answered. "Rachel's world..."

Seth smiled, "Of course mushrooms can talk; she loves mushrooms."

The mushrooms, all six of them, came up to Seth's knee, with wide umbrellas over their heads. They were brown or dark green-gray. Faces appeared on their bodies. "What did you discover?" one asked Edmund.

"Nothing about your children."

Moans rose from every mushroom. Seth felt pity for these creatures and inquired, "What happened to your kids?"

"They ran to Sasha..."

"Katarina and Evan never mentioned mushrooms..." he looked questioningly at Edmund.

"Their kids don't look like them. These guys are earth sprites."

"Sprites?" These mushrooms did not look like any sprite he had ever heard of. They could not possibly be a relative of the airsprites.

"Sprites are backwards. You know how a caterpillar turns to a butterfly? A sprite turns to a short, fat human. They keep most of their powers, but lose their wings and their beauty."

The mushrooms started shouting questions at Edmund, all of which he ignored as he continued talking with Seth. More mushrooms were piling in around them.

Edmund was not making sense. "You said human; these are mushrooms."

The shifter rolled his eyes. Not only was he surrounded by whiney mushrooms, but he was traveling with a dummy. "When earth sprites mature they are given the ability to turn into mushrooms so they can hide from attackers. Only these brilliant sprites forgot how to change back."

That brought even louder protests from the mouths of the incessantly complaining mushrooms. Edmund continued, "Their children hated the idea of becoming mushrooms, so they rebelled and refused to grow up. They hoped that if they didn't mature mentally; they wouldn't mature physically. It turned out to be a pretty accurate plan." Edmund and Seth were encircled by the still-talking mushrooms. The shifter continued grumpily, "But their children became terrors and led the way to all the other sprites refusing to grow up, wreaking havoc on and almost starting a war with Asandra."

"Don't speak of them like that," wailed a woman mushroom. "They will grow up when they are ready. They are just children; they can't be held responsible for their actions."

Edmund rolled his eyes again. Seth joined him. No accountability. No respect. No responsibility. No morals. No government. No rules. No wonder Asandra was falling apart.

"Please; you must help our children," the woman pleaded with Edmund. "You have to bring them back to us!"

Edmund ordered Seth, "Don't say anything. Just walk away. They'll never leave you alone if you don't."

More mushrooms were approaching. Seth turned to leave, tripped on some of them and did his best not to crush them as he fell. The sprites moved away from him before taking up their complaints again.

As Seth stood up and dusted himself off, he heard a grumbly voice behind him spit, "Whiners." He turned to see a dwarf. He was barrel chested with bulking arms of solid muscle. The top of his head came barely above Seth's waist but there was no doubt who was the more intimidating figure. The dwarf's twisted beard descended to his chest and held still as he spoke, "They are constantly asking for free things—just like you did last time, Edmund. And now you've brought another to take advantage of our hospitality." The dwarf sounded more whiny than the mushrooms.

Edmund seemed undaunted by the unwelcome reception of the dwarf. "Lotex, this is Seth, imaginer of Issym."

"Nice to meet you," the dwarf droned sarcastically. Seth just nodded. "We don't care here about royal personage. We don't give unless we receive. If you won't work, you won't sleep in our tunnels or eat our food."

"Who said I wouldn't work?" Seth asked, preparing himself to play his role. "The last thing I'll do is take your charity. I don't need it."

Lotex looked him over and laughed, "You, work? Hah! Scrawny lad."

"Name your task."

The dwarf thought for a moment. The mushrooms were continuing to complain, but no one paid them any attention. "Blowen stole my favorite arrow and shot it up a tree. It's stuck there. Get it back."

"Lead on."

"Not just yet. You don't think I came all this way just to socialize, do you? I'm here for water."

The dwarf walked to the nearby river, filled the bucket to the brim and then put it on Seth's shoulders. The teen felt the weight bear down, but it was not more than he could handle.

Half an hour of walking later, they saw a lone, dying tree towering above them. There was nothing else in sight, except rocks and barren ground. By now Seth's arms and shoulders were burning from the weight of his load. He gratefully set the bucket down when he saw Lotex stop. "Up there," the dwarf pointed to the top of the tree.

The trunk was thin, and almost as tall as Reesthma's tree. There were a few branches with some leaves at the very top; but there were no footholds low enough to grasp. Seth tried to get a good grip but got nowhere. He was relieved as he heard Edmund say, "I'll get the arrow."

"No!" the dwarf commanded. "You would use your shifter 'talents' and would not even break a sweat. You call that work?"

"You dwarves are bitter because you don't have special abilities. You are prejudiced against those of us who do. Together we would be stronger. We could be your allies."

Lotex's voice remained level, "The boy said he would work. Let him."

Seth did not have to search long to find his determination. Earning the dwarf's respect was his mission. Until it was completed, he could not go back to Asandra and help the others. Not to mention home. "Do you have a rope?"

Lotex shook his head. Seth decided to improvise. He took his cloak off and swung it around the tree, taking an end in each hand. He began to climb, tearing his already-tattered shoes, burning his hands, and wrenching his back. He would hurt tomorrow and that was if he did not fall. As he climbed higher, he realized that if he slipped, Ruby would probably ship him back to Earth for immediate medical care. The thrill and the exercise was welcome; the pain was not.

"Why don't you just cut the tree down?" Edmund asked. "It would be faster."

"We like having one tree left."

Seth doubted that was the reason.

Edmund asked, "It's your only tree... how will you make it through the winter with no firewood?"

"We have enough wood piled up."

"But you'll have no wood for the next winter."

"Like you care, Shifter!"

Seth continued climbing, putting all other thoughts out of his mind. He reached the arrow; now came the hard part. How could he pull it out without dropping to his death? Sweat dropped into his eye and he squeezed it shut. Taking a deep breath, he held onto the tree firmly with one hand and yanked the arrow out with the other.

"Incoming!" Seth shouted and let the arrow fall to the ground. Then he took hold of his cloak with both hands and began his descent.

Don't look down, he told himself. Down was harder than up. His muscles were tired. There was more of a chance of falling. He felt his sweaty right hand lose grip of the cloak. Seth tried to slow himself but he just did not have the strength and could not regain his hold. He fell to the ground, the impact shaking every bone in his body. When his double vision cleared, he leaned back against the tree, rubbing his shoulder.

Edmund stood beside Lotex, who fingered his arrow. Neither one seemed to care that Seth had fallen. The teen managed to gain his feet. "That hardly proves that you can work," Lotex finally declared.

"Just try and give me a task that I can't do," Seth responded in an aggressive tone. It was not the usual way he talked; but the dwarf was on his nerves, he had just fallen out of a tree, and no one had cared.

"Well, you can start by carrying the water back to the mines."

Seth sighed, but picked the container up and put it on his sore shoulders. He knew that he had a lot of work ahead of him, but he was determined to do it well.

Max kept up with Katarina a little better as their journey continued. Maybe she was taking it easy on him or maybe the snow was slowing her down.

As a frozen lake appeared in front of them, Max hesitated. In movies someone always falls into a frozen lake. "Maybe we should try to find a way around," he offered.

"You're not scared, Max?" Katarina teased him, and he was tempted to relax. He forced himself not to smile back at the pretty princess and carefully moved onto the lake.

At first the ice felt solid enough, but then Max heard a popping sound. He saw the cracks begin to form in the ice. "Katarina, we need to go back!"

She froze, then told him. "We're too far across. We'll have to finish."

Max put his steps in just the right places and distributed his weight equally. *Just like a video game,* he reminded himself.

The crinkling became a banging snap. Zara rocketed toward the sky as the ice caved in beneath Katarina's feet. She slipped into the water with a short shriek.

"Kat!" Max hollered. He dove towards the hole, his arms in the water, searching for her. The ice was rocking with her struggle. If he did not get her out soon, he would not be able to. He had no time for a prayer, but somehow He knew that God could hear him anyway. He moved his hands around and felt her arm.

Max steadied himself and pulled her up, almost losing grip of her slippery arm. The youth picked her up and ran for the shore, leaping from ice-chunk to ice-chunk. Katarina's body froze in his arms. She was not breathing. He jumped to shore as the ice fell underneath him. Laying her down, he realized he did not know what to do to get her breathing again. Why hadn't he taken the CPR course with Seth? It was going to cost Kat her life. "No. God! Not like this! Help!" He called the words out into the heavens.

He summoned the memories of the thousands of movies and TV shows that he had watched in his short lifetime and the CPR he had seen them perform. He pushed down on her chest. Then again, harder.

Sasha knew that Stewart had higher dreams than she could ever allow him to achieve, but for the time being he was proving to be a valuable aid. He understood Maremoth and Asandra. He followed her orders well. On the day she had displaced Malcon, she had appointed Stewart in his place.

Stewart had changed the way Maremoth breathed. The men stood constantly at attention and they looked fierce again. Fear marked the prisoners' faces. Good.

He had also sent out a large number of soldiers to bring in more slaves—able-bodied young men with ideals, the kind that Seth and Rachel would try to convert to their efforts. The remaining soldiers, if they were not controlling slaves, were in battle training. Malcon had let their skills slip, but soon they would meet her standards.

The crowning idea of Stewart's short period as her right hand was to dispatch two hundred soldiers to the other side of Asandra. They would build another fortress. Two homes were always better than one, and having a capital on either side of Asandra would remind the people who their leader was. Maremoth was built for a siege, not for a beautiful representation of power. Saphree, her new fortress, would display the proper prestige.

"Have you gotten anywhere with Juliet?" Sasha stared down at him. After appointing Stewart, she had had to grow a few inches. Stewart was much taller than the dwarves she was used to working with. Never let people look down on you, was the command that she remembered vividly from her father. It was the only thing he had ever said to which she had listened.

Stewart shook his head. "Nowhere."

"Do you think you would be able to with more time?"

He paused, then shook his head, "No."

"Then I believe we will need to schedule an execution. Kill Malcon then too. And that Bridget character."

After a lull in the conversation, he shifted uncomfortably.

"What is it?" she demanded.

"It's just... they say that your brother is out there somewhere, working against you. Shouldn't we try to bring him in—show that no one is above your power?"

Sasha's skin grew gray like the slab of stone she sat upon. She answered firmly, taking care not to use the term *brother*: "Edmund suffers most alone in the world and without hope. He knows he will never beat me. When I am finished watching his pitiful life, I will deal with him. Until then, make sure no one touches him."

"Of course," Stewart bowed and left.

Sasha tried her best not to think about Edmund as the gray rescinded. Compassion was weakening. Love was crippling. But that was the truth. She had a soft spot for her baby brother. She would yell at him, threaten him, maybe even beat and arrest him, but she could not imagine killing him.

In any case, she could do nothing against him now. There were no stones around. For that she was grateful.

Chapter 16

Mind buzzing, Rachel forced her eyes to stay closed. She was supposed to be sleeping. *Like that is going to happen!*

Her body was still chilled from last night's blizzard. If they had not found a cottage and met a merciful old man, she and Prince Evan might have died. Rachel knew that she should have felt lucky, sleepy, maybe even peaceful... but her mind was full. Asandra was supposed to be beautiful, full of wonder and good things. But it fell so short.

Asandra was broken.

Was this the same sorrow God felt when He looked at the beautiful world He had created?

The old man's quiet footsteps moved around the room. Rachel sat up, stretching to make sure nothing was still frozen from last night. She nudged Evan and woke him.

Standing next to the gentleman, they squirmed and waited for him to break the silence. Somehow they knew that they would not be able to keep the truth a secret. He had not asked them who they were or what they were doing. He had just taken them in. But when he found out who he was housing, Rachel and Evan would be out in the snow before you could count to ten—just like with everyone else. "Hungry?" was his first question as he began to make something in a bowl.

They nodded and Rachel spluttered out the truth. If it was dangerous, it could not be more dangerous than what they had faced the previous night.

"You said one of your companions was named Zachary..." the

old man stopped moving to ask.

Evan knew the question had significance. "Did you know him?"

"My name is Orune. My friend Aaron will wake soon. We are some of the only survivors of a school Zachary once attended."

"He spoke of you and the others often," Rachel let out a sigh—half of relief, knowing that they were safe in the cabin, and half of pain for causing the godly Orune more anguish.

Orune turned to Evan, his eyes imploring for the truth. "You said Zachary was captured. How?"

The prince glanced at Rachel, just now realizing that she did not know, "I was sitting in the tavern, watching Drainan act like an old friend to everyone there. I should have realized that something was wrong when two of them slipped out. Minutes later a young woman came in and hit Drainan over the head. As she carried him out, she turned to me and mouthed, 'Sasha's men are just behind me.' But it was too late. Zachary stayed to give us time to get away."

"Who was she?" Rachel asked.

"Vaylynne."

"The rebel-leader," Rachel clarified. Catching up on centuries of world history and current events left some names jumbled.

"And Drainan's cousin. She got him out of there and left us to be captured."

"Cousins," Rachel's mind spun. "That's news to me."

Evan's face grew darker than Rachel had ever seen him as he said, "I knew."

"You cannot take all the blame, lad," Orune reminded. "Zachary knew he would sacrifice to help you."

"But he didn't have to last night!" the prince slapped the table. The anger did not fit him. "Drainan must have known that his cousin could track him; that she would know where he would go and who he would call on. But he came with us anyway! It's his fault that Vaylynne found us and told Sasha."

"But why would Vaylynne work with Sasha?"

"Vaylynne has a special agenda most people cannot understand," Orune tried to explain. "And she will do whatever she must to accomplish it, even if that means making a pact with the shifter."

Aaron came out, nodded at the teens and dove into the not-yet-finished breakfast. He was a man in his sixties with a bald spot in the back of his salt-and-pepper-haired head. *Can't he feel the tension in the room?* Rachel wondered.

Evan was still gripping the table so Rachel put a hand on his shoulder and drew him back. "I know this is hard, but…"

"Rachel," he reeled her speech in with a single word. "I spent my life in an underground hole, watching people I loved give themselves to protect my family and me. I spent the time planning how I would be a better king than…" he did not like saying this, "than my father. I vowed to protect the people who served with me. Last night I failed."

She blinked, wondering what she was supposed to say to that. "I would feel the same way, and it is your job to try to protect them, but ultimately in a war people are captured and killed. It was up to the God of the Universe to save Zach. Maybe he will be where he needs to be now." Rachel tried to encourage him, but inside she was empty. It broke her apart that she lost people in war.

"Wise words," Orune spoke softly.

Evan shifted uncomfortably under Rachel and Orune's gaze, so she turned to study the room. It had a fire pit, a table and three chairs and four doors leading away.

"So much loss," Aaron sighed. "First the school; now this."

"The school was really destroyed?" Rachel turned back to face them.

"A few survived, but I don't know why I did. I am an old man who has outlived his usefulness," Orune groaned.

Rachel put her hand on top of his, "If it had not been for you, we would have died. God knew what He was doing."

Orune just shivered and looked outside, "You'll be stuck here for a few days, until this storm clears up."

"Why do you get so much snow?" Rachel laughed because there was no point in being upset. Like they needed one more obstacle!

Aaron nodded, "We get winter only once every three years. We have an intense snowy season for about four months. Then we begin to see spring."

"God, come on!" Max pounded in desperation again on Katarina's chest. The freezing cold was sapping the strength out of his body. She too was blue from the cold. Still she had not taken a breath.

He slammed his fist with the last of his strength. She coughed up water and began to breathe. "Thank You!" he called up to God.

Max was expecting a hug or a thank you, but she spluttered, "What did you do to me?"

Shocked, he answered, "Saved your life."

"Oh." Her eyes dazed off. She sat there limp. Hypothermia was setting in.

Max pulled off his cloak and wrapped it around her. Dashing to get some wood, he used the last of the lighter he had brought from home to start a fire quickly; Zara made sure he succeeded. It did not matter if Sasha's soldiers saw it. That was the least of their worries.

"Katarina," Max shouted. She heard his voice echoing in her head, but she could not respond. "Kat," he moved beside her, took her hands and brought her back to reality. "You need to stay awake."

"I... know."

"Tell me about one of the times you got Evan out of trouble."

She gurgled—her attempt at a laugh. "I'll try."

Seth walked through the mines, passing by dwarves who would stop their work to glare. Obviously they were not welcome. Seth hoped to change that.

In the underground hideout of the royal family, he had felt like the ceiling was secure. In these mines Seth wondered when the beams would fall. The walls were cold and rocky. The passageways were thin. Seth often had to stoop to avoid hitting his head. Neither Lotex nor Edmund seemed inclined to speak, and Seth, carrying the heavy water, had no extra energy for socialization.

Finally they entered a small room and Seth put down his load. They stepped back into the passage way and, after walking a small distance, came to a wooden door. Lotex's bang was authoritative. If Seth had been on the other side, he would have come to the door immediately. "Blowen!" the dwarf hollered. "You had better open up!" More pounding. "Blowen!"

The door opened, but Seth could not see past Lotex's bulky frame to determine who was inside. Lotex declared, "Edmund came back and brought a friend. They got the arrow you lost so I told them we'd lodge them. And by we, I mean you."

"The arrow?" questioned a voice that had none of the

gruffness of Lotex.

"Yes, you numbskull! My best arrow—the one you shot into the tree." Lotex motioned for Seth and Edmund to go in and then stormed off.

As the shape shifter and the teen bent over and stepped inside the door, a figure met them. He was considerably shorter than Lotex and did not have a beard. Thin, he carried none of the dwarf weight. He seemed only a short human. "Come in then," Blowen told them in higher pitched tones. "My house is apparently your house."

The room's ceiling was low. Edmund shifted into an even smaller size; Seth wished he could. A fire-pit stood between the bed and the table with a chair. A dresser sat right beside the door. "Not sure where I'll put them," Blowen muttered, obviously thinking out loud. "How is it that I have the smallest of all the houses and always get stuck with the company? I suppose they can sleep by the pit, but that is far from comfortable."

Seth's knees were already growing tired of the crouched position so he dropped down beside the fire. "Why did you use Lotex's favorite arrow?" Edmund asked. No one in their right mind bothered Lotex.

"Me? Me shoot the arrow? Never would I be so foolish. I don't even know how to use a bow!"

"Then why did Lotex say that you did?" Seth questioned.

"They always blame everything on me." Seth was not sure why Blowen was sweeping the room. It seemed to be in pristine condition. Not one piece of paper was out of place, and the blankets on the bed did not have the smallest wrinkle.

"But at least I get to entertain company," the dwarf said, apparently deciding to be chipper. "Now, tell me Edmund, why are you back? Come to get help to fight Sasha? I know you want to stop your sister."

Edmund took the chair by the table, and Blowen sat down on the bed, careful not to wrinkle the blankets. "I brought Seth, imaginer of Issym, to try and help me convince the dwarves."

"Good thinking," he nodded, then shook his head, "but it won't work. Words don't work with dwarves. Work works with dwarves."

"Seth's already signed up for that..." Edmund looked towards the teen.

"He has no idea what Lotex will do with him," Blowen responded. "But he looks determined and that's to his credit."

"We shall see," Edmund looked him over. "He is not used to

dwarf-sized efforts."

"They do take a lot of pride in how much they can do and he does not look all that strong."

Seth cleared his throat. Did they think he was not hearing what they said? He looked at his frame. It was thin but strong—he worked out every day after school. He was a great basketball player. He did not look strong? What were they thinking? What did Rachel think? *Focus.* "I'm tougher than I look and I'm not afraid of labor or of Lotex."

"Well, I admire you for trying. If you can win the dwarves' respect and loyalty... though I don't know how you'll do it... they'll stick with you for a while," Blowen finished.

That speech was not particularly encouraging.

"I'll get right on with dinner," the dwarf declared. "Though it will be hard on my stores to feed two extra mouths... But how can it be a bother when I have two splendid guests like yourselves?"

In her cell Bridget tried to be thankful; she really tried. After all, this was her first 'vacation' in fifteen years; but worry consumed her. Would the little girls that for months she had taken care of be okay? And what would King Remar do? Would Brooks ever come to know Christ? She tried to pray for those things, but the fact was that she was consumed by worry for something else. She did not want to die.

When someone lives in Maremoth for as long as Bridget had, death almost becomes a welcome relief and a reality that could come at any time. But something deep in her soul told her it was not time for her to go yet. There was just too much left to do.

The door opened. Her heart beat faster; she held her breath. Was this it?

Brooks entered. She looked apprehensively at him. Just because they had been 'friends', did not mean they still were. Typically, like with Josiah, when she spoke about her faith, people stopped liking her.

"You okay?" he asked.

She smiled weakly, "A little scared."

"Have they given you anything to eat?" He knelt before her and she flinched.

Go away, fear. She tried to banish the worry, but it stayed within her. She would not have been able to speak loudly if she had tried. "Some. Don't worry about it."

Brooks pulled open the leather bag that hung from his shoulder and handed her a loaf of bread. She accepted it with thanks.

As Bridget began to eat, she studied him. He looked paler than she felt. "I've never seen you this nervous before," she told him. "Are you okay?"

He paused, the question taking him off-guard. "Everything has changed since Malcon was put in prison. Stewart has us doing terrible things. I don't know if I can."

"Then don't." With the food in her stomach and the opportunity to focus on someone else, Bridget's bravery was growing.

"You know what will happen if I don't." His bravery was shrinking.

"So leave! Sneak out."

"Where would I go?" He stood up and pointed to the walls around her. "I'm just as trapped as you. Sasha is about to take all of Asandra. What do you think she's going to do with the deserters?"

"Then go to Issym; go to Noric; wherever. But go, Brooks! Don't give your life to this any longer. You do have a choice."

"You make it sound so easy, but how can you encourage me to escape when you realize just how deadly Sasha is? After all, it's your head that is about to be on the chopping block."

Bridget let the loaf fall to her lap, her appetite gone. "Was that supposed to make me feel better?"

He shrugged. "Sorry. I thought you were a fan of the truth."

"Give me some truth that doesn't foretell my demise. Is Queen Juliet..."

"Dead? Not yet. But she will be soon."

Chapter 17

Because they were stuck in the cottage anyway, Evan took the opportunity to catch up on a few hours of sleep. He was resting in the room belonging to Aaron, who was pouring over a book in front of the fire. Orune sat beside him, praying. That left Rachel to stare at the wooden walls, think... and pray.

With a deep sigh, she decided to try not to think any longer. It was just giving her a headache and not solving anything. There was not much that had actually gone well on this adventure. There were scores of problems on which she could have dwelt, but one kept coming to mind. No matter how she tried to banish it, the horrible thought returned: *It's my fault. I imagined this world—this terrible place. I caused Sasha. I caused Zachary's capture. I caused an immoral, awful place to come into existence. I caused it all—Seth and Max's leaving, the sprites' depravity, the people's cold rejection of the truth. I imagined it all.*

Rachel grew even more frustrated as a hot tear rolled out of each eye. She shook her head and the emotions that threatened to overwhelm her with it. She had to be strong... for how long? No. She had to be strong until the job was done.

But her stomach churned within her. For days she had been unable to calm it. And her neck would not stop throbbing.

Orune's firm hand on her shoulder reminded her where she was. "Is it Zachary that has you so sad?" he asked, settling himself on the hard floor with a sigh.

"It's everything," she smiled in an attempt to put on a braver face. Realizing that there was no hiding her red eyes, she swept her hair back and answered truthfully, "It feels like a never-ending nightmare. And I am so alone."

The dear old man nodded to the door where Evan lay. "You haven't lost all your friends."

Rachel shook her head. "It's not the same. I barely know him."

"From what you tell me, he was the one that kept the peace between you and Katarina for weeks. He kept you alive in the blizzard. What if Evan was a truer friend than you might have ever known otherwise?"

Despite the swirling in her head, she found the truth in his words. "Orune, I don't live here. I have a home and I have to get back there eventually. This war has to end. And right now, we're not even fighting Sasha."

"The people's hearts must change first."

"And how do I get them to do that?" There was exasperation in her voice.

"Rachel, do you realize how many *I's* you just used? *You* cannot do anything, except pray. *God* will do the rest."

"Just pray. I can do that just as well on Earth." She started bawling, feeling like an idiot. "I need to help these people, Orune! I love them and they are so lost. It's a crushing weight on me."

"Jesus already took that weight."

"I cannot rest or eat… I just need to make things better."

"Pray, Rachel. Pray like you've never done before. This isn't a cliché: 'when the going gets tough, pray'. No; this is a spiritual battle—the captures just as real as Zachary's and the deaths even more real. You taught yourself to fight with bow, sword and fists. Now let God teach you to pray."

Seth slowed down to enjoy the last spoonful of his soup. He had scarfed the rest down, hungry and exhausted from his half-day as Lotex's slave. "Yum."

"Oh I'm glad you liked it!" Blowen exclaimed, sweeping away the dishes. "But you didn't have to eat so much," he added in a low voice.

"When I was last here, Blowen, I did not see you. Why?" Edmund rubbed his forehead. It looked to Seth like Edmund's day with Blowen had been as painful as his with Lotex.

"Oh, the dwarves keep me pretty well locked up here. They say I'm too small for any good work. I suppose that is in my benefit. I don't have to fetch water or cut wood. But then again, my hands get all wilty when I wash dishes all day; and they say because I don't cut firewood, I don't deserve to have enough to make me comfortable. And I never get to socialize, except for when I'm stuck with visitors, who eat my food and wrinkle my sheets, but then, at least, I can talk to someone."

Edmund found Blowen's manner of conversation annoying, to say the least. "Perhaps we should get some rest." He shifted into a cat and curled up beside the fire. He heard Seth settle himself on the other side. The clink of Blowen's dish washing was not the only other noise that could be heard. The clunk of dwarf footsteps and the clatter of pickaxes ax meeting mine walls mixed to make Edmund wish he could turn off his hearing. Of all the insufferable creatures, why did he have to be with dwarves? They never listened. They never agreed. They were constantly obstinate.

He tried to remind himself that he did not really mind dwarves. At least most of them said what they meant; and that was something in Asandra. Political correctness meant nothing to them. They would tell you who they supported and why.

So different from Asandra. The politically correct thing to say on the continent, when asked which government a person supported, was, "I remain neutral."

Neutral! Edmund scoffed at the word. You cannot support both sides. You cannot support neither. Cowards, that is what Asandra was full of. So why was he helping the continent? He had no religious reasons for doing it. Perhaps it was his penance—penance for serving Sasha all those years. Or perhaps it was because he needed revenge on Sasha for having used him all those years.

Yes, that was it. Revenge. It was not about doing the right thing—he could care less. Or could he? He was just sick of the darkness and distrust. Why was it that he had read the Bible through if he cared nothing for doing what was right? *That was a year ago, he reminded himself. I don't care now.*

But doesn't everything I think have some counterpart in the Bible? Even my frustration with the people of Asandra. You can't remain neutral. *Wasn't there a verse in the Bible about how 'No servant can serve two masters. Either he will hate the one and love the other,*

or he will be devoted to the one and despise the other'?
You memorized it? screamed his brain. *Come back to reality.*

God was a myth and even if He was not, Edmund had no intention of 'serving' Him. But Kate. The memories of her were so sweet. He could still picture her sitting beside him, taking his hand in hers. Her hair blew in the wind; her eyes shone out at him; and yet there was sorrow in that face. The memory turned sour. She was telling him that she was leaving. Something about God. He had laughed in her face. And later, when he had let her and Seth and Rachel escape with the gem of light, should not she have returned to him then? But no. He would never prove himself worthy, to her. But to Sasha...if he could bring Seth to her. He shuddered. What was he thinking? He hated his sister.

"Guests..." Blowen was muttering. "They come into your house, eat your food, don't do the dishes and then go to sleep before a nice conversation can be had. And yet..." Edmund caused his cat ears to fold over and block his hearing. He was in no mood to hear the dwarf's double-minded words.

"Evan and I ran as fast as we could, but our pursuer was quick. We never would have been able to outdistance him. My brother, who can be amazingly brave when he has to be, stopped running and told me to go on. Like I was going to listen to him!" Katarina was saying as they walked. If talking fast was a sign of healing, then Katarina must have been completely better.

"I ran and hid behind a tree to watch the two battle. The guy was a good fighter and Evan had little practice without a weapon. He had always been trained with a sword, but he didn't have one on him that day. His opponent's had been thrown somewhere in the woods. It wasn't doing either of them any good."

"And your chaser was one of Sasha's men?" Max had a hard time following the girl with a lighting fast tongue.

"No. Just a stupid villager. We have a pretty big price on our heads." She hopped right back into her story as if Max had never interrupted. "Evan put up a really good fight but there was no way he would have beaten the guy."

"So, I circled around behind them. I jumped on the guy's back and it gave Evan the time he needed to catch his breath and grab a stick. With that, he could fight. We knocked him unconscious and ran back to our hiding place."

"That's quite the story..." Max did not mean it. It might have been interesting if she had not told stories exactly like it a thousand times before. It appeared that Kat was always getting Evan into trouble. She always added that she came in just in time to save the day. The princess had a *slight* exaggeration problem.

"And, of course, we got grounded when we got home." That was the way pretty much every one of Katarina's stories ended. So how were they outside of the underground enough to get into all this trouble if they were grounded that much? Max chastised himself for being critical. He used to be the same bad influence on Seth—only he had known how not to get caught and the stakes were not life and death.

They were coming to a town. A bed; a real meal; warmth. Maybe stopping at just one inn would not hurt. They could blend in; Max was sure of it. And Katarina should probably see a doctor. Lacerations covered her skin from the sharp ice. From time to time she would shiver. Was she coming down with pneumonia? "Kat, let's go into the town."

She looked at him like he was crazy. "One slip up; that's all Sasha needs. A small mistake on our part and Asandra will be hers for centuries; maybe forever," she shouted.

The princess was really being emotional. "Don't get so worked up," Max replied. "One night in a town isn't going to hurt anything..."

"Do you want Asandra to fall?" she asked incredulously.

Since when did you care? Max thought. *All you do is talk about yourself.* "Kat; you're overreacting!" he chastised.

"No, I'm not. You're being ridiculous. Ha-choo," she sneezed.

Max rolled his eyes and walked ahead of her. *Let it go; just let it go.* Why was she so adamant about this? Five teenagers might have looked suspicious in a town, but two?

He took out his i-pod and plugged it in. He needed some time away from the princess and this was the best he was going to do.

Stewart enjoyed the glares he got from the dwarves. He had

taken many years of abuse from them to finally achieve his position at Sasha's right hand. Now he was taking every opportunity to make their race miserable.

In his newly-made, fine clothing, he strutted towards Queen Juliet's cell. The guards parted for him and Stewart entered what once had been a nice room—fine carpet, flowing curtains, regal furniture. Now, it had been stripped of everything but a chair, upon which she sat, and a desk, upon which she rested her two arms and her head on top of them. She stirred at the sound of Stewart's footsteps, revealing the bruises on her face and arms.

"Have I not made it abundantly clear to you that I will not assist you?" she demanded, exasperation but not defeat striking her voice. She wanted him to fear all the rebels—to know that he could not break them any more easily than he could break her.

He shut the door and sat on the desk beside her. She leaned away from him, getting a clearer look into his scheming eyes. His tones were low as he said, "You have made it clear that you will not help Sasha. But what about me?"

"Why would I help you?" she questioned, keeping her voice loud.

He leaned in even closer with his enthusiasm, "I am not Sasha, but I could beat her. I could free Asandra from her rule. I can use her own army against her. Already I have started rumors that Sasha lost her mind on Issym. They know how cruel she is. But they respect me! Soon the army will answer only to my voice. If I put that force behind you..."

"Speak clearly. I know you don't want to help me."

"I want to be king, with Katarina at my side."

Juliet swallowed the emotions that threatened to engulf her. The protective mother wanted to jump down Stewart's throat, but she managed to answer coolly, "There are so many problems with that. Evan will inherit the throne. Katarina would never marry you. And," her voice rose, "I would die before I saw you seated on the throne of Asandra with my precious daughter beside you!"

"You do not know what kind of a king I would be."

She gestured to her wounds, "But I know what kind of man you are."

Chapter 18

Morning came early, but Seth welcomed it. The floor was hard and he was stiff. He stood and made his way toward the door in order to answer whoever was banging on it. He pulled open the door and squinted before the light from Lotex's candle. "Ready to get to work?" the dwarf asked.

"Are you?" Seth responded. It felt like it was still night, but Seth figured he just felt tired. When Lotex had led him to the outside world, Seth saw that it was night. He opened his mouth to protest and then clamped it shut. The cool air was helping him wake up. Good.

"See that wood pile? Load yourself up, and bring it to my room."

He began to stack on piece after piece, glad that Rachel's dad had asked for his help with their family's wood. This was an easy task. That was probably meant as an insult, but it didn't bother Seth.

A week passed for Evan and Rachel in the cottage of Orune and Aaron. The snow began to melt—a little. The time passed slowly. All the four did was pray, read the Bible, sing and eat. It was nice to be safe and warm. It was good to learn and recuperate. And Rachel's new understanding of Evan had shown her his sense of humor and decency.

But she finally knew that it was time to move on. A series of hushed conversations with Evan, who was even more ready to go than Rachel, led to their decision.

Orune asked, "And what is all this secretive counsel I hear?"

Rachel looked towards the old man, sitting in his chair. He had wanted her to pray until the path was clear. She did not want to disappoint him, but it was clear that it was time to go, so she answered him truthfully, "We think that it might be time to travel again."

Orune did not seem surprised. "And where would you go? To try to raise an army again?"

Rachel laughed at the idea, "We've pretty much given up on that. But in Joppa's tree a young girl lives alone and we promised her we would go back soon. She is the last center of the resistance and we need to tell her what has been happening. And besides, what better place to seek wisdom than in a tree full of knowledge."

"Just remember the difference between wisdom and knowledge."

"Of course," Evan answered. "Thank you for your hospitality." The prince paused and then decided to go ahead, "You seemed so hesitant for us to leave before. What caused the change of heart?"

"Now is the right time to go. Your path will be cleared for you."

Is that some kind of analogy? Rachel wondered.

Booming thundered towards them. "What is that?" Rachel asked, reaching for her sword. She would not have put the dramatic entrance beyond Sasha.

Orune opened the door. Hundreds of giant birds flocked by the cottage. They had fluffy feathers of extravagant colors and three long legs. Rachel dropped her sword and stumbled outside into the snow that came up to her waist. They were so beautiful—this was her imagination. She felt tears come to her eyes. They were so strong, so brilliant, such a testimony that they could not have been formed by chance. God had made them, not a doubt. The same God who had made all of Asandra; the same God that would save Asandra. She barely heard Orune telling Evan, "They will clear away the snow. If you walk in their tracks, your journey will be much easier."

"The tallest ones..." Rachel whispered. She looked at Orune, "Are they the youngest?"

He nodded, "They normally hibernate during the summer and come out for Asandra's brief winter."

Rachel moved forward. Now there were only a few of the big

ones lagging behind. Evan whispered sharply. "Don't! They are deathly afraid of humans. Come back!"

But Rachel, this close to the magnificent creatures of her imagination, was not about to stop. She moved closer to the birds. The animals squawked and ran from her. But one, tall, purple-feathered bird moved towards her. She put a hand on his warm chest. The feathers were soft and she leaned in to hug it. "Firil!" the animal squawked, wrapping his own, long neck around her.

Evan raced towards them. If Rachel did anything, this bird would tear her to shreds. But it seemed to be nestling her, chirping sweet things.

Rachel's foot looked like a baby's compared to the size of the bird's. Its three front talons and its back one looked sharper than her sword. Its yellow beak was just as dangerous, but the rest of him was so inviting. She realized that it was time for the bird to continue on or else it would lose the pack. She stepped back from it and walked towards Evan and Orune.

The bird croaked, "Firil!" and followed her.

"No," she said, pushing away his beak as he tried to snuggle around her again. "Go..."

"Firil!"

"Go."

"Firil!"

"What do I do?" she asked Orune and Evan, laughing.

They moved towards her and the creature backed away. The closer they came, the farther he went. "Go inside the house while you still can," Orune commanded. She did as she was told.

Orune and Evan returned inside, closing the shutters on the windows so that the bird would not see Rachel and try to stay around. Orune handed them each a bag. "It's just some food and a fresh set of clothes," he said, "but it should help."

Going to the chest on the far side of the room, Orune dug out two cloaks. They were brilliantly white and hopelessly fluffy, but they would offer good camouflage next to the snow and keep them warm on the cold winter nights. "How are we supposed to carry these?" Evan joked because words would not express his gratefulness. To keep from freezing in the cold nights to come... That was a great gift indeed. "Thank you again, Orune."

Orune shook the prince's hand and gave Rachel a hug, escorting them outside after the teens had said goodbye to Aaron. The purple bird was waiting for her. "Firil!" it shouted and got close to Rachel.

"You were supposed to go with your family," Rachel told the young bird.

"Too late now. He'll be following you," Orune declared. "See if he'll let you ride him."

Evan paled. "That is too dangerous," he replied.

"It will be fine," Rachel reassured. She carefully mounted the creature, using its neck to swing up.

"You next," Orune looked at Evan.

Rachel whispered into the bird's ears, then said to Evan, "I can keep him steady. Come on."

Evan took her hand and moved up beside her. Orune passed them their bags and cloaks.

Rachel wrapped her fingers around his neck feathers and whispered in his ear "Go." He began to run, speeding forward. Evan's arms were instantly around Rachel's waist. Rachel's hands were around the bird's neck, holding on for dear life. His body bounded up and down with each stride. Evan was constantly kicked by one of the creature's three legs. "Goodbye!" they called to the cottage as they were almost out of sight.

They moved quickly, though Evan thought that riding the bird was more effort than walking. Staying upright on the animal when it swerved to the left and right, jumped and kicked was not easy. It was much worse than riding a wild horse.

Around lunch time she told the bird to stop. He seemed to understand words, even if he could not speak them. Once off the creature, Evan put his hand on a tree to steady himself.

"You didn't like Firil?" Rachel teased.

"Riding a bird that doesn't know the meaning of the word straight and who's legs have a terrible tendency of hitting me... Surprisingly, I hated it."

Rachel looked up at Evan as she spread out some food. He really did look like he had motion sickness. "I guess we don't have to ride him."

He shook his head and cleared his vision. "I'll be fine." He paused as he picked up his food and stared at her. "You really didn't think *she* was alive did you?"

Rachel's thoughts and movements came to a screeching halt. Her heartbeat throbbed in her head. "I couldn't believe I had killed Sasha; but I couldn't believe she was alive either." She sighed. "I know you can live your life in the 'what ifs' but, it was my responsibility to stop Sasha. If I had dug a little deeper into my imagination, your country might be free right now."

"You really can live your life in 'what ifs'," he replied. "Like, what if I had stepped up a little sooner? If I had worked among my people and earned their trust, maybe we could have defeated Sasha's army while she was still in Issym."

She sighed again, "Your duty presses down upon you pretty hard, doesn't it? You really love your people."

"Kat criticizes me for it. She can't understand why my heart breaks for the people who are trying to kill us. I guess sometimes, I can't understand either."

Snow fell from the night sky. "We should stop," Kat finally decided. The princess's cheeks were bright red with cold; her auburn hair was covered with snow; and it seemed that her cloak caught more snow than it kept out cold.

"We've got to find some kind of shelter," *or we'll never make it through the night.* Max left the last words off. Kat must have known what kind of danger they were in. The storm was just going to get worse.

"If you can find us a town, we can stay there tonight!" she was willing. For once.

"Look ahead!"

It was hard to distinguish through the snow, but now that she was looking, Kat could make out the gate of a town. "Okay, let's go." They moved to the gate and banged upon it. No answer.

Katarina dropped to the ground. One moment she was fine, the next she was unconscious. "Kat." He dropped down beside her, shaking her. He was up again and banging on the door—realizing just how little strength he had.

He fell beside the princess. Both asleep.

Josiah asked for an audience with Stewart and it was granted, though grudgingly. Stewart did not like to make time for common slaves, but this one had promised information on Bridget's allies. Sasha would like punishing people who had fallen under the slave's influence. "Be quick," Stewart told him, sitting down at a conference table across from Josiah.

"I thought you should know that one of the guards has fallen in love with the prisoner Bridget."

That was even better than expected. "Which one?" Stewart demanded.

"I… don't know, but I would recognize his face."

"Well that is incredibly helpful!" Stewart clapped his hands together in mock astonishment. "Get out." Worthless people always assumed they could waste his time.

Outside the room, Brooks had lost all color. This was definitely not good. Josiah was probably talking about him. He hid his face just in time; Josiah did not see him as he stormed out of the room.

He watched Josiah go, the prisoner's eyes staring down every guard he passed. Brooks dodged quickly into the room with Stewart, making up some matter to discuss with the man just to get away from Josiah's gaze. He would have to get out of Maremoth—and soon.

Chapter 19

Seth was glad to escape to Blowen's room. From before dawn until after dusk Seth had been stacking and cutting wood, shoveling manure, fetching water. It was mundane, monotonous and degrading work. Lotex had been making a statement: *You don't deserve better tasks.* Seth refused to let it get under his skin. He would prove himself. He had to.

"Lotex worked you hard. I can tell," Blowen remarked, watching Seth ease himself into the room's chair. "He's a cruel dwarf, and yet, there is value in hard work. It will make a fine man out of you one day, as long as you don't take after Lotex. That would be terrible," he shuddered. "And yet, how miserable a dwarf I am for saying such horrible things about one of my own kind. It is true, though." And then he became silent, obviously deep in thought.

Seth had drained the mug of water Blowen had given him. He now refilled it and sat down again. "What did you do today?" Seth asked Edmund.

"Not much," Edmund replied.

Blowen offered the truth, "I made the mistake of telling Edmund that Lotex was planning something." He set a bowl of soup on the table in front of the weary teenager and continued, "That he keeps you busy only to keep your nose out of things. Edmund spent the whole day in the shape of a fly, spying! Not that I'm judging. I can see why he did it; I can also see how it could be considered morally inappropriate."

Seth looked towards Edmund, alarmed. "What is he planning?"

"You agree with his actions?" Blowen demanded in high tones.

Seth ignored him and kept his focus on Edmund.

"A council of dwarves wants to make sure you go away and never come back," the shifter told him. "Lotex stays silent."

"How much danger are we in?" Seth questioned, silently angry at Edmund. *When was he going to tell me this?*

"Not much; it seems only a few don't like us."

"Who and why?"

"You sound like you are conducting an interrogation." Nevertheless, he answered the questions, "Who? About five dwarves on the council. Why? Because they see the opportunity for gain by turning us in. When Sasha first came here, they saw her as offering only slave labor—no true gains. That is why so many stayed. But now she has power and most of the work has been done. They know that if they deliver you to her, they will be ushered into royal living. Very dwarfish. If it is good for their present they don't think about their future."

Seth sighed. "Never a moment's safety."

Max woke up in warmth. Wasn't he supposed to be in a blizzard? He refused to open his eyes. What would he see if he did? Would he be in the freezing cold, an enemy camp, Heaven, or the best possible solution—the town he had tried to gain entrance to? Max inwardly cuffed himself. Heaven was a better option than that, right? His brain knew it was, but wasn't sending the message to his heart.

Katarina. She had been worse off than him, last he remembered. Would she have made it through the night? He forced himself to open his eyes.

Fire was all he could see. The heat burned his eyes and he squeezed them shut again. He rolled over and opened his eyes once more. He was in a normal room with decrepit chairs around a rickety table and an old wood floor.

Max forced himself to get up. It seemed safe enough, but he needed to be sure. Katarina lay asleep near the fireplace. There were no windows, only a door. He twisted the handle—relieved when it opened easily. He was looking into someone's bedroom. He started to step back, but a woman who stood towards the far side of the room beckoned him to come in and close the door.

Her husband sat on the bed, putting on his heavy boots. "How did you sleep last night?" the woman asked, continuing to fold laundry, but having motherly concern.

"I... guess pretty well. Thank you." He paused. "How did we get here?"

"We heard your knocking last night. When we came, you had already passed out," the man replied. "My wife, Elizabeth, and I— my name is Harvey—brought you to our home. I am sorry we could not offer you better accommodations."

"No; believe me, we are grateful." Max liked the look of Elizabeth and Harvey. They were young, but sincere.

"What were you doing out in that storm?" Elizabeth questioned.

"It came on quickly."

The woman left her laundry and stepped nearer Max, speaking softly but with urgency, "I grew up in a town that surrounded the palace. I was just a peasant, but even so, I recognize... who you travel with."

Harvey took his wife's hand, "What can we do to help?"

"If you thought that she was... you know... it was pretty brave of you to take us in."

"It would be hypocritical to pray to God to rescue us and then, when He sends our princess, to let her die in the cold," Harvey replied, settling his feet in the oversized footwear, obviously handed down to him.

Elizabeth offered Max some kind of ointment, "This will help your skin recover, but you shouldn't travel in this weather."

Max peered out through the window, "It doesn't look like it's still snowing."

"You underestimate winter if you think you can travel during it. Everyone knows to bunker down and wait it out."

Max rubbed the ointment in, trying not to flinch at the pressure.

"Let me get you something to eat," Elizabeth said as she moved into another room.

"How far is the coast?" Max asked Harvey.

The man shook his head, "You will never make it. It would take weeks to journey there."

"Weeks?" They had already been traveling for so long! "Where are we?"

"Clidrion."

"We've been traveling the wrong way." And it wasn't an accident.

Rachel felt Evan's head fall forward as they rode on the bird they had come to think of as Firil. He jolted upright. In a few minutes, he had again fallen asleep, his head on her shoulder. She could not blame him. The night had been so cold and had afforded such little sleep. The white cloaks had offered some protection, but not enough. Perhaps they could afford a little rest during the day.

But if they stopped, Rachel was sure they would both be asleep. And how could they go unguarded? It simply was not practical or intelligent to stop.

She shook her head, trying to send the tiredness packing. The time moved both slowly and quickly—how did that work? On Earth she was so time conscious. She would check her watch every two minutes. Here she had only a rough guess based on the sun. One thing she was sure of: she had been gone from home far too long already.

Looking past Firil's furry neck, she saw they were about to climb a steep hill. At the top of that hill stood a figure. It was trying to hide itself in the trees, but as if more interested with every passing second, the form came steadily out of the cover of the forest.

"Evan," she spoke softly.

He bolted awake. "Sorry."

"There's someone up there."

"Huh?" He rubbed sleep from his eyes.

"Look. Do you see that?"

Evan blinked and stared up at the forest. "I see it. Do you think we should go a different way?"

"If we do, we'll look conspicuous."

They rode up the hill, Evan almost falling fell off Firil because of the steepness. Coming to the top, the figure—a young woman—stepped out to greet them. Rachel stopped Firil.

"Good day to you," the slender girl greeted.

"Good day," Rachel responded as cheerfully as she could. The best way to avoid suspicion was to be friendly.

"Excuse me for staring," the words came out as if politeness was foreign "it's just that I've never seen such a thing domesticated. How on Xsardis did you get the bird to obey you?"

Rachel was trying to focus, but Evan was burying half his face in her shoulder. *What is he doing?* Ignoring him, she responded to the stranger with a joke, "The question is how it got us to obey it."

"Where is its flock?"

"Gone. It liked us too much to go with them."

"What are your names?" she smiled, but there was insincerity there.

"I'm sorry. We are in a hurry—the snow has slowed us down so much. We should go."

"I think you had better stay." A whistle from the girl brought heavily armed teens to surround them. Instantly she shrugged off any pretense of kindness. "You are passing through my territory. I want to know who you are." She was staring at the part of Evan's face still showing.

"Perhaps you could start the introductions..." Rachel gripped onto Firil's feathers.

"I'm Vaylynne." At the look she received from Rachel she added, "Heard of me? Oh good! You know, even the great Seth knows who I am now."

"Seth?" Rachel tried in vain to hide her emotion.

"He really wasn't all that great. He needed my help—would have been captured by Sasha if not for me." Finally she placed Evan's face and snapped her fingers with delight at her own intelligence. "Hello there, your highness. Drainan has been quite worried about you."

Evan sat up straight. "We have been worried about him. You should not have taken him."

She shrugged, "I do things my own way."

"You led Sasha right to us—sounds like you're doing things her way."

Vaylynne's face grew dark, "Careful."

"What have you done with Drainan?"

"Get down from the bird and I'll show you. Let me think. Rachel I'll send to Sasha as a good will offering. I'll keep Evan to ransom back to his own people. The bird is mine."

Rachel froze. If they got off Firil, their lives would be forfeit. A word came strongly into her mind, the way that only the Holy Spirit of God spoke. *Run.*

Leaning closer into Firil, she whispered to his ear, "Run! Quick!"

The bird fled with wild speed and a constantly changing direction that kept arrows from reaching the teens. Vaylynne screamed at her troops to stop the bird, but Rachel, Evan and Firil were soon in safety.

Bridget tried to lie still and relax, by this time used to the smell of mold that filled the room. She was going crazy with boredom and nerves. She certainly was doing no one any good on Xsardis. She was locked in solitary confinement.

She heard the door open with quiet care. Torch light flooded into her cell. When her eyes had adjusted she saw Brooks standing before her. "Come with me," he whispered, offering a hand. She took it and followed him, questions flooding her mind.

Brooks led her through corridor after corridor. It was amazing they did not meet a guard. The two came out of the dungeons into the cold night air. Brooks shut the door behind them. Still they did not speak, knowing how dangerous it would be. Before them was the quarried wall of the fortress and the set of stairs that allowed access to it. Brooks started up.

Now Bridget grew more nervous. Security would be tightest here.

When they got to the top of the stairs, Brooks grabbed a rope and tied it to the railing. Looping it around her, he lowered her over the side of the wall. Bridget was halfway down before she realized what was going on. Brooks was helping her escape—to leave Maremoth, her home for fifteen years. She stopped climbing.

She couldn't leave. The people still trapped in the fortress were family.

"What's wrong?" Brooks whispered urgently to her. "You've gotta move!"

Bridget could not move. Far too slowly she was realizing that she was of no use to anyone in that cell. They were going to kill her. She would not be viewed as a martyr. Josiah would make sure she was seen as a failure. There was only one route left to her now. She finished the descent.

Brooks was quick to join her at the bottom, the moon and the stars offering them light to see that they were by the water's edge with a small boat waiting for them. It had blankets and a bag that Bridget guessed was full of food. She sat down in the vessel.

As Brooks paddled them away from the confinement that had been her home, the salty air and the feeling of cold water surrounded them. A slow tear trickled down her face. "Why did you do it? You didn't have to take me along."

"How much more trouble can I get in? One of the other prisoners knew I was your friend. I would never have survived if I had stayed."

"But you doubled your risk of being caught by taking me. Thank you." She held onto the sides of the boat as the water grew rocky. They were hitting some waves. "Why were there no guards?"

"I know their patterns. I was supposed to take watch on the outside of the fortress tonight. Distracting fellow guards is pretty easy."

Her body was cold from the shock. She wrapped a blanket around her and asked, "Where are we going?"

"As far away as we can. We'll land at a town and restock. Then I plan to go to Noric. You're welcome to come."

"Do you think we'd be safe there?"

He shrugged, "The dwarves there refused to help Sasha and nothing's happened to them."

They fell into silence as they both found that the freedom they had longed for fell short of expectations. Perhaps it was because neither one of them believed they would make it to Noric alive.

Chapter 20

As they rode towards Reesthma's tree, Rachel and Evan joked around and kept away from serious subjects. Rachel found it was easy to smile that morning, and in light of her glow, Evan himself felt lighter. But as Firil carried them closer to the tree, the mood grew dark.

Rachel let her smile fall, feeling that something was not right up ahead. Evan's body grew stiff. He was feeling it too.

The prince's keen ears picked up the sound of voices, angry voices. It was almost dark and they were within sight of the tree. It could only be Sasha's men. "I think it's time for the cloaks," he spoke in low tones.

Rachel nodded her agreement. Evan descended from Firil and helped Rachel down. Did he just... *Why?* Her brain gave up trying to figure it out. The prince was a gentleman. She left it at that.

Evan swung his thick white cloak around him and handed Rachel hers. "Don't let the bird come with us," Evan commanded, drawing his sword carefully so it would not make its usual sound.

Rachel told Firil firmly, "Stay here. We will be back."

She pulled the hood of her soft cloak over her head to hide her brown hair. The snow before them was lighter—partially because the blizzard had not hit as hard here and partially because of the tall trees above that had not allowed much of it in. They were able to move through it.

Once close enough to hear clearly, the two crouched behind a tree. Humans and dwarves were hacking away at the trunk of Joppa's library. Each wound to the ancient tree made Rachel feel as if they were hacking away at her.

"Are you okay?" Evan whispered. She cringed each time, by now growing paler.

She shook her head, to bring herself back to reality. Looking him straight in the eyes, she decided, "We have to stop them."

"I wish I knew if Reesthma was in there." Evan's face showed that he was working on a plan. The echoing of the army's blows was all they could hear.

Something bumped Rachel's head. She lost her balance and fell forward. Face full of snow, she turned to see Firil. "They'll see!" Evan was sharp.

"Go back Firil. Right now!"

Scared by Rachel's serious voice, Firil began to back up. He tripped on a log and fell with a loud 'thud' and a wail of unhappiness.

Evan's eyes flicked back to the dwarves and humans. Maybe, just maybe, they hadn't heard or hadn't been able to locate the sound. But all of their eyes were on him. His voice deep, the prince said only one word to Rachel, "Run."

They hurried back, Firil dashing past them. Their pursuers caught up quickly and ordered them to halt.

Rachel and Evan turned around quickly. "We're just a normal teenage couple," Evan whispered.

"Couple?" Rachel laughed under her breath, despite the danger.

"Who are you?" the bulkiest dwarf commanded, his breath showing in the cold of the night.

Rachel took Evan's hand in one of hers, putting the other on his arm. "What were you doing to that tree?" Rachel imitated what a ditsy girl would sound like on Earth. She hoped it was the same here.

The dwarf rolled his eyes. "None of your business. What are your names?"

"Oh... he's angry," Rachel hid her face in Evan's shoulder.

"Are we in some kind of trouble?" Evan demanded, sounding tough to 'impress his girlfriend.'

"Yes."

By now the twelve-man-and-dwarf group was standing in front of them. In a few moments, they would be encircled. No way out. "Don't let them talk to you like that," Rachel pouted. "You didn't do anything wrong. Did you?"

"Why are we in trouble?" Evan questioned. He broke his hold with Rachel to get into the dwarf's face.

"You ran from us. That's reason enough."

"But we stopped. Didn't we stop? I don't see why it's such a big deal. Do you?" the words rolled quickly off Rachel's tongue.

"That doesn't matter. You ran." He motioned to his men, "Tie them up. I'll decide what to do with them when we're finished with the tree."

"Oh..." Rachel trembled. "What are you going to do with us? You're not going to tell our parents we were here, are you? They'd be so mad!" And Rachel was pretty sure that her parents were going to be mad when she finally told them the truth.

One of the humans got close to the dwarf and muttered, "Come on. They're just stupid village kids. Let's leave 'em be."

But the dwarf barked at the man, "I've had enough of your kind interrupting. Because of Stewart none of you know your place."

Evan saw Rachel's hand slowly reaching for her blade. He put his hand on her forearm to stop her and motioned with his eyes past Sasha's band. At first, she saw nothing. Then she noticed that some of the snow was moving, and it was in shapes. Her brain began to process that they were animals, completely covered in snow—not an inch of their fur was showing. A slim fox, a grizzly bear, an oversized mouse, a snowman and a terrifying tiger stalked towards them.

Rachel just stared. The dwarf followed her gaze, awestruck. "Get ready!" he shouted to his troops, relishing the battle that was to come. "You," he pointed to the human who had stood up for the teens. "Guard them. If they escape, I'll take your life in payment."

The fox was the first to attack, leaping towards the nearest human. The man's slashes did not even draw blood. Some snow fell away, but no fur revealed itself. It was then that Rachel realized these creatures were not covered with snow. They were made of snow. More imagination.

But before her the carnage of battle raged as men fought for their very lives—men with families and homes. Yes, men who probably would have killed them, but still men.

After smashing the oversized mouse until nothing remained, the head dwarf surveyed his men. Some had already fallen, the others would. He turned in anger toward Evan and Rachel. "Somehow, I know this is your fault!" he shouted, swinging his ax towards Evan, but stopping in mid-swing. "What on Xsardis?" he breathed.

Rachel and Evan turned, looking up into the face of a snow-troll, carrying a huge club. His shoulders drooped, his head fell forward, his stance was low, but he looked ready to strike. Evan lost all color. Though Rachel's life had once been saved by Orvan the troll, she too paled. This creature had none of the intelligence or nobility of

Orvan.

"Come here!" someone whispered to the right of the teens.

The dwarf stared dumbstruck at the troll. They dove toward the sound, just barely getting out of the troll's path as he moved to crush the dwarf.

Before them was the opening of a snow fort. Reesthma's face beckoned them in. "That's great protection," Evan muttered.

"Not much of a choice," Rachel moved past him, following their friend deep into the tunnel.

As they rounded a corner, they saw Firil's bright form. How had Reesthma gotten him in there?

This part of the fort was just barely large enough for Firil. He was curled up in a ball on the floor, looking expectantly at Rachel. She settled down beside him, attempting to forgive him by patting his head. After all, he was hardly more than a newborn.

Evan sat down opposite her, Reesthma in between. He listened for the sounds of the enemy but none came. "Are you okay?" the prince asked Reesthma.

"I did just rescue you," she answered.

"The snow creatures… you did that?" Rachel leaned her head against the cold wall, trying to take deep breaths and release the tension. Once again her stomach burned inside her and her jaw ached from clenching it.

Reesthma nodded. Evan peered down the tunnel before saying, "But they moved."

"Of course they moved. What good would they be if they didn't?" The girl shook the snow out of her black hair. "It is really a simple technique. I read about it in the books." As if someone had just blown out the room's only candle, Reesthma's face went from chipper to downcast. "They were trying to destroy Joppa's tree."

"Is there another exit?" Evan asked, getting his bearings.

"No," she rested her nose on her sleeve. "I only started working on the fort today."

Evan opened his mouth to ask how she could have built so much so quickly, but decided that after the snow creatures, this seemed pretty small in comparison.

"We had to come in single file; so will anyone who comes after us. They won't like those odds. The safest place for us right now is here," Evan answered Rachel's unspoken questions. "Just rest." His eyes went between the two girls, "Both of you. I'll keep guard."

Rachel and Reesthma rested on Firil's soft and warm stomach. Rachel shared her cloak with the younger girl and soon Reesthma was asleep. Evan thought Rachel was resting too, but her eyes flicked open and she offered him a smile. He drank that moment in. So much struggle, but in her eyes it faded.

Hours later, Evan knew someone had to check outside. He moved quietly, but Rachel heard him. She shook her head, but he was firm and he disappeared down the tunnel.

After several minutes, he returned, "All clear."

That caused Reesthma to bolt up and run for her tree. She spent an hour examining it. Finally she declared, "I read about this salve. I can fix most of the damage."

Content, Reesthma led them into her home. Her attitude became lighter with each moment spent in her own space. As they reached the bottom the girl was ready for information, "Where is your army?"

"We don't have one," Rachel admitted. "Seth is on Noric trying to get dwarf support. Katarina and Max went to Issym. We tried the villages here on Asandra, but no one will help. We have no allies."

"Then you need new ones," she was definite. "Have you tried the sprites?"

"No. They are evil." Rachel was all too aware of that fact.

"Not all of them can be. Look; less than a day's walk from here is the sprite nest. They are powerful. Even if we can only get a few to help, it would be worth it."

"They'll probably kill us before we can say a word," Rachel answered, vividly remembering her last sprite encounter.

"They couldn't kill you, Rachel. You made them up!" Reesthma stated with childlike innocence and belief.

"Oh, if only things were so simple..."

Evan offered, "Sometimes insanity is the best course of action."

Seth eased himself into a chair and looked at his hands that were battered from weeks of work. Edmund sat down beside him, leaning forward off the table. "Tired?" the shape shifter asked.

The teen was not in a particularly good mood. He was aware of the snappy tone in which he retorted, "What have you been doing all this time? I could have used your help."

"Dwarves don't want my 'dirty, shape shifting help,'" he replied, morphing into Lotex's form for the last few words and then returning to his normal self. "Besides, you were the one who said you'd work for your keep."

Seth checked the attitude and asked, "Then what did you do last time you were here?"

"I built a small cabin away from here and kept it to myself that I was a shape shifter. When the dwarves found out, they chased me off fairly quickly."

"I take it you weren't expecting a particularly warm welcome to Noric this time?"

"No."

"Are you the reason Lotex and all the other dwarves hate me so?"

"You think Lotex hates you 'cause he works you hard?" Blowen asked.

"Hard... beyond reason! I'm athletic; I can handle pain; but Lotex dishes out more than even I know what to do with." And it was true. Night offered little rest and plenty of nightmares. Days offered labor where the short breaks he did get only served to remind him just how much the pain hurt.

"Isn't that when you are supposed to turn to your God?" Edmund sneered.

Seth closed his eyes and swallowed the less-than-godly responses that threatened to spring up. *Give me grace,* he prayed.

Edmund had moved on already from his snooty comment, "If Lotex pushes you, that means you are impressing him."

"If you can befriend him," Blowen interjected, "you will pretty much guarantee yourself an army. Lotex never agrees with anyone, so when he does, dwarves know it's important. Not that I want to sound harsh. He has his good qualities, though I can't think of what they are, right now. But..."

Seth silenced him, "Edmund, what should I be doing? You know the dwarves. I don't seem to be winning their respect. And we don't have time for me to invest six months trying." *I need to go home at some point.*

"This may be a waste of time then. So quit." Edmund meant to taunt him. It was working.

Seth gritted his teeth and bit back a sharp retort. "I'm going to take a walk." Seth got out of the apartment and escaped into the light snow. He was angry, frustrated, and offended. "Why did I let him get so under my skin?" Seth wondered out loud.

Maybe because you want to quit, Seth's subconscious answered. *He hit a nerve.*

Seth took a breath. He could not strangle his subconscious so he would have to let it go. "I don't really want to quit," he explained to the air. "It's just been weeks and I feel like I'm wasting my time. Rachel and Max are back on Asandra and…" He stopped himself. Why was he talking to the air when he had a Friend in the air Who wanted to help?

"God. I don't want to stay in this place where my faith is rejected and people are constantly telling me to go home. It was easy to be a hero on Issym—people expected me to be. Here?

"I have a life on Earth and even one on Asandra and Issym. I want to be anywhere but here. What if I spend the rest of the year on this forsaken island and don't even get their help? What if I fail Xsardis?

"What if I go home and find that time did pass normally? My band was growing. We'll have lost our following. My church and my school will have replaced me. My friends will be in college. I wanted a normal life. I earned a normal life. And I have gotten anything but. What if this island is my life? I don't even like these people!"

He paused, fell to a kneeling position in the snow and asked the question that had been burning in his heart, "What if Xsardis takes our lives? What if Rachel and Max and I die?"

Bridget felt the tension rise even as she slept. She tried to ignore it, but as the boat's rocking grew stronger and stronger, she opened her eyes and sat up.

"Bridget!" Brooks' voice was breathless, his body dripped with sweat, and his arms shook with the effort of paddling. "Pray."

Already they were swept into the pull of a whirlpool. It was larger than she could have dreamed. Behind them the sea was calm, but here the water grew fiercer and fiercer. Brooks let go of the oar. What good was it? He could not steer out of this. The vortex had them.

Brooks looked in indignation at the heavens. Was this how God would kill his dear, faithful Bridget? Would He let her taste freedom and then kill her?

Waves filled the boat with water. He gripped the sides of the small vessel. Bridget was doing the same. Her eyes were closed and her face was set tight. Was she praying even in her last moments? Would the girl ever doubt her God? Her eyes flickered open. They were challenging him to believe. That was the last thing he saw before darkness took him.

Chapter 21

Sometimes insanity is the best course of action, Rachel repeated Evan's words. They were moving through the falling snow in an attempt to find the sprite nest and win some of them over. Yes, it was insane to ask for help from a group of people who had relished the thought of killing you, but they did not have a lot of options.

Rachel and Evan walked side by side while Reesthma enjoyed a ride on Firil. Evan's appearance had returned to its typical determination. She elbowed him. He responded with an even more solemn look, but softened and offered a shrug. That was something.

It was cold. Brutally cold. Their noises were red; their ears had lost all feeling; everything ached, but the white cloaks offered so much more warmth than they would have had otherwise. The trees looked ominous in the night as if they were warning them: *Turn back. Turn back!* Still they pressed on, traveling at night because that was the easiest time to spot the trouble-making sprites.

"Rachel," Evan took her arm and pointed ahead. "Look."

Rachel followed his finger and spotted the fire spiral like the one they had seen when they had last encountered sprites. She stopped walking. Was this crazy plan the right plan? Evan's eyes bore into her. He did not want to go, but he would follow her judgment.

Nodding, she said, "We go forward."

Before long, Firil panicked at the growing closeness of the flames and Reesthma had to get down and walk. The bird ducked behind some bushes, his feathers showing on all the sides of the shrub. They would come back for the bird—if they could. The three approached on foot, weapons sheathed, trying to seem passive.

They stood as close to the fire as they could and distinguished the forms of the sprites causing it. It took only a few moments for the sprites to descend before them. "We want to talk to your leader!" Rachel called to them.

"Well our leader doesn't want to talk to you," a fire sprite answered, shooting flames that landed inches from the teens' feet. They jumped backwards and felt the heat of the wall of fire that now blocked their way out. *No turning back now,* Evan thought. *I hope she knows what she's doing.*

"How do you know unless you ask her?" Rachel called, sorry now that she had brought Evan and Reesthma into this.

"She said all trespassers were to meet death," another sprite answered. "We cannot afford to take risks. We are, after all, weak, little children."

Three fire sprites flew hastily behind each of the teens, letting a small flame of fire come out of their hands to propel their captives forward. Reesthma and Rachel moved instantly; Evan tried to resist, but even he began to inch towards the massive blaze. Understanding that they were about to be thrown into the fire, Evan reached for his blade and swung towards the nearest sprite with a roar. Fire descended onto the blade. Evan could not keep hold of it and the weapon fell into the snow, useless. He was pushed to the fire and he barely had time to glance back at Rachel and Reesthma to mouth, "Shadrach, Me..." *Meshach and Abednego,* the girls' brains filled in the rest.

Rachel cried out as Evan disappeared in the flames. Reesthma was to be next, but Rachel forced herself between the fire and the girl. And then she too was covered in the flames of the fire.

Katarina watched Zara fly ahead. The illuminescent was letting off sparks and freezing the snow so that they could walk on it. It was only mid-morning, but the creature's glow was fading.

Max kept a few feet behind, finally speaking, "We made it through that town just fine."

"You were right..." she grudgingly replied.

Sure of his hunch because of her willingness to admit her own fault, Max answered quickly, "But you *knew* we would."

She stopped walking. "What do you mean?"

The teen held his ground, despite how hard this conversation would be. He felt terrible calling *her* a liar. After all, she had not turned him in to Sasha like he had practically done with Seth and Rachel to Smolden. He went on, "You weren't afraid that Sasha would discover us. You were afraid that *I* would discover *you*."

"I'm not following," she tried to say, but it was all too clear that she was.

"Do you think I'm an idiot?"

"No!" she put on an offended tone.

Max had to laugh at that. *She* was offended? "Then why have you been lying to me? You think I have no sense of direction? Even if we hadn't gone into a town I would have figured out that we weren't heading to the coast."

"What are you talking about?"

"They said that that town was Clidrion. That's in the middle of Asandra—we're farther from the coast than when we started."

"What? We are! We must be lost."

"Not lost Katarina. You've been very purposeful in leading us here. I want to know why."

Katarina's mind spun for almost a full minute. Finally she asked, "How did you know?"

He walked towards her, not about to shout his answer to the wide world—even though no one else would hear him anyway. "Before I went to Issym... I was a master at tricking and lying and getting my way. It was an art to me. I recognize the signs of a liar."

"I'm sure you can't understand," she began. He rolled his eyes. Zara came back, glad for the break. "I didn't want to deceive you. It was just that I didn't think you'd go along with it if I told you the truth."

The silence of the wood seemed to echo in his ears as Max stared into Katarina's face. "What is the truth?"

"I..." she realized that her eyes were getting red, but she couldn't do anything about it. "I just can't lose two parents. I've been guiding us to Maremoth. I have to rescue my mom."

She waited for the storm to come from his mouth, *How could you lie to me? That is the dumbest plan I've ever heard! There's no way we can do it. What we're you thinking? You've jeopardized all of Asandra.* But the storm did not come. He shifted his bag over his shoulder and started walking, "Okay. Let's get moving."

It took her a second to realize that he was going to follow her plan. She did not move. "Why, Max?"

"I can understand better than you think."

"What do you mean?"

"You're not the only one who lost a parent, Kat. It was not easy. I was eight years old when my father died and I rebelled against everything that had to do with God. But when I came to Issym, a guy name Arvin—a prisoner of Smolden—just... he was really nice to me, and I was working for Smolden at the time. There was something about him. When Arvin almost died, I knew what I had to do. I gave myself to Jesus and tried to help save his life."

"Were you able to?"

"I only postponed his death. In the battle against Smolden, he died to save me; but truthfully he had saved me when he showed me Christ."

He continued, "Now I'm not saying that after my dad died, I always got along with my mom, but I would have done anything to protect her. I get what you're trying to do. But from now on, you *need* to be honest with me."

Seth reached for his cloak, heading for the wood room. Stacking his arms with a large armload of firewood he marched to Lotex's room with the unasked-for favor and set it in the bin.

Lotex sat up surprised to see Seth awake before he was. He had worn himself out from working Seth so hard. "I see you've finally decided to take this seriously," he huffed.

"What next?" Seth asked.

The dwarf looked him over. "I think you're ready."

"For?"

"Expansion."

Seth tried not to grin. Expansion was not a task for a nobody. It was the dwarves' most valued job. Lotex pushed past him like it was nothing special, but Seth understood. He was nearing the end of his time on Noric. These were the last steps for gaining their respect.

What had changed since the night before when he had fallen on his knees and questioned so much? He had been consumed by so much fear, but now a peace had taken hold of him.

Coming to a dead end, Lotex handed Seth one pickax and went to work with the other. Seth immediately started swinging. "No, no! You're doing that all wrong," Lotex boomed and showed him how.

Seth had long ago learned that Lotex did not like to talk while he was working, but today that did not matter. Already his arms ached from the strength it took to get even the smallest piece of rock to come from the walls. He needed the distraction in order to keep going. "Why didn't you go with Sasha?"

The dwarf grunted, but answered. "It doesn't take a genius to realize that she is up to no good. And I've never liked meddlers."

Seth wiped the sweat from his brow and went back to swinging. "Do you miss Asandra?"

"Some do. Not me. This is home. We're left to ourselves."

The teen stared at him, "Do you honestly think that Sasha will leave you alone?"

"What?" Lotex grunted, not expecting the question.

"After she wins Asandra, what makes you think that you won't be her next target?"

"Simple. What could she possibly desire on Noric?"

"You refused her, didn't you? She came to get your help and only half of you gave it. Sasha does not forget her grudges."

"You speak like you're afraid of her."

"Believe me," Seth answered, "if you looked in her eyes, you'd be scared too."

He shrugged, which meant that Seth had made a good point but he was not about to listen. "The dwarves who went with Sasha won't stand for her doing anything against us."

"They won't be able to stop her. Sasha won't need them once she has control of Asandra. She'll force them to do things you would have never thought possible."

Lotex's face became red with his anger. "Are you insinuating that the dwarves might turn on their brothers and enslave or kill us just because of fear?"

"They enslave and fight against innocent men, women and children on Asandra every day. Why wouldn't they turn on you if the right pressure was on them?"

Lotex cautioned, "Watch yourself, boy."

Someone was shaking her. Bridget felt herself be rolled over. The sun blinded her even through closed eyes. It was cold. She was soaked. A man was calling her name.

Everything came back to her in an instant. She was free from Maremoth! Part of her hoped that when she opened her eyes she would see a rugged Carpenter looking down at her, saying, 'Well done, My good and faithful servant.' Alas, only Brooks' face came into view as she peeled open her eyelids.

They had been caught in a huge whirlpool. "How did we survive?" she asked, sitting up with his help.

"I don't know."

She took her time getting to her knees and wrung out her wet hair. "Where are we?"

His eyes drifted to the cliffs behind her. A rocky castle filled the skyline. "That's not Maremoth," he muttered.

"There are no other castles on Asandra, right?"

"Sasha was building another one, but I don't know how far along she got—probably not that far."

"Brooks, that cannot be one of Sasha's palaces. I would sense the sorrow."

"How does freedom feel?"

"After fifteen years of waiting for it…" she shivered. "I don't even know how to express it."

They began their climb up a rocky path leading to the fortress surrounding the castle. Their wet clothes bogged them down and their stiff bodies slowed them even more. Bridget fell to a rock, taking a moment to rest.

Brooks stood over her, not sure whether he should be preparing for an attack or lying down to take a nap. The hot sun beat upon them. Where was the intense cold of winter?

He relived with embarrassment the moments before the current had taken them. Had he really been praying? And yet perhaps the only reason they had survived was because of Bridget's faith. "You never doubted, did you?" he inquired.

She paused to phrase her answer. "I have constantly doubted; I just didn't let the doubts rule me."

He offered her a hand, "Come on then. Let's find out what's ahead."

They finished their trek and walked into the fortress, receiving no questions from the guards. The people who moved about had no real fear on their faces. They were dressed in common but well-made clothing, which made Bridget realize how out of place they must have looked. She tried to wipe the sand off her raggedy dress but she figured that she had little hope of appearing presentable.

All of the sudden Brooks pushed her behind him. "What?" she questioned and then she saw it. "What is that?" A man-sized frog stood on two legs, wearing colorful, stone armor. It was moving. It was alive. And there were more of them. They walked around the village as if they belonged here. A female one said goodbye to a human she was talking to and approached Brooks and Bridget.

"Where are we?" Brooks breathed.

"Hello," the frog extended her three-fingered, slimy hand. "I am Lady Amber. You act like you just saw the ghost of Sasha."

"Something like that," Bridget could not stop staring; she did not even take the frog's hand.

"Where are you from?" Amber spoke in the tones of an accomplished woman relishing the mystery of new company. Her sword hung at her belt, but she did not look like she would use it lightly.

"Maremoth," Bridget answered.

"I haven't heard of that."

Brooks found that his voice was clearer now, "Where are we?"

"On Issym, in the castle of High King Galen."

"Issym. We made it to Issym? I just wanted to get to Noric," Bridget was smiling.

"Where are you from?" Amber's voice was commanding. Something was peculiar about these strangers and she was transitioning into an official court representative.

"Asandra," Bridget whispered.

Her eyes filled with wonder, then narrowed with reality. "King Galen will wish to speak with you."

Amber led them into the palace and offered them new clothes while she spoke with the king. Bridget had just enough time to change into comfortable dress before a woman walked in. She wore a pleasant garment that showed her to be well along in her pregnancy. A slender crown was almost unnoticeable in the brown curls that fell down to her shoulders, but Bridget knew this woman to be a queen. She offered a bow. Brooks, who was just glad to see a human, got to his knees. "We're not so formal here," the queen spoke. "My name is Andrea. Please, come with me."

Queen Andrea walked slowly through the halls of her palace, Amber standing beside her until they came to the throne room. There the frog waited.

Bridget and Brooks paused. "Come," Andrea gave a reassuring smile.

Stepping inside, the two saw that the throne room was simple, like the rest of the castle. In Maremoth, Sasha's throne was elevated, but this throne sat on floor level. Sasha's throne room held only her throne and elegant candle holders, curtains and rugs. This throne room had little adornment, but possessed a long table and chairs which looked well used.

The queen walked before them and approached the king, who sat pouring over a scroll, his crown sitting beside him. Andrea put a hand on his arm and whispered something to him, gently forcing the scroll out of his hands. He stood up, showing how tall and lean he was. His scruffy cheeks displayed smile lines as he put on a grin and opened wide his hands, "Welcome!"

The two travelers bowed. "No one has to do that in this kingdom as long as I reign!" his voice boomed. He put his arm around his queen and walked towards them, "My wife was telling me something about where you come from, but I couldn't quite hear her, so you'll have to tell me yourselves."

"First, may I ask one question?" Bridget began. Sasha had once come to Issym. Were these people just her officers? "Sasha..."

"Rest at ease. She is dead."

"No my lord, she is not." Bridget and Brooks proceeded to tell the king and queen everything.

King Galen stared out the window over his beautiful country. Remorse broke his voice, "Well, it seems we have another battle on our hands."

Chapter 22

Evan felt himself sliding rapidly downward on water—it might have been fun if he had not been completely stunned. Wasn't he supposed to be dead? He had been thrown into burning hot fire. Had God really rescued him like in the story of Shadrach, Meshach and Abednego?

His eyes were useless. The scenery swept past him too quickly to absorb. He felt his whole body submerge in water. The prince desperately swam for the top, but the pressure of the fall had sunk him deeply. Disoriented, he was not sure whether he was going up or down. His lungs pounded for air. Finally he broke the surface.

As his ears struggled to deal with the water that had been unwantedly admitted, he heard the muffled sounds of Rachel calling for Reesthma. Evan drew in deep breaths and kept his feet kicking to stay above water. His eyes were forced shut by the pounding of his head.

He blinked rapidly until he saw that he was in large pool of water. Rachel was not far from him, but Reesthma was missing. Feeling the dread set in, he realized the girl had not made it up. Rachel was already underwater, looking for her. Evan drew a breath and dove down, swimming hard and fast.

The prince located her small figure, descending limply farther down. He grabbed hold of her waist and struggled to pull her up with him. When they broke the water's surface, Rachel was pointing in the direction of land. He pulled Reesthma towards the gray, rock-like surface. Once they were on dry ground, Evan collapsed. He waited for the headache to pass, trying to tell if Reesthma was breathing.

Rachel knelt dripping over her. The girl's eyes fluttered open. "She's fine," Rachel reassured him.

Reesthma slowly sat up, looking around her to see hundreds of sprites—some earth and some fire—hovering nearby, leering at them. "What happened?"

"The fire must have been some kind of illusion." Evan was still flat on his back. Rachel leaned over him. "Are you okay?"

He lifted his head up just long enough to nod. It was not until the fire sprites once again surrounded them that Evan stood and walked with Reesthma and Rachel forward. They had no idea where the sprites were leading them, but they followed. Their weapons were quickly taken from them.

Rachel knew that she should have been thinking about an escape or what to do next, but she just wanted to look at the earth sprites. They were taller and leaner than the fire sprites. They wore green or brown tunics or dresses. But where the fire sprites were unadorned, the earth sprites wore bangles on their wrists, necks, ears and hair. They also had some kind of deep eye shadow on their eyes.

As some of the sprites began to turn back, Reesthma knew that they were not approaching something good. They came to a stone door that was three times as large as she was. Now all the sprites flew away. "Aren't you coming?" she called after them.

"None may enter where you now go!"

Swinging the pick with his shaking arms, Seth tried to remind himself that it was just like basketball. On the court you just kept running. In the mines you just kept swinging. He attempted to put his mind anywhere but on the pain. Sweat rolled into his eye as a thought struck him—this area of the mine had been empty for weeks. Plenty of dwarves were clamoring for the much respected mining work, so why was no one here?

"Quitting?" Lotex huffed in his direction.

Seth woke up and realized that he had stopped working. "No. Thinking."

"Think while you work!"

Seth began to swing his pick ax again, but he asked, "Why does no one else come down here?"

"All cowards," Lotex answered.

Cowards... his head repeated. Maybe it meant something different on Noric than it did on Earth? "Lazy?" he suggested.

"I meant what I said," he growled.

"Why would they be scared?" Seth stopped working. Lotex was always gruff, but there was a tone in his voice that he had not heard before—fear. It was heavily masked, but it was there.

Lotex kept pounding away at the wall before them. "We get some rumbles."

Seth understood. "Earthquakes." The apartments the dwarves occupied were well-built to withstand almost anything. But he was not in those rooms; he was in an unsecured part of the mine. If there was an earthquake, they would be buried alive. "How often?"

"Often this time of year in this part of the mines."

"Only in this part?"

"You ask too many questions." Lotex rarely wanted to talk, but he never dodged a question. So why was he this time?

Seth put his hand on a nearby beam to test it. It wobbled under his light pressure. "These beams... did you put them up?"

Lotex rolled his eyes, "Will you ever stop asking questions? This is why we make children stay with women!" He paused, then answered, "Someone else did."

"They were in a hurry. They did not do a good job." Something deep inside Seth told him that he needed to get out of there. "Let's go."

Lotex had to admit that he had a growing respect for Seth. The boy did not back down easily. If Seth was worried, so was he. "Why?"

Seth was moving backwards. "Come on!" He was far back before he felt the first rumble.

Lotex turned and ran after Seth, but the ground shook beneath his feet. The support beams fell, bringing the ceiling with them. Seth dove forward, curling into a ball and protecting his head as he landed. Chunks of rock fell from the ceiling. A few of the smaller ones hit him.

The earthquake was over almost as quickly as it had started. Seth rose to his feet and tried to make out the scene before him. When finally the dust had cleared enough, he saw a mound of rocks covering the ground before him. Lotex must have been under them.

Seth dashed to the rocks and started pulling them away, tearing what was left of his hands to shreds. He was aware of the warm feeling of blood on his arms and legs, but he did not stop. "Lotex!" he hollered. "Can you hear me?"

Before him the rocks seemed like they would never move, but

he finally shoveled enough and saw a dwarf hand. He pulled the rest of the debris away. Lotex was breathing, but barely. He had to get him help.

Seth dumped the contents of a nearby wheelbarrow. With strength that he did not know he had, he pulled Lotex's upper body into it. Pushing the wheelbarrow, it seemed like ages before he came to a small wooden door. At the sight of his destination the pain overwhelmed him and he fell to the ground. His shoulder burned, his gashes seared, his muscles ached, his head spun and he could barely breathe. He was going to pass out; he could feel it. He raced for the door and pounded on it.

Bridget moved silently into the kitchen, her stomach refusing to let her sleep with so much accessible food below her. She rounded the corner into the room and immediately wished she had told her stomach to shut up. "High king."

Galen was a good man, an attentive husband, an excellent king. He was like a sponge, constantly asking for more information to absorb. She really could not blame him. He needed to know what was going on, but she was tired of talking about the place she had just escaped.

The look on Galen's face, however, showed that he was not about to ask her a long series of questions. Instead, he set a mug of hot cider on the counter for her and poured himself another. Bridget broke a piece of bread off and sat down opposite him. "I grew up," he said, "as the future ruler of a fort. Everything was given to me, but I knew that I had to learn what want and need were if I was going to serve my people well. So I left. I wandered for years through the forest. I met so many people and was welcomed by so many villages."

He took a sip of his cider before continuing, "But slowly over those years I saw that life grew harder for those towns. Every season new criminals would spring up and take everything from them. They lived in constant fear. That was before we defeated most of those brigands in the battle against Smolden and Sasha. Even after that, the people carried fear around with them. I don't blame them. But when I became High King, the first thing I did was to promise them that I would do everything I could to keep them safe.

"I see the same look of fear in your eyes, Bridget. I can't even imagine what you've gone through, but I make you the same promise I made my people. You are safe here."

At first Bridget sat frozen. Then she let the tears come—tears she had not allowed herself to cry for those fifteen years. She felt a woman's arms wrap around her. Andrea must have been standing in the doorway the whole time.

"You were so strong. You don't have to be right now," the queen whispered. "God and I will hold you together."

Bridget found that she slept soundly that night. She did not rise until mid-morning. After getting dressed, she was ushered into the throne room. A full meal was set on the table. Bridget sat next to Andrea and across from Brooks. "This table is not set for four."

"The council is assembling," Andrea answered. "After my husband became king, he established it. Each village has a magistrate and each sector a prince over them. Those princes form this council and help him rule."

"You mean, this is a formal meeting?" Brooks asked.

"Don't worry. It will be fine."

He appeared skeptical, but stayed seated. Bridget gave him a look that showed that she was just as uncomfortable. They weren't political thinkers; they weren't military strategists; they weren't even really *they*. He nodded his agreement with all those thoughts.

The first guests arrived. Princess Valerie and Curt, the captain of her army. They were quick to engage Brooks and Bridget in a pleasant conversation. The council stopped being normal after that. The next two looked like humans, but they had wings and eyes that were covered in sparkles. "The fairy king and his captain, Elimelech," Andrea whispered to her.

In a few minutes Amber followed with a somber frog. A regal young woman who carried herself with a grace unmatched was several steps behind. "That's Universe Girl," Andrea informed her. "Call her Ethelwyn."

"Who is she?" Bridget inquired. There was an unmistakable twinkle in her eyes. Her dress was long and lean and her brown hair fell from her shoulders. How did someone barely over twenty carry such maturity?

"You'll like her."

A hawk flew in through the window, then morphed into a blond-headed woman. She nodded at Galen with a sad look, then took her seat and began speaking with the fairy king. "A shape shifter?" Brooks was ready to stand and fight.

Galen stopped speaking with Amber and answered Brooks, "This is Kate. She is as opposed to Sasha as anyone can be."

The group sat around the table, eating, talking and laughing. The council was still short two members. The first was a tall woman of great beauty with wings that extended from her arms. "An airsprite," Andrea informed them as she entered.

The airsprite was accompanied by a lively frog wearing a top hat and carrying a cane. This frog saw the winged lady to her seat then eagerly grasped Galen's forearm.

"It has been too long, Flibbert," the king spoke loudly.

"Much too long," he agreed. Before sitting at the open seat, Flibbert took his hat off and offered a deep bow to Universe Girl. "How are you, Wyn?"

As soon as he had sat down, the room grew silent. Brooks wondered if they knew what was about to be said or if they just sensed that something bad was coming. King Galen stood and put his hands on the back of his chair. "Good friends," he began, looking each of them in the eyes. "You know the victory we won against Smolden. We all hoped that this hard-earned prosperity would last for some time, but it is not to be." He paused, finding the words. "News has come from Asandra. Sasha lives."

Flibbert hopped to his feet and stared angrily at Brooks and Bridget. "What's this? Do we distrust the word of Seth and Rachel, now?"

Galen was quick to reply, "No! You and I especially know them to be incapable of such deceit. But all of Issym knows that Sasha *is*."

Kate's eyes fell shut. Opening them, she saw that the council stared at her. She answered them. "I have suspected that she is alive."

"We are to take the word of a shifter?" Flibbert demanded, looking for support from the fairies.

"Flibbert!" the reproach came from Universe Girl.

The frog opened his mouth to protest and several others began to speak. At Kate's low and un-insulted tone, they quieted. "You never wanted to know me, Flibbert, but you cannot help but know my deeds. I have nothing to gain by lying to you."

The council fell silent. The conflict over the shape shifters was not one easily resolved. It had been, by far, Galen's hardest battle. The high king looked to Bridget, "We need to hear the truth. Don't leave a thing out. Speak, Bridget."

So Bridget stood and spoke. Her words brought the threat of Sasha to reality.

The airsprite's face was filled with despair, "Then what hope do we have?"

Brooks replied, "The prince and princess are strong willed. They lead a rebellion with the help of Max, Seth and Rachel."

That simple sentence changed the entire feel of the room. The air lightened. People laughed away the tension.

Ethelwyn slowly rose. "You all seem to think," her voice was quiet but it captured their attention, "that because Seth and Rachel are on Xsardis, we have no need to fear."

The air suddenly grew stifling. A grim look settled on the council members' faces. The people of Issym had lost so much to fight Smolden and were just now rebuilding. How could they ask their people to fight another war? Yet the reality of Ethelwyn's words rang true.

She looked to Flibbert, "You remember that when Seth and Rachel first came to Issym, they lived in fear and refused to help us. But we asked them to trust God and they did. Their actions saved us all." She turned to the rest of the council, "Now that same choice awaits us."

Flibbert nodded—never for a moment having been willing to stay behind, but now convinced that he would need to bring an army with him. "Trouble will not stay on Asandra. Without my people's stones, Sasha's power will only continue to grow."

"Stand if you will fight," Galen challenged them all. One by one they stood, all of them. The tide would turn in the battle for Asandra.

A darkness had settled over Issym, deep and penetrating. As Galen gazed out the hallway's window at the stars, he thought even they shone less brightly.

They had just begun to hope for prosperity—a prosperity he so desperately wanted to bring his people. Now he would separate families for months, maybe years. Some of them would never be reunited.

He did not relish battle like the frogs. Flibbert only seemed truly alive when his sword was spinning in his hand. The two of them had spent hours that evening recalling the battles they had faced with Seth and Rachel against countless enemies. The frog was already itching to get to Asandra. He could not stand having the teens in danger and not being able to protect them. His anticipation for meeting Sasha in battle was growing with every second. *Surely he knows what that will mean,* Galen thought, wondering how the frog could be so excited.

Flibbert's passion was certainly his greatest weakness and his greatest strength. It caused his resilience to all the troubles that came, his battle fury and his protective nature that made it unbearable to be so far from Seth and Rachel. His pride, his confidence and his stubbornness could have been considered faults. They also made him relish the thought of dying in battle, Issym's best fighter and its symbol of strength and honor. Flibbert was to be honored for his sacrifice. He had given up a family to be the warrior. As Galen thought of his wife and the child within her, he could not imagine life without them.

A soft hand touched his shoulder and Galen turned to see Kate's face. He leaned back against the stone wall and waited to hear what the shape shifter would have to say. Kate was a troubled leader; with reason. There had been so much resistance to her and her kind. Now she would have to fight the old shape shifter ruler. So much could go wrong on so many fronts for Kate and the shifters.

Kate leaned on the wall opposite him and spoke softly, "I believe that Sasha is alive, but her treachery leaves us with a bad decision either way. If you take this army, you leave Issym unguarded. And if you don't, then you leave all of Xsardis unprotected. Brooks and Bridget may have been sent here to draw our army out."

He rubbed the back of his neck. "I know."

She looked grim. "There is something I did not tell you. When Edmund and I rescued Queen Danielle from where Sasha had hidden her, there was a dwarf guarding her. He boasted that Sasha had many servants on Asandra."

"Kate," stress emanated from Galen's voice, "why did you say nothing earlier?"

"Edmund went to Asandra to see if these reports were true."

"That's where he's been! How could you have trusted the fate of Xsardis to him?" he shouted at her. "The same Edmund who worked for Sasha for years; the same Edmund who captured Seth and Rachel..."

"The same Edmund that helped them escape from Sasha with the gem of light which turned the tide of the battle!" she answered him with passion. After a few silent moments, she added, "Edmund may not be trustworthy in all things, but I did not perceive this to be one of them."

"You allowed him to go to a place where he would again be

tempted by his sister," Galen rebuked gently. "That was not wise."

She nodded. "I had little choice but to let him go, but I should have been open with you. It was just that Issym needed time to heal and rumors of Sasha living and having an army would have only served to make us suspicious."

"You mean to make Issym suspicious of the shape shifters."

"In the future I will be more forthcoming. At the time I did not know what kind of king or man you were."

At first Galen thought of a few insulting remarks to throw back at her, but he let the anger out of his body. If he had been in her place, what would he have done? "Why are you telling me this?"

"I can get to Asandra much quicker than an army. Let me find Edmund and learn the truth."

"How will you communicate with us?"

Kate smiled, grateful for Galen's forgiving nature. "I intend to take an illuminescent with me. They have ways of sending messages through the water."

"You think one will go with you?" he scoffed. Illuminescents had brought him almost more headaches than the shifters. They were stubborn; they were opinionated; they had powers that were undefined; they made everyone nervous.

"Our races have become closely intertwined," Kate replied. "Two outcast species bonded together."

He understood that. "Then go; but hurry. The army will leave here in three days' time."

She flew out the window as Galen turned back to his room. Hearing shouting from Princess Valerie and Curt, the king walked towards them. "We need you here," Valerie tried a softer voice.

"I must go," Curt was firm.

Galen stepped beside them, "Curt, a word." They walked away from the princess' hearing. "I need you here."

Curt grit his teeth. "Have I done something wrong?"

"No. Valerie is a young princess, though; she needs your political and military guidance. And despite our love for the fairies, they can sometimes focus a little too much on defense and not enough on offense. You are the voice of reason I must leave behind."

Sasha walked through her palace, frustrated. How long would she wait on Seth and Rachel to come to her? She would not scour the country for them! That had been Smolden's tactic and it had certainly failed him.

She stepped behind Stewart as he stood reading a letter. He felt the dark presence and cringed, turning to meet his empress' face. "Sasha."

"It is time to draw our friends Seth and Rachel out. Announce the execution of Queen Juliet in three weeks' time. That should bring them."

"Yes, Empress." He bowed but asked, "Do you really think they'll come for her before they're ready?"

"Their consciences are sickening. They won't be able to resist." She thought for a moment. "Hang Malcon then, too. See if they won't take the rascal off our hands and let him be a spy for us."

"Of course."

"I've been away from the sprites for far too long. If I am to maintain their loyalty, I'll need to see them. Run my fortress well while I am gone."

Chapter 23

Seth felt a heavy weight pushing on his shoulder. He turned and saw a dwarf woman almost ripping it off trying to tend to the gash. "I'm okay. Really!" the teen protested. But although the debris was hiding most of the blood, he was fairly beaten up.

The dwarf woman finished wrapping his shoulder, then tore off what remained of his shirt and pulled out a jagged piece of rock that had lodged in his stomach. She bathed the wound in some kind of horrid smelling medicine.

Seth tried to move to get a better look at where dwarves stood around Lotex, trying to repair the damage. "Sit down," the woman tending him commanded. "My brother is too strong to die like this."

"Lotex is your brother?" It was an odd coincidence that this was the first house they had come to.

When she was finished, Seth tried to move towards Lotex, but she pushed him to the door. "I'll send for you when they are finished."

Lotex's gruff voice, however, came from the circle of dwarves around him, "Seth. Come here."

The dwarves parted to allow him room and Seth leaned over Lotex. Covered in blood, bandages and dust, Lotex was hardly recognizable. The dwarf grasped his hand, "It has been my privilege to know you."

"Oh, shut up, Lotex," Seth answered, communicating in a dwarfish manner. "I worked way too hard getting you out of that cave-in to have you give up. Are you some kind of coward?"

"A... coward? Watch your tongue!" Lotex protested, life back in his voice.

Seth was not finished. If the dwarf lost heart, he would die. "You owe me and I take my payment now. Fight for your life because I need you. I know you to be stronger than to give up."

Ethelwyn looked out across the open field through a window on the first floor of the castle. She was in the library and she felt content there. She liked to be surrounded by knowledge.

Outside, frogs and men practiced their fighting skills. She doubted they were preparing because they had been ordered to. Mostly, it was for pride and fun that they exerted themselves. Flibbert the frog hopped around the field like a veteran, the others unable to keep up with him. She smiled. He loved to show off.

The frog glanced in her direction and saw her staring eyes. A few moments later he looked back again, to see her still watching. Intrigued, he put away his sword, walked over to the window and in a single bound, he landed beside her.

He was breathing hard, but smiling. "You enjoy battle too much," Ethelwyn commented.

"Not the real thing, but practice—that's fun." He looked around every shelf to assure himself that they were alone. Then he sat down and propped his legs on the room's only table, flexing his six toes. "You seemed troubled, Wyn."

"War always troubles me."

"You think it is war then."

"I feel it in the air." She sat down beside him. "My whole life," she put such an emphasis on it and it made Flibbert laugh. She was in her twenties. Her life had not been that long. "I have waited for peace and we've never really had it. But Galen is a good king, he has a good council—with a decent frog on it—and our people are truly committed to God. I thought that we might at last have rest."

Flibbert saw a deep weariness in her face and wondered how long it had been since she had slept. He put his feet on the ground, leaned forward, took her hand and asked, "Are you okay?"

"I am fine," she was quick to answer. "But do you realize that we have no real sailors? No captains. We are taking an entire fleet on a journey that could last many months and we have no idea what we're doing."

He dropped her hand. "You sound like you have a solution."
"One, but you're going to hate it."

King Galen walked into the library, having been told that Flibbert and Ethelwyn had last been seen there. As he reached the window, he saw them riding away. He sighed. What were they up to now?

Hearing whispers, the man moved past bookshelves. The precious history they contained had been gifted to him from his home's extensive library.

Peering over one row of books, he saw Bridget and Brooks leaning close and whispering. He quieted his breathing to listen to Bridget ask, "Did we lose months of memory or did we get here overnight?"

"Both don't seem very likely," Brooks answered.

"There are no other possibilities. That whirlpool must have sucked us off Asandra's coast and spit us out on Issym. And if that happened, I think God saved us."

"I think you might be right."

Galen moved out of the library, leaving them to discuss the spiritual on their own. He would store the conversation in his mind and find out more when he could.

Nicholas caught just a glimpse of her. Her long brown hair, her confident walk and the corner of her delicate face brought back to his memory her melodious voice and her sweet smell. But he felt his body stiffen. She was a prisoner and they knew who she was. Life would be short for her unless he could get her out. If only he could get a message to Juliet.

If Bridget were here, she might have helped, but the girl had mysteriously vanished. The rumor was that she had escaped. The first prisoner to have ever escaped the prison fortress. The news had caused the whole place to stir and become unruly. If one person had escaped, more could. The dwarves and humans commanded by the vile Stewart brutally tried in vain to restore control.

Nicholas was so distracted by his thoughts that he did not see Stewart come out of Sasha's balcony, holding a scroll before him. At the sound of a trumpet, the prisoners stopped working and stared up at him. Nicholas' heart beat faster. This could not be good.

"Subjects of Empress Sasha," Stewart began. "Your former commander, one known as Malcon, will be punished for his misappropriation of your hard labor. He has been sentenced to death."

Most of the prisoners wanted to groan. Stewart was a much harsher master than Malcon had ever been. Secretly they had been hoping that power would swing back in the dwarf's favor.

Stewart gave a dramatic pause, then went on, "He will be executed along with your former queen, Juliet, three weeks from now."

Nicholas wanted to rush the palace, take his wife and win back his Asandra, but he had to wait. The time would come.

A golden throne sat on an elevated rock, a beautiful waterfall as a backdrop. Stone walls filled the rest of the room and the stone slab door shut as Rachel, Evan and Reesthma walked in. A small fire sprite girl sat engulfed on the throne, a golden crown upon her head. She seemed sad.

"Who are you?" Rachel asked gently.

"The queen of this sad race," the sprite introduced herself. "And I need your help. Are you not Rachel, who saved Issym? Can you not help me save my people from the flood of moral decay?"

Her words caused a hollow feeling to wrap around Rachel's stomach. She moved her body in front of Reesthma's. Evan's eyes scanned the room for anyway out other than the door and back through hundreds of sprites.

The fire sprite before them began to giggle, then laugh. Her laugh turned venomous as the sprite formed into something else and before them sat a woman, still laughing. It was fairly easy to determine by process of elimination that she was Sasha.

"Oh Rachel, you truly thought you killed me, didn't you? You, kill me? I may once have been your 'imagination', but you no longer rule me." Sasha stood. Her form changed to the appearance that she had maintained when she had tried to kill Rachel on Issym. Sasha stepped forward quickly, pulling a dagger from her boot. With one hand Sasha grabbed Rachel's hair and with the other she held the sharp tip of the dagger to the teen's throat. Rachel breathed shallowly, not wanting her throat to expand into the cold blade.

Most likely Sasha would spend minutes gloating and then would take her captive to lure Seth out. Somehow that seemed worse than death. Evan might survive for the same reason—maybe. But Reesthma was the one in danger. Even so, fear coursed through Rachel's body at the sight of Sasha alive and holding the power of life and death over her and the others.

In a strange state of shock, time slowed for Rachel. She could feel Reesthma and Evan ready to charge Sasha in a futile effort to save her. If they did, they would have no hope of life. She opened her palms in an expression to tell them to wait.

Sasha spoke, "Pathetic. That's what you are. You really think you can change people's hearts? Surprise! They don't want to change—that requires work. These people are lazy scum. That's why they're so easy to control. Why would you want to save them?"

"For the same reason Christ wanted to save me..." Rachel answered. "Believe me, I was pretty scummy myself."

Evan's eyes had been darting between Rachel and Sasha. Now they rested completely upon the friend he enjoyed learning more about every moment. She was not going to die like this. He shielded Reesthma with his body and got ready to attack the shifter.

Chapter 24

Kate and a red illuminescent landed on a beach, the sky dark and the land covered in snow. Kate shifted to a human form, whose face showed how tired she was. It had taken her days but she had crossed the ocean.

The illuminescent shot off sparks and buzzed so quickly Kate could not keep up. "Calm down Tias!" the shifter tried in vain to slow her. "Tias!"

Finally Tias spoke clearly, "I sense an illuminescent. I think it's Ruby!" Tias was Ruby's best friend.

"Where?"

"Due west. A long way. You should rest first."

"No. We do not have much time. We should go on."

Kate took three deep breaths, then shifted into the form of a polar bear. The little illuminescent, who was very trusting, hopped into the bear's mouth.

They had been traveling for hours when Kate began to feel something. The sensation grew stronger. Finally she stopped, let Tias out and turned back into a human. She was dressed in warm fur. Her skin was still sickly white. "I feel a shifter presence north of us. It's probably Edmund. We should check it out."

"But Ruby..." her voice was sad.

"We'll find her; but Edmund is nearby and that is why we are here." Kate was ill enough without the thought of finding Edmund so soon. Their parting had not been on the best of terms. She probably was not on his good side.

A snowflake half the size of Tias landed on the illuminescent and the creature fell close to the ground. "We hate snow!"

Kate returned to her polar bear's shape and let Tias back into her mouth. She found the strength needed and raced towards the other shifter. In the distance a pillar of smoke rose into the air

It did not take long for Kate to draw close to the presence and realize that he was below ground. She turned back to her human form and knelt directly above him. Water rushed down through a small opening. "What is he doing down there?" she wondered out loud.

Sparks fell from Tias beside Kate and a large opening formed. "They can see us now!" Kate whispered sharply.

"No. You can see, but they cannot," Tias answered.

"How did you do that?"

"Red illuminescents have many special powers."

Kate turned her attention down the hole. With dread she saw Sasha holding a dagger to a teenage girl's throat. Recognition dawned. "Rachel." Kate turned desperately to Tias. "What other powers do you have? We've got to do something... and fast."

The dagger still at Rachel's throat, Sasha's focus changed for a moment. Her eyes flickered to the ceiling of the cave in which she held Evan, Reesthma and Rachel as prisoners. Rachel's hand gestures become more violent as she motioned to Evan not to do anything. She could feel his desperation growing.

Her eyes turned back to Sasha. What was distracting her?

Sasha put her focus back on her captives. "Beg for your life, girl," Sasha ripped Rachel's hair backward, sending pain through her head and forcing her throat dangerously close to the tip of the blade.

Rachel's anger at the woman who had led her world to such disgrace and who now threatened their lives exploded. "I'll beg God for my life, but not you!"

Sasha was still distracted by something up above and her grip on Rachel's hair loosened. Seizing the opportunity, Evan tackled Rachel to the ground with one arm, bringing Reesthma down with the other. He would have been up to fight, but pieces of the ceiling were falling behind Sasha. From the new hole descended a bird which took Sasha's attention from regaining hold of Rachel. The bird turned into a blond woman dressed in leather armor and a fur cloak. Her beauty doubled the best Sasha could have hoped for despite the tiredness that marked her face. "Kate," Sasha sneered.

"That's a friend," Rachel smiled. The three rose to their feet.

Kate spoke in a low and steady voice, "The stones are coming, Sasha. You can feel it, can't you?"

Sasha turned her dagger to Kate, but she batted it away. Kate's hand was sliced but healed in seconds. It was the first time that Evan and Reesthma they had seen just how powerful shifters were, and they both sat wide-eyed.

Kate said, "You know that they are coming and I'm not about to let you kill these youths. You should go while you still have the chance."

"Your life will be in danger too, Kate, if you stay till the stones get here," Sasha spat. She had felt the presence of the stones and of Kate. Why had she let her archenemy get so close? She knew she had been cocky, thinking that it was Edmund returning to beg for her forgiveness.

Kate shrugged, "My life has been in danger before and will be again. But you, Sasha, will you risk your life and your empire? You can already feel their affects."

Sasha had no time to stand there and banter with Kate. The stones were getting closer. In all likelihood her more difficult abilities were already inhibited. "This is not the end," she spewed and morphed wings onto her back.

Before she flew upwards, she offered one last attempt to show her rage. Her newly-made dagger spun towards Rachel. Evan dove in the way.

Rachel caught his falling form, his head landing in the crook of her arm. He was already struggling to breathe; his color fading. Blackness oozed from the wound.

"It was poisoned," Reesthma began to hyperventilate. "I know this toxin."

"Oh, Evan. You shouldn't have done that," she whispered, leaning her head against his clammy one. In a second she was sitting upright again, taking command of the situation. "Are the others here?" she asked Kate.

The shifter shook her head, "Just an illuminescent who helped me fool Sasha."

"A blue one?" Rachel hardly dared to let herself hope that one with healing powers might have come.

The woman shook her head with compassion. She saw that the

wound was almost hopeless. "Red."

"Can't you shape shift into something helpful?"

"I'm not familiar with healings. By trying to heal him I would probably kill him."

"Then we need to find someone who can help."

"I'll locate the nearest dwelling and come back."

Rachel said to Reesthma, "Do anything that shifter asks you to do. And pray with all your might."

Looking into Evan's glazed eyes, Rachel promised, "We're going to get you help. Just hold on!"

She swung her cloak off and covered the prince with it—the red and black from his wound staining the cloth. "Do you know what?" she whispered so close that her tears fell into his ear. "If I could pick a king for my Asandra, it would be you."

Reesthma fell by the door, rocking herself as silent sobs fell from her small form. Kate returned quickly with Tias. "I found a cottage. The illuminescent will help us move your friend."

Seth cleared his dishes after dinner. Beatrice, Lotex's sister, had cooked a hearty meal and Lotex's color had brightened from it. There was no doubt now; he would be fine.

"Whoa..." Seth stammered as his eyes landed on a guitar made of what seemed to be pure gold.

Beatrice spotted his look. "That is Lotex's guitar—a family heirloom passed down to the men."

"Do you play?" Seth asked Lotex.

"Hah!" his sister scoffed. "Have you seen his fat fingers?"

"The first man to own this guitar... he was a great musician, wasn't he?"

"He brought it over from..."

"Issym," Seth finished.

Lotex raised a brow. "How did you know?"

"There was once a young boy who dreamed of being a famous singer, the first with a golden guitar. And so he had imagined this guitar with strings made of dragon's scales."

"Then take what is rightfully yours," Lotex offered, waving towards it from his bed.

"No."

"I owe you a great debt for saving my life."

"Not this."

"Then what would you have? Certainly something of high value, in payment of both my life-debt and the work you've done."

What *did* he want? He wanted to go back to Asandra—to fight alongside Rachel and Max. And then he wanted to go home. "What I want you cannot give to me in payment."

"And what is it?"

"I want to stop Sasha."

Chapter 25

Flibbert was infuriated as he rode along a woods path beside Universe Girl—the cause of his vexation. "How could you not tell Galen and me?" he demanded.

"He deserved the same deal that Galen offered the others," she reasoned. "And I knew that you would never give it to him."

"He's a traitor and almost got Seth and Rachel killed!" It was not the first shouting match the frog and the woman had had, but Flibbert could not remember a time he had been so angry.

"Yes, he was a traitor. And so were all of the other undergrounders. This one, however, managed to settle down and stay out of trouble—a remarkable feat when you consider how long he'd been on the other side of the law."

"Ethelwyn, you had no right."

"Check *yourself*, Flibbert," she challenged before he could say more. "What kind of frog are you to go against our king's promise?"

He rode seething on his horse until Ethelwyn stopped hers. "What now?" he asked.

She led her horse to turn and face him. Looking into her face, Flibbert could, for a moment, envision them out of all this strife and war. But the quiet tones she used next were far more frightening than her shouting had been. "If you are looking for revenge Flibbert, I'll not lead you to him. I thought you realized that we needed his help. Think about what you will do when you meet. Answer me carefully."

Several moments later, he looked her in the eye, "I'll not harm him."

They rode the rest of the way in silence and pulled up to a little, freshly built cottage. Flibbert and Ethelwyn descended from their horses and knocked on the entrance.

A bulky man in sloppy clothes opened the door. "What do you want?" he growled at Flibbert. When Universe Girl stepped into view he moved back. "Come on in, then."

"You let us in for her?" Flibbert questioned. How many times had Wyn been there?

"She," he pointed one of his bulky fingers, "never wanted me dead."

The man sat down on a stool by an empty hearth. It was cold enough for a fire, but he was not burning one. The cabin had low ceilings and not much room. It was clear to Flibbert that he did not intend to stay here long.

"Philip, we've come to ask for your help," Ethelwyn sat cross-legged on the floor.

"Go on," he answered, glaring at Flibbert.

Ethelwyn drew his gaze off of the frog as she said, "You told me once that you sailed with your father throughout your childhood. And when he died, you captained his ship. We need your skills as a sailor."

He stroked his beard. "I haven't sailed in a very long time."

"I don't think the sea ever leaves your blood," Ethelwyn whispered for emphasis.

She had won him over. "It is possible I could help," he said.

"And we'll need the men who worked with you before," Flibbert put in, trying to show to Ethelwyn that he could not only let Philip live, but also have a civil conversation with him.

Philip nodded, "Perhaps if you gave me a few months, I could find my old crew."

"We need your help *now*," Ethelwyn countered. "Our fleet is leaving in only a few days."

"A fleet? A fleet going where?"

"To Asandra."

"Why?"

"Possibly to war."

"Oh. No. My battling days are over. I've come too close to death too many times."

Ethelwyn stood up and walked towards the door, asking, "Is it only that you refuse to fight?"

Philip nodded and she pronounced, "Then you shall not fight."

"No!" Flibbert was firm.

"Then I cannot help you," Philip returned.

"Flibbert," Universe Girl stared him down. "This is the only way. Seth and Rachel need us, *now*. Not a year from now when we finally figure out how to get the sails up on our ships!"

The frog nodded.

The house looked like a small barn; and judging by the large amounts of open, snowy space behind it, it probably was the homestead of a farm. Smoke came through a chimney. Instantly Rachel realized the trouble she was bringing to these people's door, but it could not matter. Evan lay dying.

Along the short hike between the sprite nest and this cottage, Kate and Rachel had filled each other in on all the important things. For a few moments they had been silent with only Evan's shallow breaths and Reesthma's controlled tears to listen to.

Rachel walked up to the door of the cottage and knocked gently, then loudly, then more gently. They did not need to scare these people.

A weathered man opened the door just enough to see her in the light of his lantern. He opened it wider. "Are you hurt?" he asked, gesturing towards Evan's blood that had soaked parts of her clothing.

"My friend is dying. It was the sprites," her voice trembled.

The farmer flung open the door and called to his wife, "Rasee! Get the spare bed ready and boil some water. Quick!"

His eyes grew wide as Evan's floating form followed Rachel through the door with the illuminescent hovering above him. "What on Xsardis?" he breathed.

A petite woman hurried down the steps, her feet not even making a sound. Her lantern cast a new light upon the room, but Rachel did not have time to take in her surroundings.

Rasee had Evan moved into a room and laid on a bed. Kate forced Reesthma to stay outside as Rasee took control of the situation. The woman thrust her light into Rachel's hand. "Hold it here."

She cut off Evan's shirt and took away a large blue gem from his neck. "You," she gestured to Kate, "get hot water." She spoke to her husband, "I need a needle, thread and all the medicines you can find. Hurry!"

Rachel witnessed the desperate attempt to stop Evan's bleeding, get rid of the poison and sew him up again. As her body was wrapped in a chill, she knew that they had only prolonged the inevitable. "Say something to him sweetheart. He needs to hear a familiar voice," Rasee whispered, forcing the lantern out of Rachel's hand and putting it beside the bed.

Rachel stepped beside the prince and took his hand. "Evan, Asandra needs you. I need you." She trembled. "Keep fighting. We'll find a way to save you." She slipped off the blue vial from around her neck and put it on his. "They say this no longer works, but it saved my life once. Maybe… maybe God will do a miracle."

Before Rachel knew it, she was sitting beside a newly-lit fire, staring into its orange flames. At some point in time she had changed her clothes and washed up, but she couldn't remember much. She was aware of childlike whispers coming from the loft above them, and of the conversation of the farmer with Reesthma, and how Kate sent Tias to give Issym a message. Everything seemed so meaningless and Rachel found herself bent over and whispering, "God please. God please. God please."

She found the strength to stand up and talk with Rasee and Kate. "He's lost too much blood, hasn't he?"

"I've never seen a poison like that." Rasee put a hand on her arm. "The girl thinks that there is a certain root that will help. Inan will try to find it tomorrow, but even so."

"Is there anything else that can be done?"

She shook her head. "I'm sorry."

"How long did it take you to get from Issym?" Rachel looked to Kate.

"Days… and I'm too worn out to travel that fast."

"Edmund, Seth and Ruby are on the island of Noric. You could probably get there in a day."

Rasee did not question her, believing Rachel to be in shock.

"I already asked Tias," Kate replied. "Red illuminescents cannot heal."

"But that's our only hope. Please Kate! Ruby's not like the others. She's from generations ago. Maybe they knew things then that they don't know now. Please!"

Kate sighed and looked to Rasee. "How much time does he have?"

"I wouldn't even give him three days," Rasee responded. "You'll never be back in time."

"I can do it. I will do it."

Seth held the *borrowed* golden guitar in one hand. With the other he reached for the door to Blowen's quarters, but it opened and Edmund stepped out. "Believe me, you don't want to go in there," he shivered. "Blowen cannot make up his mind about anything tonight."

It did not sound that bad, but Seth nodded.

"If I hear the words 'but' 'however' 'on the other hand' or 'still' again, I'll leave you on this forsaken island forever!"

"Where are you going then?"

"The cabin I lived in last time I was here. I want to get a few things."

"I'll come with you."

"You had a rough day. Are you sure you're up for it?"

Seth thought for a moment about his sore body. "After a cave-in, I don't really feel like being in a cave."

As they emerged into the cold night, the two plodded through the snow that covered the land as the only decoration. The dwarves had made a path just large enough to walk single file. The heavens were full of storm clouds, but Edmund did not seem concerned as some light snow fell. "What were they thinking cutting down all their trees?" Seth wondered out loud.

"Dwarves," Edmund rolled his eyes, then changed the subject. "I found out some things."

Seth nodded, turning his mind on. "Okay."

Edmund answered, "We should leave here."

"Without their help?"

"Of the eight dwarves who hold power on Noric," Edmund explained, "those who want to get rid of you are getting anxious. The others won't be able to stand up against them much longer."

"What about Lotex?"

"He stays silent. I think he would have let them do what they wanted but now you have saved his life and he will return the favor."

Seth turned back. "Where are you going?" Edmund called.

"To talk to Lotex."

"Did you not hear me? He would have let you die. He might have even helped!"

"Perhaps."

"Lotex will need his rest. At least, don't go right now."

Seth sighed, but continued walking with Edmund. After a mile of silence, Seth risked a dangerous question, "Why did you let us escape with the gem of light?"

Edmund grunted. That was so long ago. "Is that important?"

"Rachel thought it was crazy for me to come with you. And I don't get the feeling that you're helping me because you like me. So why did you let us get away before? Was it for Kate?"

Edmund decided to answer. "In part. I never could refuse her anything. But I wanted to stop Sasha. That's why I'm here. That's why I let you go."

He answered the rest of Seth's query too. "And the reason I don't like you is because you're a meddler. You know nothing about this place or my life or Kate and you pretend like you do! Like you can rely on your knowledge and your God, sweep in and save the day. And after you have won your glory, you leave us! But we are no longer your play thing to pick up, then throw away. We don't need your help. And your God has no place here. He just muddles people's minds, like my Kate."

Seth stepped backward. First Vaylynne, now Edmund. This was the second time his imagination had told him that he was not wanted here. He cleared his throat and replied, "God didn't confuse Kate; He gave her clarity and a purpose. She's happier than she ever was."

"I'm here to help and so is God," he continued. "You may not want that help, but you need it. That's why you're helping me, isn't it?"

They finished the walk in silence. Finally coming to the cabin, they saw the snow blocked the door and the roof had caved under the pressure of the snow. "I'll be a ladder. You climb inside and I'll follow you," Edmund told him

In a minute they were inside the cottage. Edmund shifted his hand into a torch that lit up the one large room. Half a straw bed stuck out of a pile of snow. The other side of the room was completely buried. It took Edmund several minutes to dig out a cabinet. When he had opened it, a tattered book and a leather bag spilled out. He took both in his hands. "This is what I came for. We can go."

They began their walk back, the snowfall heavy. "The way those clouds are moving, this storm is just going to get worse," Edmund admitted. "We have much too far to go."

"Okay. We need shelter."

"I looked at a map once that showed an abandoned dwarf mine from a century ago. It's not too far. We can head there."

"I'm sick of this manna," Katarina declared as she sat on her cloak and chucked away the food that they had dug through the snow to get.

Max looked around, searching for a rock or tree branch to sarcastically offer her to eat. He saw mushrooms, tall and with large umbrellas, behind her. "Hey, do you think we could eat those?" he asked.

She turned to face them. "I wonder if they're really mushrooms at all. They could be earth sprites hiding as mushrooms."

As she spoke, a blue glow emanated from the mushrooms, danced past him and began to sink into her skin. Her look became dazed as faces appeared on the mushrooms. One asked, "What are your names?"

Kat answered, "Katarina and..."

Max jumped towards the princess and put a hand over her mouth. "Shh!" he commanded. "Don't tell them!"

The mushrooms glared at Max and told her, "He wants to harm you. You must stop him."

Kat reached for her sword. It took Max a second to realize that she was actually drawing her weapon to harm him. He quickly pulled his hand away and drew back from her. "What are you doing?"

"Stop him," she murmured. Something wasn't right.

The blue glow grew stronger around her as Katarina stood and turned her weapon on him. The mushrooms were controlling her, somehow. But why not him? He was closer. "Katarina; stop this! It's me, Max. I'm helping you rescue your mom, remember? Remember!"

She charged towards him. Max refused to draw his own blade. He could not and would not hurt his friend when she was so obviously not herself. He dodged her attack easily. Her mind was not in the fight.

"Kat, stop this, please." He moved to a safer distance and spoke to her calmly. "See, I'm not even drawing my weapon. I'm not going to hurt you so you don't have to fight me."

She did not seem to hear his words but moved forward again to attack. Max dodged again. A third time she attacked and nicked his arm. Her coordination was growing and he could do nothing. The blue glow was becoming darker and darker. Why wasn't it affecting him?

God, why isn't it affecting me?

And the answer seemed obvious. It could not affect him, because he was already *e*ffected by something much stronger and much more powerful than mushrooms could ever hope to be compared with. But Katarina was not *e*ffected by God. He had to clear her mind.

Max charged the mushrooms and took off the first one's head. The other mushrooms yelled orders at the princess. "Stop him now!" the chorus arouse.

Max defeated two more of the six mushrooms before Katarina came so close that he needed to move away. He ran from her; and when she charged him, he doubled back and finished off the last three sprites. A hollow feeling came over him.

The blue still surrounded her. "Kat, come back to reality!" He had to pull his sword out. Hers clashed against his, her eyes showing the inner struggle. He dropped his weapon. "You don't have to live like this. Jesus can save you!"

Kat fell to the ground, the blue receding from her skin. Max moved towards her. She was already sitting up and was struggling to surface. "What happened?"

"The mushrooms affected your mind. You tried to kill me." It made sense that the mushrooms would glow and have psychological effects. They did that on Earth, too.

"It... feels like a dream." She looked at him. "Your arm is bleeding."

"Your fault."

"Not my fault; the mushrooms' fault." That was the old Katarina for sure. "Why didn't the mushrooms affect you?"

Max answered matter-of-factly, "Because I'm not empty."

"What?"

"Each of us have a hole in our hearts. Mine is filled."

"You mean with Jesus," her tone betrayed her irritation. "Max, you know I'm a Christian."

"You claim to be, but think, Kat."

"About what? I'm helping Asandra! And I'm rescuing my parents; I pray before my meals. Do you know how hard those kinds of things are on this continent? What more could you ask of me, Max?"

"But who are you doing it for?"

"Who are you doing it for?" she retorted. "Why are you here Max? You just wanted glory and adventure so you tagged along with Seth and Rachel."

Max steamed, but answered, "I'm here to help because I think God wants me here."

"I'm helping."

"Say what you like; but you know what's really inside you. You've claimed to be a Christian to please your parents, your brother, your country. But how would you live if they were all gone?"

She stood up, infuriated. "Why do you believe you have me figured out?"

"Because I've walked where you're walking."

"Shut up Max! I'm saved and I don't want to hear any more about it."

Chapter 26

Rachel woke from her fitful rest to hear Rasee's soft steps in the cooking area of the cottage. She sat up and instantly began praying—not just for Evan, but for Asandra. God needed to change the hearts of the people if they were ever going to take Asandra back and Rachel was determined not to let his sacrifice be in vain.

She walked into the kitchen and asked quietly, "How is he?"

"Same as before," the woman answered, dumping manna into a bowl. She ground some of the seed Rachel had come to know as Sasha's bread and added it to the manna. Rachel put one of the seeds in her mouth. It would make her feel full, even if it offered nothing for her body.

Rasee looked to Rachel, "A sprite would not have been large enough to hold the weapon that hurt that boy. You lied to me."

"We were taken to the sprite leader, who turned out to be a shape shifter."

"You encountered Sasha? And you lived to tell the tale?"

"For the time being we live."

Rasee sighed, "I don't want to ask questions, but I have children to look out for. Who are you?"

"My middle name is Beth—call me that. My companions and I are on the run from Sasha."

"You've brought us more heartache, haven't you?"

"I'm sorry."

"Our life has been full of it," Rasee went on, mostly to herself. "Inan let you in because we know the devastation sprites can have."

"What did they do to you?"

She began to beat her dough. "Took our crop—not half of it, all of it. We have nothing. Inan spends his days and his nights hunting manna, but it's so hard to find in the winter. We've sold all our animals—the ones that survived. Even if we make it through the winter, we won't be able to rebuild after this."

The woman stopped suddenly. Judging from the sound of prancing feet behind them, Rachel guessed one of her children was coming. A blond haired, adorable, six-year-old girl stepped beside her mom. Her eyes were squeezed shut. "Tethy, open up."

Tethy complied. Her entire eyes were solid brown. Rachel swallowed hard and fought the urge to step backwards. Before she could say anything, the mother had sent her daughter upstairs to wake her sister. "It was acena," Rasee informed before she could ask. "Her eyes had always been weak, but now... she's blind and the village doctor says she's dying, that the disease is spreading to her brain. Her sister caught it too—her heart is so weak we could lose her at any time."

The mother beat the dough harder. "Those girls, if they even make it to adulthood, have no hope. Who will marry them as they are? How will they provide for themselves?"

Rasee looked deeply into Rachel's eyes, not angry but frustrated, "Do you know what it is like to have *no* hope? And you have only brought us more despair!"

Rachel sighed, "I know what it is to face acena."

"Someone close to you had it?"

"I had it. In my lungs."

"But you appear fine," the farm wife looked at her skeptically.

"On Issym the dust of the fairies cured me."

Rasee stopped working. "You say there is a cure on Issym?"

"Yes." Rachel nodded, glad to deliver some good news.

The doubtful look returned to her face. "How much did it cost you?"

"Nothing. They do not charge for the opportunity to do good."

She looked hopeful for a moment, but then shook her head, "We could never afford the fare there."

"Maybe you won't have to," Rachel said out-loud without thinking. The army from Issym was coming. Soon, she hope! But she could not tell this woman that. If word got back to Sasha, she would attack immediately, and they would not be able to offer even a covert resistance.

Seth's cheeks burned with the cold of the coming blizzard. He followed Edmund into an opening and closed the hatch behind them. Edmund formed his arm into a torch and lit the torches on the walls on either side of him before letting his own disappear.

"I thought you said this was a mine?" Seth asked looking around him at the narrow and short hole they were in. It was more like a crevice.

"It was supposed to be, but the dwarves lost interest in it."

Seth sat down, not particularly enjoying the thought of staying there all night. How would they get out in the morning? Wouldn't the snow weigh down the hatch so that they could not open it? He asked Edmund, but the shape shifter assured him that nothing could keep him below ground.

The teen rested the golden guitar on his lap and tested the strings. Even the slightest touch produced a sweet but somehow eerie sound. This truly was the ultimate instrument. He placed his fingers on the appropriate strings and played a G chord. The sound reverberated around the small mine. Next he tested out Em and D. His hands had already begun to lose their callouses from the short time he had been away from his own guitar, and the dragon-scale strings were much sharper than he was used to. His fingers yelled at him, but he ignored them and began to play one of his own songs. At first he did not sing, but finally Seth began the chorus and then whole thing. "Is that a very popular song on your world?" Edmund asked.

"I wish. I wrote it."

"Really?"

"Yes."

"It is a very good song, even though it's a little preachy."

Seth was about to answer but some kind of sound was coming from the other side of the wall. "Do you hear that?"

Edmund nodded. They both squeezed themselves toward the far end of the tunnel and leaned against the wall. Someone was singing on the other side. It was hard to be sure, but it sounded like Seth's song. Edmund shifted his arm into a pix ax and began pounding away.

It was not a thick wall. He had broken through with his third swing. A few more swings and they stepped through. The singing was immediately gone and the room was only barely lit from the light of the other room. "Maybe it was just the wind," Edmund declared as Seth kept moving forward.

"Ouch!" squealed a shrill voice. Seth pulled his foot back. He had stepped on the corner of something small and fleshy. "Oh," moaned the voice, definitely small and female. "Oh no!"

"Did I hurt you?" he squatted down and tried to make out the slender figure lying on the ground.

"No... but now I'll be in so much trouble," she bubbled.

"What do you mean?"

"You'll go and tell my parents and they'll be so angry and we'll all get caught. Then the others will go and... oh!" After a moment, she sat up and rubbed her eyes.

Light flooded the room as Edmund formed another torch. A tan-skinned, brown-haired sprite who was wearing a green dress down to her ankles and brown slippers looked up at him. "Humans!" she gasped. "Here, on Noric?"

Edmund chose not to correct her. He did not particularly like the little sprite. He hated emotional women.

"But, why?" she questioned. "Unless..." she whispered, panic returning to her voice as she stood up. "You don't work for Sasha do you?"

"No; just the opposite."

"In that case," she declared, now hovering above the ground, "allow me to make a proper introduction. I'm Abigail."

"I'm Seth and this is Edmund," Seth spoke gently, as he did with the younger kids at his church. "But why were you so afraid that we'd tell your parents you were here?"

"You don't know much, do you? Have you ever seen an earth sprite?"

"I've seen mushrooms," Seth answered.

"But not sprites. Our parents forgot how to be anything but mushrooms. What child wants to grow up and be a mushroom forever?"

Seth remembered this part. "Yeah, I know."

"When Sasha came and took the dwarves, she took young sprites too. She promised that if we ran away we would never be considered adults and would never have to transform into mushrooms. Many of us left. Our parents are scared to death we'll leave too. So they keep us hidden, separated even from each other." She looked into Seth's eyes, "Do you know what that was like for us? They were forcing us to *have* to leave." A tear dripped down her cheek. She was just a kid; but one with a tender heart.

"I couldn't think of all my friends joining Sasha so I started meetings for us. Twice a week we slip out after our parents have gone to bed and hang out here. It is the only thing we have to look forward to!"

"So what's the problem?" Seth asked.

"If they find out, they'll be furious. They'll stop the meetings; we'll fight with them; and then all of us young sprites will leave!" her whole body shuddered.

"We could talk to your parents," Seth offered. "Try to get them to see your point of view."

"If they find out we'll be in a lot of trouble..." Abigail replied, burying her head in her hands.

Edmund finally tuned into the conversation as he saw opportunity knocking. With a little manipulation they just might get some help out of these sprites. "What if Sasha was no longer a threat?"

"Huh?" the girl looked up.

"If Sasha was defeated, your parents would have nothing to fear; then you and your friends would be free to live life again."

"But Sasha's too powerful! No one can stop her."

"It can be done, but we'll need your help—and all your friends, too."

"What would we need to do?" her body steadied, her tone leveled out.

"It would be dangerous..."

"We're not afraid!" a male sprite flew out of the shadows to stand beside Abigail. He sounded definite and cocky—very much like the average pre-teen boy.

"I don't know," Edmund replied. "Maybe you sprites are too young for such a dangerous mission."

"We'll help," Abigail was firm, making the decision for everyone. Large numbers of young sprites gathered around. "We have no choice."

Edmund smiled and warned them, "You will have to fight against the sprites who left."

They slowly nodded in unison—at least two hundred of them. Edmund felt a little guilt not telling them that many of the sprites who had gone to fight with Sasha had turned into mushrooms. When they had chosen to fight for evil, they had made an adult choice and therefore turned into adults. The shape shifter just hoped Seth would not figure things out. If he knew, he would tell the sprites and they would lose the creatures' help.

The sprites began talking with each other. Seth whispered to

Edmund, "How can they just choose not to grow up? It is not natural. Certainly, someday they have to grow up, whether they want to or not."

"It does seem unnatural that they would choose to be neither children nor adults; serving neither good nor evil; neither disobeying, nor submitting. I tried all of that back when I was serving Sasha, but it didn't matter. Somehow I still ended up working for evil."

Seth stared at him, "Do you really think you've made the choice now? Sure you do brave things, but you run from God. You run from really making the decision to serve good or evil."

Edmund's eyes narrowed on Seth. "I don't run from the decision, Seth. I've made it. Even if your God is real, I won't serve Him."

Seth shook his head. "That's an extremely dangerous position."

"I know."

Flibbert, Ethelwyn and Philip rode into the castle, each unhappy for their own reasons. They dismounted from their horses and headed straight for Galen's throne room, only to find that the high king was not there. "Where is he?" Ethelwyn asked the guard at the door.

"In the field, practicing with the troops," came the reply.

They soon found him, matching, if not besting, some of Issym's best fighters. He saw the three out of the corner of his eye and immediately stepped back from the battle, moving towards them. The four walked together through the field. Galen did not recognize Philip—he had never seen the face, though he would know the name.

Ethelwyn spoke first, "We went to hire a captain and a trained crew for your ships. We found Philip."

Every muscle in Galen's body tensed. The man who had almost gotten Seth and Rachel killed. And he was going to have to trust the entire country to him unless he acted right now. This might push him too far. He had only a second to make the decision. "Philip," he extended a gloved hand.

Philip gripped it hard. "King Galen."

Galen gestured to Universe Girl, "Ethelwyn can show you the supplies we have. Be sure we have what we will need."

Ethelwyn received the message in the king's eyes. He was not happy. He knew that she had kept Philip hidden, brought him out and had gotten Flibbert involved. The frog would give him quite the lecture later. She offered an apologetic shrug.

"Can I see the vessels?" Philip questioned.

"There is no time to build them. The shape shifters are going to form themselves into boats for us," Galen responded.

"This voyage will take months! Can they maintain their shape for that long?" It seemed ridiculous.

"The stones will keep them stuck in the form of our transport vessels. It will be painful, but they are willing."

They began to move away, but Galen brought Philip into his throne room. "Is something wrong?" Philip asked, not blind to the difficulty with which the king had controlled his anger.

"This all started when two travelers came to us from Asandra. They said they boarded a vessel, were sucked into a whirlpool and woke up on our beach. I need to know if they can be trusted. Have you ever heard of such a thing?"

Philip smiled. The king already trusted him enough to ask his council. He sat down on one of the councilmen's chairs and put his feet up on the table. "My father was a sailor all of his life. I went with him some of the time, but mostly I heard his stories. He told me many tales about the sea between Asandra and Issym. He said that the dangers were beyond imagining. After a while, he wouldn't even sail there."

"What kind of dangers?"

Philip told what he remembered and made some stuff up on the spot, "That dragons would attack vessels; that singing maidens would lure men to their deaths; that whirlpools were a common occurrence; that the air would make the men go mad. Not many vessels have made the trip in one piece. Why do you think we stopped having contact with Asandra?"

"But where does the legend stop and the truth begin?"

Philip shrugged, "If I thought any of it were true, I wouldn't be going. But there is the matter of payment."

"They promised you money?" It did not sound like his friends. Flibbert did not even want him here and Ethelwyn would have appealed to his 'good nature'.

"Not money; a village." Philip was a pretty good liar—that was how he had gotten Seth, Rachel and Flibbert to trust him so long ago. This king was far too trusting. It was true that he had learned sailing from his father; but the best thing good old daddy had taught him was how to ask for the moon so it would appear that you were settling for the stars.

"A village?"
"All to myself and those who live there with me. You'd have no jurisdiction there—that was the bargain."
"They would never have said that," Galen barked. "I won't... I can't do that. If I did, it would be as if Mt. Smolden were revived. It would destroy everything Issym stands for."
"You promised all of us a second chance. Trust us."
"Then why do you wish to be free from the same authority the rest of Issym accepts? Take gold. With as much as you will receive, you will be able to build your own city. But it will be under Issym's laws."
Philip smiled and offered his hand, "It's a deal."

The stupid boy! Katarina muttered. *Pretending like I am not a Christian. What does he think? That I'm the enemy?* She was sputtering and pounding her fists. At least Max was away getting some manna so that he did not see her outburst. He might have been suspicious if he had. They were only two days from Sasha's castle. She could not give up now. *He deserves what's coming to him.* She wished she could really believe that.

When Max returned, the princess put a smile on her face, "I told you that I didn't want to go into any of the villages because I didn't want you to know that we weren't on the right path. Now that you know, can we stay in one?"

He was quick to answer, "Yes!"

Chapter 27

The first thing Evan saw when he opened his eyes was Rachel staring down at him with concern. He thought that she had never seemed as truly herself. She was not acting for anyone.

He felt her hand in his. His consciousness faded.

Rachel looked to Reesthma, "That seemed to have worked a little."

The young girl had applied the herb Inan had retrieved from the forest. "I remember the scrolls saying it would help, but it cannot cure him. Kate has to succeed."

Rachel put her free hand on Reesthma's shoulder. "It will be okay. Evan will keep fighting and Kate will be back in time."

Afternoon found Seth and Edmund back with the dwarves of Noric. Lotex boasted that he had not been in the least concerned that they had been lost in the blizzard. Beatrice, however, informed them that he had been nearly ready to get up from his bed and go after them.

That evening Seth and Edmund walked slowly into Blowen's room, unsure if they were ready for his company. But they had to sleep somewhere. "Oh, finally they come back to me," he moaned, putting a hand to his head. "They, of course, have no idea what a strain it is on a host not to know how much supper to have ready or how disturbing it is to one's sleep to have guests rising early in the morning and coming home late at night. Not that I'm complaining! Of course I love the company. And you two work hard, well at least you, Seth. But the other dwarves aren't willing to house you, of course. That's dwarves for you. However, they certainly have a good work ethic; even if they act like I don't exist. I just wish..."

"Blowen!" Edmund interrupted suddenly. "Why don't we all go to bed early? Seth and I already had dinner and we're quite tired."

They all lay down and Seth waited until his companions' breathing flowed rhythmically, then he pried himself up and moved quietly towards Beatrice's dwelling place. His body had stiffened from the few moments of rest. The teen knocked and Beatrice opened the door, huffing. "What can you want at this hour?" she demanded.

"I need to speak to Lotex, alone."

"You do, do you? Then come back in the morning."

She tried to shut the door, but Seth got his foot in the way and found that his tone had an edge to it, "No. Now."

Lotex's voice came, "Go, Beatrice. We'll just be a minute."

"Go? This used to be my house until you came in here! Who do you think you are?" Nevertheless she moved into the hallway, muttering, "I don't know how your wife puts up with you."

Seth entered and closed the door. "What is it?" Lotex questioned, sitting up.

The teen's candle illuminated Lotex's weary face as he moved close. Seth pulled the dagger he carried in his other hand from its sheath. He put the weapon in Lotex's fingers. The dwarf let his calloused hand close around the weapon. Seth spoke, "If you wish me dead, then kill me."

"What are you talking about?" the dwarf's gruff voice filled the air.

"No one will believe you had the strength to kill me. And all your problems will be solved."

"You shouldn't believe everything a shape shifter tells you," he answered.

"You knew Edmund was spying on you?"

"I guessed. Did he tell you that I did not say anything on your behalf before the other leaders? That does not mean that I want you dead! You are Xsardis' hope, boy; I need you alive. But it takes time to convince dwarves. If I had a hasty opinion I would not have a chance of convincing the others. They would have cut me out of their loop and then they would have gotten rid of you anyway. This was the best way to protect you."

"You want to protect me?" Seth found that hard to believe. "You've hardly acted like it."

"What do you want? More pats on the back? I like you lad, but there is no value in praise."

"No value?" Seth laughed. Lotex liked him? That was difficult to believe.

"Now can you let me rest?"

He had an ally. "Listen Lotex, we're running out of time. I have to get back to Asandra. How do we get the others to help?"

"If you challenge the dwarves that you—a puny human—are willing to fight Sasha, and they—tough dwarves—are too cowardly, many of them will follow you. Tell them that when Sasha is done with Asandra, she'll come after Noric—that'll get them moving. I can get them together. All you have to do is challenge them. I will make sure they take you up on it."

Max and Katarina approached a village. The city walls looked like they had seen battle, but that the town had quickly surrendered. The gate appeared to be wide open but as they walked through it, they realized the gate was gone. The villagers barely glanced at them, the atmosphere tired and gloomy as if it was a rainy day. Snow covered the ground—people had not bothered to shovel most of it away.

At the sight of one disreputable-looking man, Max looked instinctively to make sure Zara was hidden away safely and moved closer to the princess. He put a hand on his pocket, realizing that the golden coins the illuminescent had formed for them were jingling and attracting attention.

They walked into the busy inn and tavern. The rest of the town was dead; this place was alive. Men wearing armor filled the room— Sasha's men. He tugged at Katarina to get her to the door, but she kept moving.

They were soon sitting at a table in the middle of the tavern, meat and bread on the plate before them, steaming cider in their mugs. Kat was devouring her food; Max picked at his. This was not a safe place to be. "Let's just eat in our rooms," he spoke softly.

"Wait till I'm finished," she commanded. Was the proximity to the powerhouse of Asandra making her more bossy? *Was that possible?*

Finally, they went up to the second floor of the inn. They sat down in Katarina's room to discuss the next day's plans. "Tomorrow we'll be there," Max voiced, realizing how disinterested Kat seemed with him. Her mannerisms were asking him to leave.

"So?"

"Do you have a plan, Genius?"

She scrunched her nose, "We're going to have the element of surprise. No one ever willfully goes into Maremoth. What more do we need?"

Max studied the princess. Her cloak hung from behind her; her legs were swung to the side; her brown boots were still on—there was energy flowing through her. She was keeping something from him, he was sure of that. Hopefully it was a crazy plan that she did not want to admit to; or perhaps one that would only work if he was in the dark. If not, they were in trouble. He accepted her silence.

Galen and Flibbert stood at the palace entrance in the cool of the night. Scores of tents were set up, but no one was sleeping; people were savoring their last night on Issym. But Galen and Flibbert had an entire country to think of, and savoring that evening was not an easy task.

"I made a mistake once, Galen," Flibbert broke the silence that had taken them both. "I left Philip with Ethelwyn and Seth and Rachel. I went away because I thought that my mission was more important. But you knew that Seth and Rachel were kids who just needed a little encouragement. I trusted Philip with our heroes, and if it wasn't for you, they might be dead right now. I'm not trying to be a thorn in your side, I just don't want to make that mistake again. I can't trust him."

Galen nodded, "I don't think we *should* trust him. He's on a short leash."

As he leaned on his cane, Flibbert looked jolly in his top-hat and colorful armor, but his heart was heavy for more reasons than he was willing to admit. Galen reminded him, "When I asked you to come onto Issym's council, I thought I would be constantly fighting with you. I was right." Flibbert laughed. It was true. "But I did not know you would become my greatest ally. The two of us together in God have not met an enemy we could not handle—from stubborn princes to ferocious dragons. We will protect our people, Seth, Rachel and Xsardis."

That picked Flibbert's spirit up. Talking about battles always did that.

"King Galen!" the call came from the lookout tower.

The gates were wide open. The cry told Galen that an enemy was coming. He and Flibbert sprinted to the gates, blades drawn, top-hat left behind. Ten minotaurs and a couple of rough looking humans stood just inside the fortress, armed to the teeth. Even a dozen well-armed, well-trained enemy warriors inside the camp was not a big problem tonight. They were not about to attack.

Still, Galen kept his guard high. Minotaurs had had the most trouble acclimating to normal life. They had spent a century as undergrounders in Smolden's service. They did not want to be around civilians and civilians did not want to be around them.

One of the minotaurs took a step forward. "King Galen," his voice was deep but there was no malice in it. "My name is Joeyza. We wish you no harm."

"Then what do you want?"

"To fight for Xsardis."

"Why?" Flibbert questioned.

"I was born in the underground and I witnessed the atrocities committed by Smolden. Even so, I know enough about Sasha to realize that she is a far greater enemy than the leviathan."

Another minotaur declared, "We don't want darkness to consume the world again."

Joeyza finished, "And we desire to earn your people's respect."

A dozen enemies on a ship. Galen shook his head, "I can't."

"I speak for the minotaurs," Joeyza grew louder. "No one trusts us. There is no way to earn a living. What choice do we have but to rob? You promised us a second chance. Let us earn it!"

Galen was about to say no again, but something held him back. A thought resonated in his mind: *You'll need them.* He nodded, "Come."

Flibbert's jaw dropped open and he croaked. "You're kidding, right?"

King Galen walked inside his palace, leaving the frog to his amazement. He loved being a husband and a king, but there were days when he longed for his wanderings. The noise of the birds and wind to sing him to sleep; the ability to go anywhere and do anything; and visiting Valinor, a garden God had blessed as a refuge for his people... No heavy weight had rested on his shoulders during those years, unlike now.

Galen passed by a widow, hearing a rush of wind as he stepped beyond it. Turning his head, he saw an airsprite descend. She gave a quick nod of her head, "High King."

"Jennet," he greeted. "Are the other airsprites here?"

"They are on their way. I was just about to tell Queen Danielle," her tones betrayed her young age.

"The airsprites once lived on Asandra?" The tall woman nodded, allowing her wings to retract. "Why did you leave?"

Her face lost its glow. "Airsprites were not always as peaceful as we are now. Our government split. Most of us followed Danielle's ancestors to Issym. Those who stayed above Asandra soon regretted it. All the airsprites eventually moved here. By the time the evil ruler of Asandra's clouds died, we were happy here and did not want to go back to a place of such bitter memories."

Something about the way she said it made Galen pause. "Are there other kinds of sprites?"

"Oh yes; earth sprites, fire sprites. A delegation of water sprites just came to inform us about a most joyous wedding. We didn't even know they existed," she laughed, then turned heavy again. "And then there are sound sprites—the horror of our people."

"Tell me," he commanded.

"They live in and around and above the ocean between Issym and Asandra. We know of only three. They use their songs to manipulate the people around them."

"How?"

"Have you noticed that Flibbert's mood changes based upon the song that's played? Amplify that a thousand times. Their beautiful melodies lure men in and change their hearts and minds."

"Certainly something can stop them."

"They do whatever they please and are subject to no man."

Queen Danielle, dressed in a long, white robe, stepped into the hallway, "We are not proud of the heritage they bring. Luring, then killing sailors. They love the high seas because the other races are at their weakest. But they prey on the weak and strong alike."

"It is said that they possess great wisdom," Jennet put in.

"And many a young man has gone looking for it, never to return," the queen contradicted. "Water sprites hoard shiny treasures. Airsprites can't live without light. Earth sprites need to be ever near the dirt. Sound sprites... they can't live without knowing that they can have anything they want. It is a sad history."

"Perhaps things have changed."

"Perhaps. Goodnight, Galen."

Galen slipped into his room and wrapped his arms around his wife, feeling the baby kick as he did. Andrea sighed and whispered, "I love you."

Those words, he knew, would sustain him for the half a year he would be gone.

Chapter 28

Seth woke with a start as he felt a clammy hand on his shoulder. "What?" the youth whispered, making out Edmund's shape hovering over him. The deep and loud voices of dwarves filled the air outside the door, but their room was dark and Blowen's heavy snoring still permeated the small space.

"Don't you hear that?" Edmund asked.

"The snoring or the shouts?" The teen could feel Edmund's glare. "Alright, alright. I'm getting up."

Seth knew what was going on; he just had not guessed Lotex would act so quickly. He reached for the door, but Edmund pulled him back. "Don't you realize what's going on? That mob is coming after you!"

"Not exactly. Trust me." Seth slipped out of the apartment before Edmund could reply.

Edmund followed him as he rounded a corner into a large, open space, with scores of torches lighting the faces of countless dwarves. The two made their way towards the center of the crowd, which was still growing. Edmund saw Lotex standing with the other seven members of the unofficial council of dwarves. While everyone else was moving and shouting, these dwarves held perfectly still, not a sound slipping from their beard covered lips.

Lotex turned and looked straight into Seth's eyes "There's the boy!"

The mob turned in on the teen. A very loud voice asked, "And what does he have to say for himself? Let him speak!"

The noise dropped off so that Seth could answer. He took one breath of the heated air and planned what to say. Dwarves did not want a flowery speech; they wanted quick, concise information. "Not long ago, Issym called for my help because a dragon and a shape shifter were trying to take over their continent. That shifter knew no end to her cruelty and now she is trying to take Asandra. She is after the world! When she is finished with Asandra and Issym, she'll come after you. Do you really think you'll offer her any resistance then?"

"What do you want from us?" another shout came.

"While I have been here, Rachel has been on Asandra, raising an army and preparing to fight Sasha. Come with me to join her ranks and together we will stop the shifter once and for all." Seth refused to say, *I'm not too scared to fight. Are you?* In this mob, they would tear him to shreds for that.

The dwarves began yelling at each other. Several elbows accidentally hit Seth in the stomach. Things were getting dangerous. He looked to Lotex and saw his nod. "It's time to go," Seth told Edmund.

They took their things and left the mines.

"It's just over that hill," Kat almost moaned the words.

Her particularly low spirit this morning made sense. Being this close to Maremoth would make anyone nervous. In fact, Max was impressed that she wasn't excited for the adventure. She actually realized the gravity of what they were about to do.

They stayed low and hid behind the hill. Craning his neck, Max saw the black-walled fortress and the single guard that stood by the entrance near to their hiding place. "There's just one guard," Max returned to a more comfortable position, puzzled. Just one guard and no one had ever tried to take the fortress? "What's the plan once we get in there?"

"You can pass yourself off as a guard, find out where my mom is. Okay?"

"What about you?"

"I'll go through the prisoners. Maybe, just maybe, my dad… will still… Never mind."

Max felt as if a vine had sprung up from the ground, wrapped itself around his will and was keeping him planted. It was not panic; it was his gut that refused to allow him to move.

"Are you ready?" the princess asked him before seeing how pale he was.

"Something's not right."

"We have to go, now!" she gripped his arm. "Maybe the other guards were called somewhere else, but they will be back any moment. This could be our only chance." She stared at his face, then into his eyes. She was losing her own courage.

He looked back at her, "Okay, but stay here. I'll clear the way first in case there's an ambush waiting."

Her hands were violently shaking. He had never seen her this nervous before. He jumped over the hill, but stayed low to the ground, not wanting to be seen until he had to be.

Katarina felt her stomach do so many circles that she thought she would faint. She just could not go through with it. "Wait!" she whispered urgently. "Come back!"

Max dropped down beside her. Hopefully, no one had seen him. She was bawling. "What's wrong?" he demanded. He was in battle mode; and when you were going into battle, you did not stop to cry. She was risking their lives by having this episode.

He whispered harshly, "If this is fear, buck up. But if this is something else, tell me now. This is dangerous territory. We had better not stay here too long."

"I... tricked you..." she finally managed.

They went back into the cover of the woods. "What are you talking about?" he needed information, quickly and clearly.

"When we were in the town, I sent a letter to Sasha..." She attempted to compose herself before continuing, "Telling her that if she would let my mother go, I would give her one of the heroes of Issym."

A cold feeling wrapped around his heart. His voice was creepy and low as he said, "You were leading me into a trap."

"I'm sorry."

He paced through the woods. This had been her plan from day one. Every day they had spent together she had been using him. The anger boiled inside Max, along with frustration and sorrow, but now was not the time for feelings. *What next? Focus on what's next.*

Max glanced back at the princess before marching away from her. "Wait!" she cried, following him. "At least I didn't go through with it."

He turned and got right in her face, "This isn't a game! If you had handed me over to Sasha, do you realize what she would have done to me?" his voice cracked. "I would be grateful for the day she executed me. All along you have been manipulating things to go your way." Max's voice got louder: "Don't you realize what is at stake? People's lives are on the line here! We were supposed to go to Issym; without their help we will never stop Sasha. So don't think one of your 'I'm sorry that you *felt* my dagger in your back' apologies is going to patch that one up."

"You agreed to go after my mother," she answered weakly.

"It was a little late to go to Issym and I assumed you had a plan! Now we don't have Issym's help and we can't rescue your mom because Sasha knows we're coming."

"So you're just going to abandon me here?"

He turned to face her. "Yes." He walked away.

"What happened to good, old-fashioned Christian forgiveness?" she asked after him.

"The Bible also talks about not casting your pearls before swine," Max just kept walking.

"You dare compare a princess with a pig!"

"What kind of princess are you? You have betrayed your country."

Katarina fell to the ground, her eyes open wide as the truth of his words flashed before her. She was buried in the snow and her arms were wrapped around her knees. She looked sincere. But was it repentance on her face, or just another gag?

After a moment she looked up at him, the redness in her eyes not covering the control it took to speak, "I know I did wrong, Max," she began. "But I just can't leave her there. Sasha is going to execute her. You go ahead to Issym. Take Zara with you. I'm staying here."

Sasha was going to execute the queen. That changed things. "When?" he asked.

"Two weeks." Her watery eyes looked up at him.

Come on. She's just using you, man. But Max knew what he had to do. "I am going to rescue the queen. If you want to help me, you can, but I'm in charge."

For once, Katarina was completely submissive. "Fine."

Sasha sat upon her throne, just waiting. In two weeks' time she would rule Asandra. In the first place, the executions of Malcon and Juliet were imminent. In addition, she had gotten a letter from the princess Katarina, saying that she was going to lead one of the heroes of Issym into a trap. Sasha did not care whether it was Rachel or Seth—one would trap the other. The executions had been meant to force Seth and Rachel to make hasty mistakes, and they were. Sasha would all too gladly capture the princess after she had turned in one of the so-called heroes.

With Seth and Rachel out of the way, Issym would not be difficult to capture. She smiled, a luxury she did not often afford herself. The hard work and sacrifice of her life was about to pay off.

The ambush was set; Stewart was in charge of it. But the hours of the day passed and no one came to her with good news. She called Stewart to her side. "Where are they?"

"They have not come, Empress." The man's eyes flicked towards the door. He needed to be there when the princess came or else he would receive no glory for the capture.

"Search the woods," Sasha ordered. "Perhaps the princess lost her nerve and is hiding there."

Rachel was actually sleeping, never mind that it was on Evan's arm. Something about his steady heartbeat that pulsed through the limb and his rhythmic breaths had allowed her to rest.

She woke to Firil's squawk and bolted upright. She must have been dreaming. "Firil!" she heard the noise again. The teen ran outside and there he was. Giant, purple-feathered Firil had tracked down her scent. She ran to hug him.

"How did you find us?" she asked.

Inan stepped beside her. "You should be careful. That thing has some very sharp parts."

"I know," she replied.

"All our animals are gone. You might as well keep him in the stables."

"Thank you." Rachel led Firil there, but found him following her back to the house. "No. Stay here!" She had no time to take care of a bird. She needed to look after Evan and Reesthma.

The bird gave a disappoint sigh, but remained.

Rachel walked into the cottage, burdened and praying as

quickly as the thoughts came into her mind. Zachary and Drainan. Evan. Max and Katarina. Seth. Inan and his family. Asandra. She could not change anything for any of them.

Orune's words resounded through her: *Pray, Rachel. Pray like you've never done before. This isn't a cliché: 'when the going gets tough, pray'. No; this is a spiritual battle—the captures just as real as Zachary's and the deaths even more real. You taught yourself to fight with bow, sword and fists. Now let God teach you to pray.*

And so she prayed. For hours upon hours as she sat by Evan's bedside, she talked with God about everything. As darkness set, Reesthma came beside Rachel and prayed with her. Before she went to bed, the fair-skinned girl gave Rachel a piece of paper. "Evan is a writer—that's how he processes things. He wrote this while he was in my tree. He threw it away, but I kept it. I think you should read it."

Rachel waited several moments before finding the courage to unfold and read the short note:

Kiash. People have forgotten the true meaning of the word.
They think that it only means victory
And faith that God will grant that victory.
But that is not how it was meant to be used.

Kiash is complete and total surrender of yourself
And the things you hold most dear to God.
It is acceptance of death
And of the loss of the war, if that is God's will.

It is trusting God
And following His orders in every way.
Kiash is a challenge and a commitment.

So today I say this to my God:
Kiash! I submit!

Chapter 29

As Seth waited in the cave for the sprites to assemble, he watched Edmund grow more and more agitated. "What's going on? What's wrong?" Seth finally asked.

Edmund sighed. "I was trying to ignore this, but I have to go. I won't be back."

"Why?" They would be leaving in an hour. Something had to be really wrong for Edmund to dash away all of the sudden.

"I can sense a shifter—she's headed for us. And if I'm not with you, Sasha won't be able to find you."

"No. We need to stick together." How would he get back to Asandra without Edmund? Maybe Ruby could help, but he had not heard from her since they had first landed on the beach.

"Sasha can't do much to me yet—no stones. But she can do a lot to you." Edmund turned into a blue jay and left.

After half an hour, the blue jay returned with a robin. Edmund and Kate turned into their human forms.

"Kate," Seth gave a sigh of relief. "You have no idea how good it is to see you."

"I do not come with good news," she answered. "Rachel sent me. The prince is dying."

Seth attempted to absorb the grim news. "What can we do?"

"She wanted Ruby."

"We have no idea where she is."

"Edmund," Kate spoke without looking at him, "I can't become an illuminescent or a fairy—can you?"

"You're far more talented than I," he replied. His eyes seemed to be locked on her.

Kate grimaced, "Either way, I need to get back there; Rachel won't move until I return."

"How far?" Seth asked.

"More than a day," she answered.

Seth had to be there. He might not be able to help, but he had to get there. "Will I slow you down?"

She looked him over, then shook her head, "Not too much. So let's go."

Seth asked Edmund, "Can you bring the sprites?"

The shifter responded, "We'll head towards Maremoth."

"He's slipping," Rasee's urgent voice came from Evan's room. Rachel was there in an instant. The prince could not stop coughing.

"We have to be able to do something!" Rachel pleaded.

Evan stopped coughing. He stopped breathing too. Rachel looked toward Rasee, but saw that she had already given up. The teen let her head fall to his chest as the tears began to come.

A calloused hand touched her shoulder and sent electricity shooting through her body. She turned hopefully and saw Seth. She stood up, her chair falling to the ground underneath her.

Seth's eyes flashed as they landed on the bedside table and the gem upon it. He drew his dagger and slammed the butt of it into the stone. A blue illuminescent rose from the pieces. "He needs your help!" Seth buzzed urgently.

Rachel could hardly believe that she had not realized what had lain beside Evan the whole time. He might die because she hadn't remembered. "How did you know?" Rachel breathed to Seth.

"I didn't forget all of our childhood," he answered with a smile meant to give her some comfort. Together they watched as sparks poured from the illuminescent for a full minute. The creature was shaking when it finally fell onto the bed.

Evan took a breath. Rachel pulled back the cloth on his wound—a small red welt remained, but it was not serious. "You're going to be okay," she whispered.

"What changed your mind?" Max asked as they sat in the middle of the woods, racking their brains for some plan and hoping that Sasha was not looking for them. "What made you decide not to give me over to Sasha?"

Katarina liked him, but she had liked plenty of boys in her time. Certainly that had not been the only reason. She searched for another. None offered itself. "I don't know." That was a good enough answer. "I'm sorry I even thought it, I just couldn't pass up the one chance I had to save my mom."

"But you did."

"I guess there was just something wrong about handing the guy who saved my life over to Sasha on a silver platter."

He laughed at that.

"What's so funny?"

"Do you know where that phrase comes from?"

"No."

"I guess it's not that weird that you guys use it here too. You have the Bible."

"It comes from the Bible?" she asked.

"You know John the Baptist?"

"Of course." The name sounded familiar.

"He was pretty awesome. He was Jesus' cousin and he did a whole lot of preaching about Jesus and baptized a lot of people. But John ticked off an important person and landed in prison. While he was there, a girl was offered anything she wanted. And she asked for his head on a silver platter."

"Yuck. Why would she want that?"

"A lot of people do a lot of dumb things for a lot of dumb reasons."

"She must have been a sick person inside."

"Why? Because she had somebody killed?"

The princess glared at him. "I didn't have you killed Max."

"You were going to. You were the one who said that was the plan."

"But... I'm not that bad."

"I know. I've spent a lot of time with you and you were no worse than I was. But what you've got to recognize is that life is never going to slow down. I kept telling myself that I would deal with the whole God-thing later. First it was when my school slowed down. Then it was when summer was over and I wasn't as busy. When I came to Issym, I kept saying I would think about God when I got home. But life will always be crazy and Satan will always throw things at you that distract you." He really did not like this part of being a Christian. Witnessing was at the bottom of his to-do list. But some things had to be done. "God is real," he continued. "And you, no matter how bad or good you are, have to realize how deeply you need Him."

"Don't you get it?" she shouted as loudly as she dared. "We're running for our lives! If I sit down to ponder life, I'll be dead before I even begin."

"You know better than anyone that death lurks at every corner. Where are you going to go when your head gets put on that silver platter?"

"Come on Max, is it really that dramatic? Don't you think that all the good things I've been trying to do or the craziness of my life will get me a break? I think God understands."

"He's very understanding. If He wasn't, we could never be forgiven. But you have the opportunity today to take God seriously. If you reject that opportunity and you die tomorrow, what excuse will you have before God?"

"Don't make me regret saving you."

The early morning came and Galen found his body going through the motions of leaving. Most of the newly trained 'sailors' were already on the 'boats'; it was time to go. But the king heard Flibbert shouting at Ethelwyn and knew he had a few more minutes. He returned to the throne room and hugged his wife once more.

She felt the tension. "Is it this trip that troubles you?"

"Why has Kate not returned? I wonder if Sasha..."

Andrea put her fingers to his lips, "Don't say it. They don't have stones there; she can't be dead."

"Sasha may have captured her."

"Do you not know how powerful Kate is?"

Galen took her hands and looked into her eyes, "If this is a trap..."

"If this is a trap, you've left us enough of an army to defend ourselves. Issym will not fall. Are you not following God?"

"Be careful."

"You trained me well. I will."

Galen kissed her goodbye and walked out of the room to be met by Bridget. He understood the look in her eyes, but let her speak. "I want to come with you."

"Are you sure?" he asked. "You are welcome to remain here."

"No. Asandra is my home and I am going to face it. Brooks is already heading to the ships. We will help you once we arrive on Asandra."

In another room of the castle, Flibbert had calmed down enough for Ethelwyn to try to reason with him, "Do you think I made the decision easily to stay behind? You shame me with your talk."

"We need you Wyn; I, better than anyone, know of your battle skills."

"Did I fight with blows in the war here on Issym?"

"No."

"You said it yourself, you know me better than anyone. You should understand this. I cannot come."

"Why?"

She shook her head. He did not understand and she could not explain it to him. "Just go to the boats; they need you."

"They need *you*."

"Not this time, old friend."

"You're only twenty—you're not old enough to have an old friend."

"I'm older than you think."

"Oh, so you just look great? You have the unchanging beauty of youth."

"You should go," she told him, not even blushing at his compliment.

He wanted to fight with her, to convince her to come. But Amber appeared in the doorway and all he said was, "Keep the kingdom safe."

Chapter 30

Evan had woken up for a few hours, only to be ordered to go back to sleep. At that point, Rachel left his side, to sit by the fire and talk things over with Seth. There was a lot to report. "What happened to Evan?" Seth inquired.

"He took a dagger Sasha had meant for me," she answered.

"You guys saw Sasha?" What had he left her to face?

"Kate's illuminescent came up with a little trick that made Sasha think the stones of the frogs were coming. She ran after that. What happened with you? You look pretty banged up."

"Thanks," he laughed sarcastically. "I was trying to win the dwarves respect and was mining with one of them when there was a cave-in."

She stared at him, "And you survived?"

"I'm sure God had everything to do with that. The dwarves are thinking things over right now—trying to decide whether to help or not. But we did get some sprites to come."

"Sprites? We've had a couple encounters with them. They are almost as evil as Sasha."

"These ones seemed kind of nice," Seth replied. "Did you get any kind of an army?"

She looked down, "No... These people—I don't think they want to be rescued."

"Hey," he drew her eyes back to him. "Are you okay?"

"Yeah; it's just been really hard here. I mean, Drainan and our friend Zachary were both taken. And I have lived amongst the misery of these people..."

He knew exactly what she was feeling. "It's not your fault, Rachel. Don't let anyone tell you it is."

Five humans and two dwarves surrounded Kat and Max. There was no resisting them. "The empress desires your presence," one dwarf said mockingly. He looked at one of the other dwarves, "We found them without Stewart's help! This should put us in good favor with the Empress." The two humans snorted and rolled their eyes.

Zara flew from Katarina's bag and disappeared in the woods.

The group entered Maremoth and were led into the throne room of Sasha. The woman on the throne wore an elegant dress and an extravagant crown upon her head—neither seemed like they truly fit her presence. The smug smile she wore turned into rage. "Who are they?"

"The... humans you sent us after," the head dwarf answered, pushing them forward and trying to back out.

"Really?" Sasha scoffed. "Because I don't recognize either of them. Get me Stewart."

The dwarves rushed to exit, leaving Kat and Max to stare at Sasha. After a few moments, Stewart entered the room breathless from his run. "Empress," he said, bowing to please her. Things were not going well today. Someone was going to get in trouble.

"You," the shifter pointed to Katarina after staring at her for several moments. "You look like your mother. Why did you lie to me?"

"What?"

"You said that you would bring me Seth or Rachel."

"I said a hero of Issym; this is a hero of Issym," Kat protested.

"I've never seen this boy before."

"This is Max..."

She grabbed Katarina by the chin, "I did not want the sidekick!"

Sasha shoved Katarina towards Stewart, "Take her away and find out what she knows. She may be of use yet."

Stewart gently led her out. No need to make an enemy of a potential ally. There were many rumors about the princess—even more now that she had almost turned on this boy Max.

Max wanted to stop Stewart, but there was nothing he could do. Katarina was gone.

Sasha settled into her throne as she waited for a drink to be brought to her. Max studied her during the time of silence. She was less impressive than he had thought she would be. There was no doubt that she was pretty, but it seemed fake. And her arrogance was almost amusing. Still, he felt drawn to her, and he knew why. He had always craved power. It lured him in. *Snap out of it!*

She took a sip of her drink, then narrowed her focus on him as the servant shut the doors behind him. "These are the rules," she began. "I will tolerate no sermons about how God will protect you. He can do what he wishes with you—I don't care. But as long as you are alive and in Maremoth, you will work for me."

"What exactly do you want?"

"The truth. That should be easy enough. Are Seth and Rachel here?"

"I think so, but I haven't seen them in a while." Max was going to answer the questions that would cause Sasha to be afraid. He would tell her nothing important.

"What are they planning?"

"To defeat you."

She laughed, "Not likely."

He shrugged, "We shall see."

"You are a bold one. No wonder Smolden," she spat, "liked you."

"In the end, he wished he'd never met me."

She wanted to slap him for his confidence, but she reined herself in and spoke calmly as she descended her steps: "I had heard rumors that you caused that mighty earthquake. But looking at you, I can't believe it's true."

Max felt the hairs stand up on the back of his neck. She was testing him, looking for his weak spot. And as soon as she knew where it was, she would strike. He needed to get out of here. Prison, anywhere, but not here, standing helpless before her. "You'll wish you never met me too," he said.

She grabbed his hair—her sharpened fingernails bringing blood from his skull—and forcing him to look into her creepy eyes, "Do not test me, boy. I have no need to keep you alive."

She yanked him to the other end of the room and threw him into a wooden chair she had brought in especially for the occasion. Forming herself a larger chair, she sat down beside him. "I know," she whispered.

"What do you know?" he asked, slicking back his hair, trying to retain his composure.

"I know," she answered, "that you are bought and sold. When Seth offered you the opportunity to move up in the social circle of Earth, you befriended him. When Smolden provided you with the life of a prince, you moved onto his side. And when God seemed to hold the keys to a happier you, you took Him up on that."

Max's throat felt suddenly dry. She offered him her drink and he took a sip.

She continued, "When the pretty princess gave you her friendship, you readily agreed to follow her through the continent, oblivious to the fact that she was using you to get her mother back. Just like Seth used you to promote his own welfare, Smolden used you to help conquer Issym, and God used you to promote 'his kingdom.'"

Max winced. Her lies were so closely intertwined with the truth... he was having trouble telling them apart.

"Are you still listening?" she asked as he stared at the floor.

Max nodded.

"This is the sad truth of your pitiful life: you are nothing but a pawn in other people's schemes. Seth, Katarina, God—they're not your friends. Even that prisoner you rescued, he was just using you. God was just his tool as you were his tool."

His hands were shaking now. His whole life he had felt lost—God had brought him peace. But what she was saying made sense. "What do you want from me?" he asked.

"Oh Max, I'm sorry. I want to use you too. But I also want to teach you something."

"What's that?" he growled.

"That when other people use you," she circled his chair and gripped his shoulders, whispering in his ear, "you can use them right back."

Max took in the fragrance that encircled her. Where had he smelled that before? In Smolden's lair? It could not be. This beautiful, intelligent woman was totally different from the stupid, vile beast.

"I will not put up any pretenses around you, Max—you could see right through them," the shape shifter complimented him as she sat back down. "You have greatness in you, but will you use it?"

Adrenaline shot through his body. He had greatness in him?

"No one else recognizes this, but you are so important. Once you were unpopular—then you latched onto Seth and have risen to popularity. Here, you have captured the eye of a princess—I saw the way she looked at you." Her voice rose, "You are the key to this battle, but will you just be used to turn the lock? Or will you start making decisions for yourself? Will you forever be used?"

Max's tongue felt even more dry and numb. He wiped his hands on his pants—they were drenched with sweat. There was only one question to ask: "What do you want me to do?"

"It's not about that. It is about what you want. Do you wish to help your friends—those that have used you? Or do you want to help me and become the right hand of an empress? For once, it is your choice."

Max's eyes fell closed, the cup falling from his hands. So many thoughts! They all swirled around in his head. His head slumped to his chest. "Max?" the empress called to him. And then he fell asleep.

Sasha smiled; the concoction in his drink had obviously confused him—hopefully enough. She might have to have him executed with Juliet and Malcon, but he would give her plenty of information before then. His execution would get Seth and Rachel out of hiding! A guard came at her call and took the teen to the room prepared for him.

Flibbert was not the captain of the ship, but he was the first mate and he was a leader to the people of Issym. He knew he needed to control his temper. Galen captained this ship, while Elimelech and Queen Danielle were in control of the others.

How did I get stuck on a boat full of illuminescents? Flibbert wondered. He'd never liked the little creatures, having distrusted them from the beginning. But now... they'd been at sea for only a couple of days, and already their buzzing and glowing and buzzing and flying and buzzing and instructing him was grating on the frog.

Truthfully it was not the illuminescents that were the problem. It was Ethelwyn. How long had they known each other? And yet, she still was keeping something from him. There must have been a reason she stayed behind. Was she sick?

A yellow illuminescent was dancing around his head, bouncing on his shoulders and buzzing incessantly. Flibbert waved him off to Galen.

The creature flew to Galen's side. "King, King!" he exclaimed.

Galen tried to focus his eyes on the creature, but the toss of the waves allowed him to barely focus on large objects, let alone on this little creature that continually moved.

"King, King!" the illuminescent repeated.

"What is it?"

"Did you not see the change in the water?"

Galen immediately focused. Was the creature trying to tell him that they were in danger? As if sensing his fears, the illuminescent responded, "It was Tias communicating with us. She flew to the water's edge and there sent a message—the sea carried it the rest of the way, until I saw it."

More illuminescents were heading Galen's way—apparently this yellow one was not the only one to have seen. The king felt the urge to run away before the others arrived, but he was too late.

"What did her message say?" he asked one who was bigger and older and would speak more slowly. Out of the corner of his eye, he saw Elimelech, the fairy captain, descend on the ship. He was heading Galen's way, obviously aware that news was being delivered.

He arrived just in time to hear a red one say, "Tias says that Sasha lives and has almost taken the continent. The king and queen have truly been captured. The prince lay dying when the message was delivered. She knows nothing of the princess."

"And what of Seth and Rachel?" Flibbert asked.

"They are fighting for Asandra."

The shout of joy went up from all three ships: "Kiash!"

Chapter 31

Seth and Rachel's light-hearted conversation, and the children's laughter as Reesthma played with them, filled the house with pleasant sounds. A knock to the door did not quiet the happy noises. Inan opened it only partway to hear a woman say, "What are you going to bring to the festival?"

"What festival?" Inan responded.

"You haven't heard? Sasha has declared herself empress and is having a celebration. Every town is to have its own dinner in honor."

"Where will she hold this celebration?"

"In Maremoth. Of course, we're not invited! Only the lucky people who have been working for her and her army are going to be there."

Lucky? Rachel thought. *She thinks the prisoners are lucky?*

The woman kept going, "Three people have been sentenced to death by hanging. One is Queen Juliet, the second is a dwarf who betrayed her, or so I hear, and the third is someone called Max—apparently an old enemy."

Seth drew a sharp breath. "What was that?" asked the woman at the door.

"When are the executions?" Inan questioned, shutting it a little more.

"One week's time exactly."

He closed the door in her face. Rachel and Seth just looked at each other. "He's supposed to be on his way to Issym, isn't he?" Seth asked. It was the only question he could think of.

Evan was still confined to his bed, but it had been a week since he had first woken up, and he spent most of the time awake and talking. He called out, "If he's sentenced to death, what about Kat?"

"Maybe she got away," Rachel pondered, moving with Seth to stand in the doorframe to his room.

"This sounds like a challenge. One I can't refuse," Seth admitted.

"No," Kate was adamant. "You cannot give Sasha what she wants."

"We're not just going to let them die," Rachel answered.

"This isn't just about your friend or about the queen. It isn't even about Asandra, anymore. This involves all Xsardis. You two just can't get yourselves killed."

"Kate, Xsardis will survive without us," Rachel declared. "We need to accept Sasha's challenge."

"Evan can't even move yet," Reesthma joined them.

"With what army will you storm her fortress?" Kate asked.

"This isn't a one-encounter war. That was a blessing in Issym, but that is not normally how things work. This is a rescue mission—one fight amongst many."

Seth nodded. "Speed will be our ally. Once Sasha turns herself into hundreds of deathless forms, we will have to run."

Reesthma smiled, "I brought the blueprints of Maremoth."

"If the dwarves come to our aid," Evan began, "we can win this fight."

"We need to leave now, but Evan..." Rachel did not know how to word her sentence.

Hector, the new blue illuminescent, said, "I can help him travel. It will be okay."

"Then let's get going," Seth decided.

"What can you possibly want from that idiot?" Stewart questioned.

Sasha took a moment to decide whether or not she would explain it to Stewart. "Max knows things he does not even know he knows. He knows what Seth will do when he is confronted with every situation. He knows the plans they currently have and the ones they are likely to make. And Seth trusts the boy completely. He will lure Seth and Rachel out just by being here. Max is a valuable tool for the time being."

"Do you fear them so?" Stewart questioned.

Sasha could have killed Stewart right then for that question, but he was a skilled commander. Once her kingdom was firmly established, and she had taken both Asandra and Issym, and the cursed stones of the frogs were destroyed, she could afford to get rid of her entire army. But until then, Stewart and the others would live as long as their usefulness outweighed their inconvenience.

"You are a fool if you do not fear them," she answered. "They may just be teenagers, but do not underestimate their God or their knowledge."

Now Stewart grimaced. He tried to hide it, but it showed on his face. Sasha knew that look to mean failure. "Joppa's tree is destroyed, correct?"

"One man returned and said that they were overpowered by... snow creatures."

Sasha leaped from her chair, turning into a wolf and pummeling him to the ground. She was about to kill him when she heard him say, "*All* the men are dead." Stewart added, "I was going there myself when we got the princess' message."

"It has been a few weeks since I sent them to Joppa's tree," her wolfish voice scared him more than any other he had yet heard her use.

Stewart had no answer. He just kept staring her in the eyes, waiting for her to choose whether to kill him or let him up.

The shape shifter moved off him, going to the throne and curling up on it, "Burn it or *you* will burn!"

Stewart and a group of fast-riding humans quickly reached Joppa's tree. They doused the bottom with oil and threw their torches upon it, but the torches died out and did not set the tree ablaze. Stewart watched as his men tried again and again to get it to light; nothing happened.

"Perhaps it has a magic enchantment," one of the men said.

"Maybe its wood is just fire-resistant," Stewart answered. "Climb it; find a way in."

Precious time ticked by. Sasha wanted them back in time for the celebration. He had already angered her enough. One of the men came down, protesting, "There is no way in."

Stewart threw his torch at the man, who quickly patted out the fire. He answered, "There has to be a way in—one that a thirteen-year-old girl could find. Keep looking!"

More time passed. Stewart could tell that the men were no longer actually searching for an entrance. They were just keeping busy. "We will return to Maremoth," Stewart finally decided.

"Will Sasha kill us?" one asked.

"Only if she finds out." But how could a secret of this importance be kept by six fools? Stewart told the men, "I'm looking for a new captain, boys. The last man alive will have earned that position."

The men drew their blades. The last man alive would fall at Stewart's hands—secrets were much more easily kept that way.

Chapter 32

Seth tried not to think about home as they moved through the woods, but the truth was he missed it. It had been a long time since he had talked to his parents or been to his church or driven in his car with the music blaring and the windows down. Rachel's presence reminded him just how he longed for Earth and for Max. Max could not die. He would not let it happen. He steeled himself for the battle to come—one they were in no position to win.

Firil's noisy squawk and scrambling feet jolted Seth back to reality. Evan had fallen asleep—again—then slumped to one side and thrown the large bird's relative balance off.

Kate returned from her scouting. "I see no one for miles—no enemies and no friends. We can camp nearby and build a fire. I can protect you from whatever comes."

She sat down and leaned against a tree, eyes closed. As Rachel, Evan, Hector and Tias went to sleep, her breaths grew rhythmic, but she was obviously on high alert.

Seth stayed up, taking first watch. Reesthma moved next to him. She started, "My uncle turned himself in to Sasha's men to save me. For a long time I have been trying to pretend like he's okay, but I saw what Sasha did to Evan. That blade wasn't meant to kill quickly but to make people suffer. A woman like that would never have let a great man like Joppa live."

Seth could not promise her that everything would be okay. She was probably right, so he got her telling a story. "Did Joppa raise you?"

"Most of my life. I don't know what happened to my parents.

Joppa won't tell me much about my past—I just remember that we were farmers. It's odd to live in a place where you are surrounded by history, but you don't know your own. I guess that now I'll never know."

Kate was instantly on her feet, her eyes sweeping through the woods. She looked to Seth. "Shape shifter," her voice became deep and gravelly as she turned into a wolf.

It could have been Edmund, Seth knew as Kate ran past him, but there was no way to be sure. He could have woken the others, but any noise they made would only make things worse. As time passed, Seth grew more and more anxious.

Rachel felt the tension as she dreamed and sat up, slowly and quietly. She took in her surroundings, then had an unspoken conversation with Seth and understood what had happened.

They waited for almost an hour for Kate, sitting in the silence and praying that Edmund had come, that Sasha had not found them out so quickly. Kate's wolf padded back to them, turned human and smiled. "Edmund brought the sprites *and* the dwarves."

Max woke up on a soft bed. He was home. No, he was on Issym. No, he was on Asandra. But where? At Sasha's palace. He was a prisoner? Not exactly. He was a prince? Not yet. He opened his eyes.

His stone walled room was small, but the bed was much softer than the ground he was used to. Wrapped around him was one very warm blanket. Across from the bed was a desk. His eyes passed over the paper, quill pen and ink to settle on the plate of bread, meat and cheese. His bare feet were instantly on the cold floor, but he barely even felt it in his rush for food. After stuffing his face, he noticed a jug beside the plate; he drank right from it—something his mother would have yelled at him for doing. His mother... that was a strange thought. It had been so long since he had thought of his family.

Searching around him for his bag, Max realized it was gone and with it his now uncharged iPod, his lighter, his Bible and the other traces he had had left of home. He kicked the chair in frustration. *I shouldn't even be here. I should be on Issym.*

It was then that he noticed the clothing sitting on his chair. Fine black-leather boots and standard black pants, but the shirt... He dropped his roll. It was actually a gold-colored satin. Real crystals, as far as he could tell, embroidered the top. So what if it was girly by American standards? It must have cost a fortune. As he pulled on the shirt, something tumbled to the ground. A gold ring with a large ruby centered in it. The outfit was fit for a prince. *Am I a prince?*

Remember, said a Voice, *who Sasha is. Remember Who I Am.*

Yeah, I got it. He put on the pants and the boots, then slipped the ring on his right hand ring finger. Only then did he finish his meal.

His conversation with Sasha from the night before began to swirl around in his head. Was she right or was she wrong? She had not seemed to lie about anything. The shape shifter had not put into question the reality of God, or of his friendship with Seth, but she had called them the same as Smolden and Katarina. Were they? Were they truly manipulating him like Kat and the dragon?

Sasha had made sense. She was right that Max had befriended Seth because he was popular. Why wouldn't other people treat him the way he treated them?

Even if everyone else had used him, God had not, right? But then again, hadn't He protected the apostles as long as they could do good on the Earth *for Him.* When they had outlived their usefulness He had let them die like the vilest of criminals. How was that unconditional love?

He was so dizzy he fell back into his bed. That was not the God he knew. God had protected the apostles from death hundreds of times, but all men die. They could not live forever. The God he knew worked all things 'for the good of those who love Him.' After all, He had sent His son to die on the cross, hadn't He? He had saved Max when he had seemed beyond saving. God hadn't had to do that.

Max's thoughts fell onto Princess Valerie, the sister of the man who had led him to God. She could have been mad because Arvin died to save Max, but she wasn't. Instead, the princess had reminded him before he left Issym that her brother had died for his physical self and that Christ had died for his spiritual one. Max, therefore, could no longer waste either of those lives. His life was no longer his.

One thing was clear: Arvin had not used him. Max was incapable of believing it.

Another thing became clear: Christ had not used him. Max was incapable of believing it.

Truth came rushing into his mind—wiping out the confusion, if not the dizziness. Max found once again the line between right and wrong, between falsehood and truth, between justice and injustice. Sasha was wrong, false and unjust. God was right, true and just. "I remember Who You are, God," he whispered.

You have the potential to be great, Sasha's words rang in his head, *but will you use it?*

He could accomplish great things. But if he chose God over Sasha and over himself he would be giving up the accomplishment of great things. No. That was another lie. Maybe he would never take over the world, but he could definitely help save it. Max made up his mind.

The teen paced his room, knowing it would not be long before someone came to get him. He was ready for the next encounter with Sasha.

The door opened and a guard ordered him, "Come with me. The empress wishes to see you."

Max followed him out, where two dwarves joined them as they proceeded into the throne room. Sasha had set up a table and two chairs on the balcony of the palace. She sat there, arrayed in her regal clothing, food and drink already set out. She smiled at Max, "Come join me."

He took his seat beside her. The guards went away. "Did you have a good night's rest?" she asked pleasantly.

"I don't think I stirred." He tried not to look over the people suffering in Maremoth. Was Katarina now one of them?

"And your breakfast was pleasing?"

"Yes."

Why had he thought that she had been trying to confuse him? She had opened his eyes to truth, hadn't she? His brain could not process his own thoughts. Why could he not shake the numbness that clawed its way through his insides?

"I'm so glad that you are not afraid of me, Max. I can see in your eyes that you're not. And you look so nice in those clothes," she complimented sweetly, putting a hand on his forearm before pouring him a drink. Her hair was arrayed in ringlets and her face appeared a bit younger. "Shall we eat?"

"Yes." After the meal he would tell her what he really thought about her. Which was what? He couldn't remember.

They feasted while she talked. When they were finished, she took him by the arm and they began to walk through the palace. "You do remember the conversation we had yesterday?" she inquired.

"I do." There was that aroma again—the same one from Smolden's lair, and though it masked itself as sweetness, the truth was that it stank. He was determined to keep his mind alert. *A little help would be nice,* he prayed.

"I'm sure you understand that my time is short. I would dearly love to work with you but we must make our plans quickly. Do you like my palace?"

Everything looked spectacular to him. "It is very nice."

"It could be yours, Max. I need a building more regal. This one could be your own. Think of it: Max, lord of Asandra!"

"And what would happen to me once I have served my purpose?" Max had no idea where that question had come from, but it deserved an answer.

"Oh Max, don't you remember anything I said yesterday. This is about what you want! You can reign here as long as you desire. You can help me without betraying your friends. Help me, Max. I need you."

Now that was a lie. His mind locked on the truth and it showed in his eyes.

"What is it?" Sasha inquired in her sweetest tones. "Can't you see what I'm offering you?"

"I can taste what you put in my food to cloud my judgment. And I know what the likes of you did to Arvin! Where is Katarina?"

Sasha took a moment before she answered. Stage one of her plan had obviously failed. Things for stage two had to be set in place. While her duplicates were doing the work, she looked deep into his eyes.

Max squirmed under her gaze. It was like she was staring straight into his soul. What did she discover there? "Where is the princess?" he repeated.

"I will show you," she replied. Sasha led him farther down the hall and then took a key and unlocked a door. As Max began to enter, the shape shifter put an arm in his way. "You aren't going to be helping me, are you?"

"No. You blend lies and truth very well, Sasha; but God's light is much stronger than your darkness."

"Go on then and see your pretty lass. It may be the last time you ever do." She smiled, "You are going to hang with Juliet in a few days' time! And your girl? I'll send her to work with the common prisoners until I need another victim for a celebration." Sasha let him in, then pulled the door shut behind him—he heard it lock.

Katarina sat on the floor, quietly sobbing. Her hair was disheveled and her clothes dirty, but other than that she looked fine. When she saw Max she stood and ran into his arms. At first he did not put them around her. "I'm so sorry, Max! I know this was all my fault."

There was sorrow in her voice and perhaps even repentance. Max gave into the hug, "This was my choice."

She put a hand on his cheek. He pulled back, confused. That

was not the Katarina he knew. He even had to stop her from giving him a kiss.

From the cracks in the door, the real Katarina watched what her shape shifter double did. She turned to look at Stewart and Sasha, disgusted, "I wouldn't act like that. He knows me better."

Stewart whispered to her so that Sasha could not hear, "You know I can get Max free from this."

She shivered and stepped closer to the crack.

"Oh, Max," the fake Katarina exclaimed, "Sasha said that she is going to kill you and me too eventually. What are we going to do?"

"Seth won't let us down. He'll come and rescue us." He was buying time with the answer—things were not right. Kat was confident, never looking to him for guidance. And there was one thing that always held true to Katarina. She never admitted that anything was her fault.

"But how can he hope to defeat Sasha?" she asked as she stroked the back of his neck.

Max stepped farther back, rubbing the area of his neck that she had touched—it felt gross.

"What's wrong?" she moved towards him.

He took her chin and stared into her eyes. He shuddered at what he saw. "When was the first time you got your brother into trouble?" he whispered.

"What?"

"You heard me."

Katarina disappeared. Max looked at the door, "Nice try."

It opened and Sasha admitted, "You are intelligent. It is a pity you won't follow me. I could have put that intelligence to work."

The true Katarina, slightly less disheveled, called to him proudly, "I was two and it involved stealing a sword from a sleeping sentry."

"That's my girl," he smiled despite the circumstances.

"I am not your girl."

"Just had to be sure."

"You just had to be arrogant."

Chapter 33

"You better speak to them," Lotex huffed.

Seth's brain stumbled to catch up with the dwarf. They had been marching for almost two weeks. They were practically at Maremoth's doorstep, but the crowd of sprites and dwarves were getting nervous. Many wanted to turn around and go back home. They needed someone to rally their courage. "What can I say that I haven't already said?" Seth questioned.

"You have to try something," Rachel pressured him.

He knew she was right. The dwarves did not like being led by a few teenagers to the heart of Sasha's power with little hope for success. They had come expecting to join an army, not to *be* the army. Seth needed to remind them that he was no ordinary teenager and that his God was no ordinary God.

Edmund stepped behind him, the shifter's mood having been growing darker and darker with each step they took closer to his sister. "I spent way too much time and energy getting these dwarves this far, Seth," he reminded him. "Make it count."

Seth shuffled through the snow and stood before them, receiving their attention after Lotex's holler. The young man prayed, then knew what to say. "I know you all want to go home," he began. "I would love to give you a brilliant speech that promised not one of you would fall tomorrow, but I can't. All I can say is that tomorrow is not our battleground; today is. Today you decide the course of Asandra. For too long, this country has hidden from the fight against Sasha—the fight against evil. It was happy to believe that life was better letting her and evil rule. You know that to be false. So, what will you do?

"When you go into battle, you face the reality of death. And today, you know where you're going—to Heaven or to hell. There is no middle ground.

"Asandra's problem is not Sasha; it is the lack of God in our hearts and souls. As long as we try to fight this battle in our own strength we are going to lose. We think, 'God is so terrible. How can He let this happen?' But have we actually asked for His help? We blame God for a problem that is a result of our own sin. And until we take the blame and say, 'God, I am sorry. I have done wrong and I need you to be my Lord and to change me,' we are going to lose to Sasha.

"If you can't trust Him, if you can't give your life to Him, go home. We don't need your help. My God is enough and He will find another way. But today is the day when we need to ask Him to come to our aid. Today's the day to make your choice. Are you for Him or against Him?"

Seth turned around and walked back. The next thing he knew he was on the ground and someone had gotten in a very hard hit before being dragged off him. Rachel and Kate's voices were the loudest in the shouting that followed. It took him only a moment to sit up and few seconds longer to realize that Kate was restraining Edmund from taking another swing.

Some blood, jarred by Seth's movements as he stood, fell from his lips and stained the crystal clear snow. He wiped it away, aware of Rachel's glance to make sure he was okay. "What was that for?" Seth asked, taking command of the situation. Edmund stopped struggling. Kate let him go.

Edmund got in his face. "I have slaved, I gave up my life on Issym," his eyes flicked to Kate, but the anger in her eyes forced him to turn back to Seth, "to get those dwarves to come to Asandra and fight. And what do you do? You send them home!" He shoved Seth, but the teen barely stumbled. "I brought you to Noric to lead. I helped you so that you could help Xsardis. But you are too cowardly to even ask the dwarves to stay. You are no warrior!"

The shifter turned to Rachel. "This is your country, Rachel. Stand up and lead it!"

Rachel stared into the man's desperate eyes. She answered, "Seth is right. Don't you know the story of Gideon? He went from an army of thirty-two thousand to three hundred after God sent them home."

"I know the story. You are going to let Xsardis fall because of a *story*?"

He moved to Kate, imploring her. "Please. You know Sasha. Don't let them do this."

Maybe Edmund saw the look of remorse and love. Seth and Rachel certainly did, but Edmund looked away quickly and shouted at them all, "Who do you think you all are? Your blind faith in the Almighty is going to get us all killed! I'm done. I've tried to help you people, but you just won't be helped. Let Sasha massacre you then."

Moving close to Kate once more, he took her hands and stared into her eyes. "We had something Kate. Give it another chance. I can't ever love your God, but I will love you forever."

In that moment she knew he would never be saved. She gripped his forearms, searching for some other option, trying to stay upright under the grief from the horrible reality that there was none. She spoke with a quivering voice, "Then you can't really love me. There is no us anymore, Edmund, and there never will be." Kate pulled back from him.

He disappeared and a large tear rolled out of her eye. "But I did love you," she whispered.

Evan stepped beside Seth and Rachel. "Seth, you okay?"

He nodded, but in truth he wasn't. Edmund had been one of those annoying, difficult, stubborn friends, but a friend nonetheless.

Seth felt Rachel's hand on his shoulder as he wiped away the blood from his chin. What if something like Kate and Edmund's blowout happened to them? What if one of them died in the upcoming battle? That was a seriously possibility. She meant far too much to him and he had never even told her that.

Lotex shook his head grimly, knowing the damage that someone like Edmund could do if he carried a grudge. Reesthma stood next to him, absorbing everything.

"Guys," Evan broke the silence that had taken the group. "No one is leaving. No one."

"Good," Seth answered. "I don't want to sleep any closer to Maremoth than this. We will camp here."

As they sat down to discuss the strategy for tomorrow's fight, Rachel was glad that Firil was off bothering the dwarves. The jolly creature would have no place in the grave conversation they were about to have. So much suffering would take place tomorrow. She and Seth were in the middle of a civil war and it wasn't even their country. It was not Max's either, and she would not let him be executed. "We've got to do this right," she voiced. "Where are those blueprints, Reesthma?"

Reesthma set them out in the center of the circle of leaders.

She shivered. She had read about councils like these. Now she was in one.

The sprite Abigail flew to them. "Where have you been?" Seth asked. The young girl had been gone for most of the day. These woods were not as safe as the home she was used to.

"I found the sprites that left Noric and the others that had joined them," Abi answered excitedly. "I convinced them that we wanted to help. They are expecting me to bring back my sprites and join them tomorrow when they go to Maremoth. We can get inside the fortress *and* stop them from serving Sasha." She paused to take a breath. "But we need to leave now. That's okay, right?"

Rachel nodded. Seth said, "Go." Abigail dashed away.

Lotex knew that they had tossed around several plans in the last few days but only one had real merit. "We have to wait until the executions are about to take place. Then the guards will be distracted and the prisoners will be assembled, so we'll have a bigger crowd to blend into."

"All reports say the execution is at noon. We'll have to move quickly," Evan added.

"Even though dwarves are accepted into Maremoth, a group this size is sure to arouse suspicion. You'll send them in throughout the morning?" Kate forced herself to ignore anything that had to do with Edmund. Lotex nodded.

"Someone is going to have to sneak into the palace," Seth added. "I will lead the team."

Rachel wanted to say no. That was practically a suicide mission, but she had no right to stop him. Max was his best friend. He had to do this. But what if something happened to Seth? "We need a distraction."

A fearsome grin came over Lotex's face. "I will start a brawl. Without a doubt the prisoners will try to escape. The guards' focus will be anywhere but on you," he assured.

"We need to try to release as many prisoners as we can. Sasha's wrath will be great after tomorrow if we succeed," Evan reminded.

Rachel's attention lingered on Evan. He loved his people. It was so admirable. *I'm glad he's okay. So glad.* She shook herself back to the present. "Our window of opportunity is small. As soon as Sasha begins to multiply, we need to pull out." She stared at each one of them, "All of you; no exceptions."

Seth recognized her look and realized there was a backup plan. "What's the other plan?"

She looked at him nervously, "You're going to hate it."

The hair's stood up on the back of Seth's neck. "What is it?"

"I will get her attention. She will use her full force and come after me. The rest of you will be able to get to safety."

"No way," Seth snapped. "That is not going to happen." In that moment it was only Seth and Rachel as they stared into each other. "You are the one who said this is not a one-battle war. We'll need you for the rest of it."

"It's only the backup plan," she offered. Rachel was terrified of it. In battle Sasha would show no mercy.

"I'm not going to lose you like that."

She found no words to answer him with. They might have kept staring at each other if Kate had not said, "I cannot go to Maremoth." That broke them out of their trance.

The shifter gave her statement time to sink in before adding, "Sasha would feel my presence and any surprise we would have had would be gone. Tomorrow I leave you. I'll return to my own people."

Reesthma tugged Rachel's attention away, pointing on the map to the back wall of Maremoth, "Rachel, there is a guard up there that will let us in. You and I can go in from there. If you need to catch Sasha's attention you can do it from this tower," she gestured to another building. "You can stay safe until then."

"You can teach me to make those snow creatures," Rachel murmured. Kate had to come with them. It would be a slaughter without her help. What had just happened in those moments with Seth?

Something warm wrapped itself around Rachel's arm and pulled her up. She traced the arm back to Seth's face and together they walked into the woods. "Seth, I don't..." she began, but he cut her off.

"Only if it's necessary." It took her a second to follow his meaning. His eyes kept boring into her; his hand rested on her arm. "Promise me. Only if it is necessary."

Of course I'll only do it if it's necessary, she thought. *I don't want to die!* She looked down at his hand on her arm. It did not move. She stared him in the eye and realized he needed to hear her say it. "I promise."

"We don't know what's going to happen tomorrow and I don't want to leave any regrets." He took her hands. "When I met you again in Issym, you changed everything. You inspired me to stop half-living for God and I took that challenge seriously. You are amazing. We're not average teenagers. We've fought battles together and been through the fires of life and the Valinors. We've handled long distance and close-proximity and every time we're apart, I want to be together. You fit, Rachel."

Rachel smiled, then laughed gently. "You fit too." She leaned her head against the good heart that had just spoken the words she had longed to hear.

Katarina scowled as she took the plate of absolutely disgusting food, doubting she would be alive long enough to get used to it. She plopped down on a log, every muscle tired. "What's Sasha doing to you, Max?" she whispered.

An old man sat down beside her and offered his name, "I'm Nicholas."

She looked into his eyes and saw an odd twinkle. It caught her off guard and the scowl fell from her lips. "Nice to meet you."

"It seems hard at first, but it gets better."

She kept staring at him. Something about him was sending electricity through her.

"What's your name?" he asked.

It did not matter anymore. She could tell the truth. "Katarina."

He blinked several times as if making sure he had heard her right. Joy and sorrow mingled in his expression, but she saw how feeble he was. Nicholas would not make it much longer in Maremoth.

Her father was probably dead too. Kat looked out over the people and saw no one who reminded her of him. She had held onto hope that he was alive for her mother and Evan's sakes, but she had always known he was dead. Now she was sure. This work would have killed him.

The two sat lost in thought—neither eating, neither speaking. Nicholas knew that he should not tell his daughter who he was. He needed to keep his distance. Sasha had probably put Kat here to draw him out and as soon as she found out who he was, they would both be dead.

Nevertheless, it had been years since he had cast his eyes upon his daughter. The curly auburn hair was slightly tamer than before. Her eyes were just as defiant. She was leaner and more confident, but there were the traces of the timidity that she had always worked so hard to hide. Katarina would know about Evan, too. He opened his mouth to tell her who he was, but he found that the words would not come.

Max sat in his cell with only one picture in his mind—that of a battered and worn prisoner in once-nice clothes that were now destroyed. His wild beard and determined eyes showed that although he had been in the mud cell for a long time, his spirit had not yet been broken.

"Arvin," Max whispered, the scene in his mind changing to the conversations the two had had, then resting on a battlefield where the man lay dying. The blood covered his shirt. The sounds of battle surrounded. Max still felt the anguish as the man breathed his last.

Is this to be my fate? To rot in a cell, save one stupid teenager, then die in battle with the one who imprisoned me? How could You do that to Arvin? Max questioned severely. The grief for Arvin would overwhelm him at random times. "He trusted You."

Max kicked the stone wall in front of him. His room was small and musty and the four walls were already closing in on him. "He was torn and tattered and broken. And he was there so long he lost track. His family and his country were terrified for him. And when he finally got free... God, is that what my future holds?"

Sasha was threatening a dwarf when Stewart was carried in before her on a stretcher. "What happened to you?" she scowled.

"We were attacked," he lied. He hadn't even had to kill the last of his men off—they had killed each other on their own. Sasha would find out if he told her he had burned the tree, so he would have to come up a different lie. Self-inflicting a few wounds, spreading his blood around and ripping his clothes, he forged a tale that he hoped would satisfy the shifter.

"By who?"

"Vaylynne." He paused. Useless people did not live around Sasha. "I'll be up on my feet by tomorrow. I just need a little rest. I dragged myself all the way here to tell you."

"A little rest," there was that growl in her voice again. "You should have fought Vaylynne until you were dead."

"I was unconscious. They dropped me somewhere—probably thought I *was* dead."

Sasha weighed her options, "I'll send someone else to do it, after the executions. Seth and Rachel bring the battle to us tomorrow and we must be ready. I require someone strong. If you are better by the morning, I may keep you around. If not..."

"I'll be fine," he assured.

Considering the fact that he was still alive after his enormous mistake, things were going very well. And after the executions, she would be in a better mood. Death always did that to her.

Chapter 34

Galen lay on his bed and took steadying breaths. After some time at sea, his army was beginning to get anxious. No one in their lifetime had ever sailed this far. Flibbert kept arguing with Philip. The crew was nauseous and tired. Everyone wondered what they were getting themselves into. His own thoughts for the family and country he had left behind were heavy.

"Land!" the surprising shout echoed through the ship.

Galen was instantly on his feet, listening to make sure he had heard right. Land? There was no way they had reached Asandra after only a few weeks at sea. "Land ahead!" the call was repeated.

The high king sprinted to the deck, launching to the right as the helmsman swung the ship in an effort to avoid a towering boulder that they had not seen in the thick mist. He righted himself and had a conversation with Flibbert through their eyes. The frog knew no more than he did.

Then Galen heard it. A melodious noise seemed to wrap around him, simultaneously warming and freezing his insides. Everyone was silent; no one moved. The sound was so beautiful. The frogs were squatting in a trance; some even croaked. At that moment they looked more like animals than like people.

The noise's pitch rose; the mist intensified. Galen allowed his eyes to close for a moment. When he opened them, the second-most beautiful woman he had ever seen stood before him.

Her clothing was rich, colorful and flowing. The young lady had the same angelic blond hair, the same cute nose and the same slender features of his wife. She was just a hair taller than him and he looked instinctively for the wings of an airsprite, but this woman seemed completely human. How had she gotten on the ship?

As her mouth opened a song came forth. All his thoughts disappeared and he took a step towards her. The others were moving closer too.

Flibbert jumped over them all and landed before her with a bow, his top hat in his fingers. A harp materialized in her hands and she stroked it gently. Peace covered the ship, dulling Galen's senses. A woman this gentle would need help. "Who are you?" he tried to ask.

As she laughed, her hair seemed to dance from her shoulders to her back. The harp's song intensified and the ship rocked a little. Galen reached out a hand and she reached for his, tears in her eyes. Their hands were inches away. The king felt himself tackled to the ground by a slimy frog. Flibbert was on top of him, enraged, "How dare you?"

"What?" he shouted, confused. As the melody grew darker, Galen's mood turned black. He shoved Flibbert and got to his feet.

"She is a goddess among frogs. No human should touch her."

"Frog? She's a human!" Galen boomed. Who did Flibbert think he was? He had always tried to control Issym. At some point it had to end. "Get below deck. That's an order!" he snarled.

The sound of the other sailors bickering with each other over the descriptions of the woman joined with the harp's unhappy noise. The woman sang along now.

"You've impugned her honor." Flibbert shouted. "Now face me!"

The noise of the swords coming out of their sheaths was indistinguishable from the chorus of sound. Galen and Flibbert stared each other down, vengeance in their eyes. Each used their full strength as they began their duel. They were accomplished swordsmen, dancing across the ship.

"You were always so prideful!" the king shouted, his ears thudding with the song and his heart matching its beat. "Do you care about anyone but yourself?" Galen almost got a blow to the frog's heart, but Flibbert jumped to the helm. "So like you!" Galen called. "Run away when you can't fight."

"You are a selfish king! Can't you see how happy she would make me?" Flibbert retorted.

The frog jumped down upon him, the pressure sending the king to one knee. Flibbert's blow missed its target, but drew blood from Galen's side.

"Happiness!" Galen cut one of his enemy's legs before he could get away. Flibbert limped back. "That's all you frogs care about!"

The frogs and humans each fell behind their race's leader and fought with fists and weapons. By now the song was so loud that not even the battle could be heard.

Galen and Flibbert's swords locked together. They were close enough to hear each other as Galen spat, "Did I ever tell you that you were prideful scum? You've only ever made my job harder, Toad."

"I never would have picked you as king if I had known you!" Flibbert countered. The insult of being called a toad erased any mercy he might have had.

The king gained the upper hand. He pinned the frog to the wall, his sword at Flibbert's throat. Flibbert dropped his weapon in surrender. "Kill me then. It will be my privilege to die defending her honor!" He chuckled as he smiled and accepted his fate.

Galen hollered and almost brought the blade forward, but something held him back. They had been friends, good friends, but Flibbert had made him so angry. What had he done? Was it really bad enough to kill him for? He squinted at Flibbert and refrained from finishing him.

A mighty roar from a minotaur snapped the king's mind closer back to reality. He lowered his blade and turned to see. The minotaur charged towards the singing lady and brought an ax close to her throat. "Stop that music," he growled.

Flibbert's body grew stiff. When the woman's music ceased, he pushed Galen back and ran to her. The king was not far behind.

Galen tried to think logically. He saw a human woman. Flibbert saw a frog. She was why his whole ship was fighting. He had to restore order. "What are you?" he asked. The other sailors had stopped fighting, for the time being. Some of the mist rescinded.

She cocked her head. "We are sound sprites." Her voice erupted into a booming and shrill note until every creature on the ship fell down, crying out at the noise and trying to cover their ears. Only the minotaur stayed on his feet. "Stop now or I will make sure you never sing again."

"Hah!" The volume intensified. Many of the frogs passed out. "Who do you think you are?"

"My name is Joeyza. I am the minotaur who is going to save this crew." He pulled a dagger from his belt and put it through her side. Her voice fell silent for a moment and then a cry of anguish broke from her. The crew relived every loss they had ever felt and they wept— grown men and women sobbed on the deck of their ship.

She crumpled to the ground and Joeyza caught her and laid her back. "Be silent and we can help you heal," he promised her.

The sound sprite gave up her music and whispered, "How did you resist my song?"

Flibbert and Galen struggled to their feet, both of their minds now grasping the desperateness of the situation. Their ship had almost destroyed itself. What about the other vessels?

They looked upon the sprite and, without her song, saw her growing older. Only Joeyza saw the true form of a shriveled hag.

"I am a minotaur. We care nothing for sound."

She let out one small chirp. From the mist came two others just like her. A sprite with white hair and a sprite with silver hair arrived simultaneously, hovering over the bow of the ship. They tried to sing but at Joeyza's warning growl, they shut their mouths. After a moment, the silver-haired one said, "Give us our sister and we will tell you whatever you desire to know."

"Take your sister. Tell us nothing," Joeyza decided for the ship.

A wariness sparked in Galen. The minotaur was giving orders on his ship. *The same minotaur that just saved us.*

"We intercept all messages of the sea and of the air and of the fire," the white-haired one proclaimed.

"We heard what your illuminescent said. Sending a message through water is easy, but bending light and therefore time—that is difficult," added the silver-haired sprite.

"Still, we can do it. I see a child…"

Galen longed to know about his family, but he did not need to hear the news from these sprites. "Just get off my ship," Galen commanded.

The ones in the air screeched. Flibbert barely kept on his feet, his sensitive ears threatening to burst. "I will tell you this at no charge!" spat the silver one. "I see a vision of a girl you," she looked at both Flibbert and Galen, "consider a sister. I hear a boy weeping her name, 'Rachel, Rachel!' She will burn this very day."

"Get off my ship!" Galen shouted. "Take your sister and leave us!"

Flibbert understood the intensity. Such words would demoralize the whole army.

The gray-haired one looked pathetically at Joeyza, "You are like no other. Let me stay. I can tell you things, help you."

Joeyza stood, "Go away. You have done enough damage."

"But there is more to the prophecy," she tried. "A boy…

named Max..."

Joeyza walked below deck. Her sisters began to laugh and it caused the three of them to rise and disappear.

Nicholas was reminded of the early days of Katarina's life, when he and Juliet had patiently tried to teach her how to be nice. Maybe she had learned that skill over the years, but she was not using it with the guards. She was mouthing off. It was reckless, perhaps, but at least it showed that she was not defeated inside. She was struggling, no doubt, but she was strong.

"That is utterly ridiculous!" Katarina shouted. "No one could do that."

Nicholas tried to get closer without showing that was what he was doing. What had sparked the fight this time? He peered from behind a building and realized. Kat was defending another worker—not even a child, just someone who looked like he needed a little help.

There was a human guard in front of them. Prisoners, dwarves and other humans were watching. The guard's face turned cold. Katarina had defied him in front of all of Maremoth. He would have no choice but to punish her in someway.

Back off, Kat. Recognize the look in his eyes.

Katarina understood what was coming, but glancing back at the other prisoner, she knew she had to stand her ground. Her body stiffened. *How many times have I gotten Evan into this kind of trouble and allowed him to take the beating? Now it is my turn.*

The guard spoke, "Get back to your own work!" He was giving her one last chance.

She had already made her decision. "No! I won't let you do this to..."

He gripped her hair and shoved her into the building nearby. Her head slammed into the door post and her vision faltered. The sounds blurred; time slowed.

"Anyone else want to challenge me?" the guard shouted to the crowd as they went back to their work.

Nicholas tried not to run to his daughter, but before he even knew it he was kneeling over her. He checked the wound and realized she would be okay. The father looked to the guard, then stood up and waited for orders.

"Get her to her bed. She'll need all the rest she can get for how hard I will work her tomorrow."

Nicholas scooped his thin-framed child in his arms and carried her to the building. He stared into her face and smiled. She looked so much like Juliet. The same Juliet who was going to be executed tomorrow. How long before Kat was? Something had to change.

Katarina was beginning to revive as Nicholas put her down and walked out. Her tears began to fall, but not for the pain or the fear. She saw herself in all her wretchedness. She had terribly mistreated a much-loved brother. And Max. What had she done to him? Her decisions to mislead him would mean that Issym's help would not come. Without them, Sasha would never be stopped. The country had fallen apart and she, its princess, had betrayed it. The guilt threatened to swallow her.

Katarina lay in its grip and sobbed. Max had been right. She had never truly trusted in Jesus. He was real and she knew that, but He did not seem to care about her or her country! *People say all the time that you have a 'greater plan', but what about reality? My world is drowning. You won't fix it. What good is there in serving You? You don't want to look at me and I don't blame You. I am despicable. So why don't You just take my life and finish it?*

Katarina's thoughts ran out as she tried in vain to stop her tears. She had ruined everything. There was no hope that anyone could love her after that.

I love you, Katarina, the Voice of God whispered. She froze. What was that?

I have always had a plan and I am still working it out. Trust Me, the Voice insisted.

The princess began to shake. God was talking back. *What about all I did?*

My Son's death cleared you. Just ask. Just submit.

"Where has Your love been?" she spoke the question with trembling lips. Was it just the emotions speaking or was it really God?

Working. Bringing you and Xsardis to this place. I pursued you and Asandra even when you pushed me away. Now trust Me.

I don't trust anyone! It was all-too-true. The guilt weighed down so heavily and her throat choked with the pain. She could not change sufficiently.

Trust!

She gasped for air. "God!" *I'm sorry. Take me.*

Rachel rolled over one more time. It was cold. The ground was hard. Her stomach was nauseous with thoughts of the coming fight. She guessed it was still hours before dawn when she got up and took large steps over snoring dwarves until she reached the forest and was out of sight.

She had regrets. And right now, every one of them was making her feel inadequate for tomorrow. "What are we even doing?" she whispered, fighting through the snow. "On the one hand, all odds are against us. I just want to get Max and go home."

"But on the other hand... I'm so sick," now she spoke louder, "of being told that the things I want to do are impossible. I'm so tired of *feeling* like they are impossible. On Earth all I'm told is that I'm wasting my youth by spending it the way You want me to. And here on Asandra... they tell us the same thing in their own way. 'Try to ignore the evil and everything will be fine. If you confront it, you will lose everything.'"

She turned her eyes up to the brilliant stars. "What if I do lose everything?"

As if a ghostly vision, Seth emerged from the trees before her. "I thought I heard you," he moved beside her. "I was taking the same walk, saying the same things."

"Even the part about just wanting to go home?" she asked, embarrassed but curious.

"Especially that part, but you're right. People need to believe that the impossible is possible, that there is value in living for God."

"At least we know what the right thing is to do here. On Earth there are times when I don't know, and I think that scares me more."

She slipped her hand into his... He prayed.

A red illuminescent swept past Seth and cuddled up to Rachel's cheek, buzzing incessantly. "Ruby. Where have you been? Seth said he couldn't find you when he left Noric."

"I came back as quickly as I could!" she answered.

"You made it just in time."

"Empress, the sprites have arrived," Stewart seemed frustrated by them already. That was fine with Sasha.

"You know where to hide them."

He nodded, then turned back. "Why do you need them?"

Sasha stared into him. "I don't *need* anyone. I brought them here because I appreciate beings who are created to be wicked. Sprites have an unnatural amount of intelligence for children, without an abundance of wisdom. Their abilities are strong. I like this combination."

Sasha loved sprites. They were devious and easy to manipulate if you understood their delicate nature. She had, of course, invited them to the celebration she was holding for herself. When Seth and Rachel did show their faces—stupid as it would be for them to do so—the sprites would be of significant help. When dwarves and men fear for their lives, sprites were stupid enough to believe that they were invincible. Flying high and fast, they could attack and then retreat and attack again. A powerful weapon.

"There are a lot of them," Stewart mentioned. "More than we were expecting."

"Did you think my power would not draw them in?" Sasha snapped.

"I will do as you asked." Stewart escaped. After today, if Sasha was still alive, he might need to rethink his strategy. She would not keep him alive forever.

He returned to the sprites and let them into one of the towers. "Follow Sasha's orders. You know what to do."

As soon as he had closed the door, a silent and swift battle took place. Most of the sprites were unconscious and tied up in minutes. The others waited for the riot to break out and for Abigail's command.

Chapter 36

Maremoth. A prison of death. Sorrow and pain could be felt, seeping out through every crevice. Just one look upon the high stone walls with the cruel spikes on the top and Rachel knew—their mission was more important than she could have ever imagined.

The sun seemed to shine blood orange upon the fortress, making for an eerie feeling that sent shivers up Rachel's spine as she made her way through boulder after boulder, brook after brook, and flesh ripping tree after flesh ripping tree. She, Reesthma and Evan tried to stay low. They had to move quickly, but it wasn't easy going, especially as the coldest wind they had yet felt on Asandra bit at their bodies. How could anyone deny that Sasha was pure evil? It was evident on the outside of her home, for goodness sake!

The executions were scheduled for noon. The three had been walking since the sun had come up and now they feared they would not reach the fortress in time. Firil would have made the journey faster, but he also would have attracted a lot of attention. They had left him behind and, for once, he had not followed. Rachel, Evan and Reesthma could see their destination, not far away, but there was no safe place for one's foot, or elbow or head to go and they moved slowly as a result. Ruby's abilities to freeze the snow could only help them so much. They did not speak, nerves and tensions were too high.

Rachel had forgotten what armor felt like. The stiff leather protecting her torso; the studded bracers guarding her wrists. The bow and quiver slung over her shoulder, the knives in her boot and around her waist, and the sword strapped to her felt normal enough. She was glad that chainmail had not been an option. The weight and sound would have slowed her down even more. Her cloak flapped in the wind they fought through.

Rachel's thoughts drifted back to Seth, his group and the rest of the army. How many would die? Was she leading them to their deaths? The responsibility pushed down on her. But a soft voice inside her head dispelled the fear and said, *It's not on your shoulders. I took it on Mine.*

Finally they reached the wall. Evan swung a rope towards the top and it grabbed on a spike. "I don't like how easy this was," Rachel murmured.

Evan made to climb the wall, but Reesthma touched his arm and pulled him back. "I need to go."

"You're thirteen. You shouldn't even be here," he answered.

"The guard will only let us in if he sees me and I'm a better climber than any of you."

Evan stared her down, glanced to Rachel, then let Reesthma go. "Be careful," he said.

She scaled the wall quickly. After disappearing for a few moments, the girl motioned for them to come. Rachel followed Evan up.

They were met by Reesthma and a poorly dressed but well-armed guard. The young man extended his hand.

Evan looked skeptically. "Who are you?"

"He's my cousin, Codon," Reesthma answered.

"I haven't seen Ree in a couple years, but she's hard to forget." He put an arm around her. They acted more like siblings than cousins.

"If you serve Sasha, why are you helping us?"

"You didn't even tell them that?" Codon asked, looking down at his cousin. The two looked nothing alike. His attention turned back to Rachel and Evan. "I came here to take care of Joppa. Sometimes I think he takes care of me more than I do him."

"He's alive?" Reesthma jumped. "I didn't think..."

"Maremoth's old leader built some dwellings just up through those trees," he directed Reesthma's eyes. "I convinced him to take Joppa there. Sasha thinks he's dead. The dwarf knew the prestige knowledge brings. He was having Joppa write out all the scrolls he could recite by memory." He got down on his knees to look Reesthma in the eye, "All Joppa ever talks about is you. He loves you a lot. He kept telling me to leave and go take care of you, but I could never escape the fortress. And I would never have left him. Are you okay?"

Reesthma nodded. "I'm just so happy."

"Are you Joppa's son?" Rachel asked. They hardly had time for pleasantries, but she could not help inquiring.

"Might as well be. He took me in," he stood up. "Now what do you guys need?"

"The plan is to stop the executions," Evan answered him. "How much time do we have?"

"It's getting close to twelve," he replied.

"We need to stay hidden for now. We're the backup plan," Evan declared.

"Follow me." Codon led them down a set of stairs and behind one of the fortress' towers. "This should be safe enough. We never expected anyone to be stupid enough to go through the brambles."

"No one probably ever thought Sasha had a spy either."

Reesthma bent down and began to make her snow creatures.

Rachel looked around the corner as she huddled in the snow. The nooses were around the prisoner's necks. "Come on, guys. Move!" she whispered.

Seth had chosen a small group of dwarves. He had dressed himself as Kate had instructed him, so that he would look to everyone like just another of Sasha's army. Then he and some dwarves had marched into Maremoth. It was gross inside—smelly and dirty. He could hear the chains of some of the more difficult prisoners clanking together, the sound of whips against men and women's backs, the barking of orders and the whimpers of children.

All around him were huts, ready to fall in at any moment. He was enclosed by the rough walls of the fortress and to his left was the 'castle.' The structure was made of wood and stone and spikes, with men and dwarves walking through it. Seth struggled to walk like he belonged. He did not want to belong to a place like this. He wanted out.

He caught a glance of some of the prisoners—dirty, barely clothed, malnourished, heavily burdened with objects to carry into the castle. Those people deserved to be liberated as much as Max and the queen—and what of Katarina? They had heard nothing of her, but if Max was Sasha's prisoner, Kat must have been too.

Seth and the dwarves entered the castle. It was dark, with torches every few feet. What had they been thinking—walking themselves into Sasha's grasp? For all he knew, the shape shifter could know what they were doing, and simply be waiting for the right moment to close in her trap. There were too many people involved to really keep such a secret.

They must not have looked out of place, because as they passed by man after man after dwarf after dwarf, no one paid them any special attention. Reaching the entrance to the throne room, they saw that ten men and dwarves stood watch. Only ten? That was insulting. Sasha knew they were coming, but only stationed ten men?

One of the dwarves, Dibri, winked at Seth and then turned and hurried in the direction of the guards. "Let me in. I need to speak to the empress."

"Oh, then go right in. She loves unexpected company," the guard answered, his voice dripping with sarcasm. "Get out of here!"

"The empress commanded us to watch for that boy, and I think I've found him."

The man's face changed. He quickly opened the door. Dibri glanced back at Seth, then rushed to him, shouting, "I told you to watch the boy!"

Seth had never enjoyed improvisation, but he gave it his best shot, "We were, but then..."

"Spit it out!"

"He slipped into the crowd and we lost sight of him."

Another of Seth's dwarves spoke up, "We hoped to catch you before you told Sasha."

"You what!" the dwarf launched himself at the group. "You almost had me chopped up into little pieces! Thank goodness I hadn't told the empress."

The guard's face turned hard. "Oh, you're going to tell the empress, alright—every last one of you. Get in there."

"No, I'm begging you!"

They were thrust through the door and the guards shut it behind them. "Nice work!" Seth whispered.

"I didn't expect that to work."

There was no one in the room. *Sasha must already be on the balcony,* Seth knew. Time was so short. They stepped as softly as they could through the throne room. It did not strike any of them as impressive, but they did not take the time to dissect it. Seth leaned against the wall to the balcony and risked a glance out. Three nooses had been set up, with a guard placing the prisoners behind each one. Five enemies: three guards, Sasha and some other man.

The prisoner closest to Sasha was a dwarf Seth did not

recognize. Something told Seth not to trust whoever it was.

Then Max. Seth's heart beat faster. His friend was so close to death. Why had they waited so long? What if something went wrong? Seth found he suddenly had all the adrenaline he needed to do this. He would not let Max die.

Beside Max was a woman dressed in regal clothing, who held herself with dignity even as she was about to die. Queen Juliet.

Sasha was ranting on and on about how evil Remar and Juliet were, and how they had robbed the people in order to afford their style of living. She spoke about what she had done for the people, but how Max had come to stop it and the dwarf had used the people's money and labor for himself. "And so, for our progress and peace, these three must die. Today, I officially become your empress. I am glad you all are here for this festival," she proclaimed.

The nooses were strung around the three prisoners' necks. Seth racked his brain for some plan that would not get Max and Juliet killed. Sasha was standing mere inches from him. What was he supposed to do?

Sasha's head turned his direction. Seth ducked back, hopefully in time. Sounds rose—there was some kind of commotion. The teen heard the clanking of weapon against weapon. The dwarves were attacking.

Lotex did not doubt that Seth now stood ready; he had full confidence in the boy. He hollered with all the breath in his body before launching himself at a dwarf in front of him. All eyes turned to the fight because dwarves often fought with humans, but never with other dwarves. Lotex's dwarves attacked. He tackled a human to the ground. The battle spread through the ranks of both races.

Still Sasha droned on, oblivious to the fact that she had lost her audience. It was time to capture that attention. Wildly Lotex slashed at anything around him. "The prisoners are escaping!" he shouted, thinking, *Prisoners, it's time to escape.* Maybe they would get the idea. Judging by the surges of sickly humans to the gates, they were understanding.

Reesthma's snow creatures—tigers, elephants, snow men, giant squirrels—began to join in the battle. Somehow they knew who to attack and who not to. That finally captured Sasha's eyes. They narrowed, then closed. She was preparing to multiply.

Seth saw the slightest change in Sasha's posture, but he understood what it meant. She was distracted. He crawled silently passed the dwarf and cut loose Max's hands. His friend waited until Juliet was released before slipping off his noose and escaping. Together the three ran.

Chapter 37

Abigail's sprites joined in the battle. For one breathless moment it looked as if they were fighting the good dwarves, but it finally became evident whose side they were on. Abi's form spiraled through the air, yelling a battle cry that spurred her troops onward. Sasha shouted angrily at the sprites. The shifter turned sharply to where her prisoners should have been. They were gone. Only the dwarf remained. And her right hand guard stood there oblivious. The shout of rage shook the ears of everyone in Maremoth.

Sasha was about to join the battle. Things were going to change in her favor.

Evan kept his sword ready. His job was to make sure that Rachel stayed safe long enough to sacrifice herself. Every fiber within him turned. He needed to be out there finding his family, helping his mother, leading his troops and rescuing his people. But he was still weak. He had been ordered to keep Rachel safe so that she could sacrifice herself if they needed her to. The prince looked at Rachel. With a white face and eyes full of determination, she was ready for whatever was coming. He was protecting her only so she could die. He couldn't let her go through with it.

Rachel tried to speed up her hands as she made snow creatures, but they were growing stiff with the cold. Ruby got right in her face. The teen swatted the creature back. She needed to keep her mind focused on the battle. She longed to be fighting alongside her troops, or helping Max, Juliet and Seth, but she had to stay safe. For now.

"I have something to tell you!" Ruby flew right into Rachel's forehead to make sure she got her attention.

"I'm busy."

"You are my dearest friend in any world. I love you. That's why I have to do it." She showered her with spark after spark after spark. Rachel was temporarily blinded by them and felt the energy rushing through her. "It is what red illuminescents are meant to do," Ruby added, flying lower after exerting so much power.

"What did you do?" The teen had a sickly feeling. Her memories and her heart told her Ruby had just sacrificed much.

"Now any wound you take, I take for you."

Rachel remembered putting that into a story after she had seen something similar in a movie. How could she have imagined something so painful? "No, Ruby. Take it back!"

"I cannot. But be careful. I am much weaker than the others of my kind. I may not be able to protect you from everything."

"Ruby!"

Evan put a hand on his friend's shoulder. "Rachel, there is no time to argue with the creature. The tide of battle has been turned. Look. We're losing."

Katarina stood with the other prisoners of Maremoth. When the fighting had first begun she had tried to stay out of the way and to keep her eyes on Max and her mother. Surely Seth and Rachel were going to do something! Would they truly let the queen and their friend die? Nicholas, a fellow prisoner, was beside her. He was just as absorbed, just as teary-eyed.

God. You must save them, she prayed with all her heart.

The battle changed sides. The snow creatures were demolished. Many of the sprites were retreating. Their rescuers seemed to be falling.

Many of the prisoners had run to the gate out. Several had escaped, but now versions of Sasha blocked the way. They were trapped. There was only one thing to do.

A soldier fell before Katarina. She grabbed his sword and charged into the battle. Nicholas ran after her. Some of the other prisoners took up arms and fought anyone who fought them as they made their way to the walls. They would climb up the stairs and jump over the edges if necessary, but they were getting out of Maremoth.

The fresh wave brought strength to Rachel's troops, but it was only temporary. Sasha stood on the balcony. She jumped onto its ledge and stayed there with the balance of a cat. Her eyes were closed. When they opened, hundreds, perhaps thousands, of new forms were battling. New dwarves, sprites and humans joined in the fight.

Lotex tried not to attack any of Sasha's versions of these creatures. What point was there in attacking something that couldn't be hurt? His dwarves were falling. They needed to get out of there. *Come on Seth.*

Inside the castle, Seth, Max and Queen Juliet raced for their lives. The dwarves Seth had brought with him had joined in the fray outside. It was just the three humans, hiding from versions of Sasha at every turn.

As they rounded a corner, Max saw her. He pulled Seth and Juliet into a side room. Hopefully the shifter hadn't seen them. *I guess that's up to You, God,* Max thought.

Seth waited all of a minute before going for the door. Max blocked his path. "Sasha won't waste time checking out rooms when she knows we'll have to come out eventually. We should lie low."

"No. We don't have much time." Seth looked ready to barrel through him.

Max knew he was missing something. "What's going on?"

"There is a massacre going on out there and they don't know if we're captured, dead, or running and need a distraction. Rachel won't wait much longer before giving that distraction. And it's going to cost her her life."

Rachel looked at the carnage before her. It was a death trap. There was no way out for the prisoners or the troops. She had to act, now. Even if Seth didn't need help, the people of Asandra did. She turned to Evan.

He saw the faraway look in her eyes. "What about the illuminescent?" he inquired.

Ruby lay sleeping in a hat. "If I'm remembering right, she'll be fine. As sick as she is, her form will only accept my minor wounds. Death shouldn't touch her."

Evan stood as she rose. "I'm coming with you."

Putting a hand on his shoulder, she answered, "This is my task. Asandra will need a good prince."

"Give them more time," he implored.

"Thanks for everything, Evan. You made the last few months bearable." Rachel saw that he still wore her fairy dust necklace and was glad that he had it. She looked towards Reesthma. The girl's attention was elsewhere. Good.

Is this to be the end to my influence on the world?

They embraced for a moment. She took in his strength.

The stalling feeling abandoned her. Energy surged and she took the stairs of the tower two at a time. Sasha hated Rachel. Fact. Rachel was going to die. Fact. She would be with God. Fact. But at that moment, she was still frightened.

Rachel made it to the top and stood on the open, unfinished area. She shouted, "Sasha!"

The word echoed in the shape shifter's ears. Her nemesis was calling her. All her forms melded into one giant fire sprite. Sasha flew towards Rachel, feeling the twinges of illuminescent power. It didn't take long for her to understand what she needed to do.

Max nodded to Seth. "We all go different ways out. It will make us harder to spot."

Juliet agreed. "It is our best option."

Seth was the first out the door. He escaped the palace. Seth moved through the mob, sword in hand, running straight towards the far tower where Rachel stared Sasha down. The shifter was almost upon her.

Max waited a few moments, then left the room. He made it to the top of the wall and walked around to the far end. He would come at the battle from the other side.

Dropping to the ground behind a tower, he saw Reesthma crying and a guard trying to comfort her. Evan's back was turned. Max drew the knife Seth had given him and was about to attack the guard when Reesthma saw him. "No! He's a friend."

Evan turned back. Max understood the look. "She's already gone. Hasn't she?"

"Up that tower," Evan nodded. "A few seconds ago."

"Then maybe there's still time. Let's get her down."

Nicholas' strong voice compelled Katarina to listen. *Why?* she wondered. *I have never listened to anyone in my life!* But something about Nicholas made her obey.

"Let's get some horses from the stables. We can fight better on those."

Again, she was not sure why, but she nodded.

Nicholas desperately wanted to keep his daughter from the fighting. Whatever was going on was not going to end well. Katarina was not the type who was going to sit around and watch, no matter the circumstances, so the best he could hope for was to get her out of the fray for a few moments.

They reached the stables and Nicholas opened the stall of one horse, pulling him out. His heart leapt. There in the hay, sat Juliet. "You're just as beautiful as ever," he whispered, kneeling down in front of her. Juliet's arms wrapped around him and they shared a kiss. "Mom!" Kat rebuked. She looked disgustedly towards Nicholas, "That's the queen!"

"And should not the king kiss the queen?" he asked, smiling.

"You're... the... you're my..." Katarina stared at his twisted body.

"Father," he suggested.

Remar got up and hugged her. It was difficult to believe. She mouthed to her mother, "Really?" She got a nod in reply. The emotions that swirled in that moment were inexplicable, even to the usually talkative princess. She stepped back and straightened herself. "We have to get back to the battle. There is work to be done."

"I don't want you two in harm's way," the king replied.

"I won't hide." Katarina jumped onto the horse and raced back to the heart of the battle.

"Go after her," Juliet nodded.

"Stay safe."

"The word safe has no meaning in Asandra."

"Your illuminescent friend did put a good charm on you, Rachel, but not a strong enough one. I have found my way through it," Sasha's voice rumbled through the fortress.

Seth stopped running. He was nearing the tower, but was not close enough. He could do nothing but watch. Max and Evan appeared behind Rachel, reaching to pull her back. "Get out of there!" Seth shouted, although he knew that they could not hear him.

"Goodbye, Nemesis," Sasha called.

Rachel saw Seth standing below. It was too late. They stared at each other from the uncrossable divide, knowing that it was the last time they would see each other on Xsardis or on Earth.

Max took Rachel's hand. Evan grabbed her waist. They tried to pull back.

Katarina saw her brother and Max appear on the tower. She moaned with the terror of what was about to happen, "No!"

Fire flew from Sasha's hand. It consumed the teens.

With the fire dissipating, Seth stood breathless and empty. He just knew he would see her there, okay, somehow. Surely she could not be gone. Rachel. Max. Evan. Smoke just kept billowing out. He would not wait.

"Just like Shadrach, Meshach and Abednego," he chanted to himself as he raced to the tower. "Please God, just like that."

Seth scaled its steps with lightning fast speed. He reached the top. They were gone, completely gone.

Seth sunk to his knees. Sasha was already elsewhere, gloating in the glory of his misery. They were dead. Now? When they had been so close to the happy ending?

They were gone. His stomach ejected everything within it. No. No. No. This was not right. This was not how it was supposed to be. He could not breathe.

Seth felt the cry of anguish and anger come from him. He

clenched his hands and swore, "I won't stop until I have finished what you guys started."

Lotex was calling for a retreat. Sasha's distraction had left the gates open. The wounded and many prisoners had already escaped. For the others this might be their last chance.

They had accomplished their main purpose. They had rescued the queen.

The battle had been some kind of success. But so many had died!

Rachel, Max and Evan were gone.

Epilogue

Joppa let out of a heavy sigh. "I am sorry you had to go through all of this, my girl. I desperately wanted to keep you away from such heartache."

Reesthma stood up from straightening her bed as the tears resurfaced, "The pain is all around us. You could not keep me from it forever."

"I suppose not. But this war has only just begun. Things are going to get much worse."

For their generous financial support of Asandra, Jessie Mae Hodsdon and Rebirth Publishing would like to thank the following people by naming characters after them:

Abigail the sprite: Abigail Desrochers, donated by Andy and Kelly Desrochers

Zachary the traveling preacher: Zachary Desrochers, donated by Andy and Kelly Desrochers

Vaylynne the independence fighter: Valene Whitty

Joeyza the minotaur: Joey Wright, donated by Valene Whitty

Nicholas the prisoner king: Nicholas Galloway

Interested in **Xsardis, Book Three of the Xsardis Chronicles**?

Then go to www.issym.com where you can find out more about the chronicles, Jessie Mae Hodsdon and Rebirth Publishing. Sign up for the Xsardis Insiders and stay informed!

Check out the author's blog at
issym.wordpress.com
Or follow on Twitter:
ISSYMXSARDISCHR

Rebirth Publishing

Adventure with a purpose

Rebirth Publishing, Inc is committed to using adventurous literature and high quality writing to shine Christ in a dark world.

About the author:

Jessie Mae Hodsdon is a freshman at Columbia International University in South Carolina, where she studies Bible and business. She serves as an inspirational speaker at churches, schools and youth groups and she holds writing workshops for children and teens.